John Andrew Hamilton Sumner

Life of Daniel O'Connell

John Andrew Hamilton Sumner

Life of Daniel O'Connell

ISBN/EAN: 9783337416324

Printed in Europe, USA, Canada, Australia, Japan

Cover: Foto ©Raphael Reischuk / pixelio.de

More available books at **www.hansebooks.com**

STATESMEN SERIES.

LIFE OF
DANIEL O'CONNELL.

BY

J. A. HAMILTON.

LONDON:
W. H. ALLEN & CO., 13 WATERLOO PLACE,
PALL MALL. S.W.

1888.

LONDON:
PRINTED BY W. H. ALLEN AND CO., 13 WATERLOO PLACE, PALL MALL. S.W.

PREFATORY NOTE.

THE only complete Life of O'Connell hitherto published is Miss Cusack's, a bulky and uncritical book, founded, however, upon a considerable quantity of unpublished materials, chiefly correspondence with Archbishop McHale, not all of which was used. John O'Connell began a life of his father, which he brought in two thick volumes as far as 1824. Of this book it is difficult to speak temperately. A son, writing of his father in the father's lifetime, is not expected to be impartial, but that is no reason why he should be grotesquely eulogistic of his father and his party and indecently abusive of his opponents. Such merit as the book has is due to its being a kind of scrap-book of the speeches and resolutions at the meetings from 1810 to 1824. The same author's edition of his father's speeches is carried only a year or two farther. He also published a volume of " Parliamentary Reminis-cences " from 1833 to 1842, which contains a number

of his father's letters of the years 1829 and 1840.
William Fagan's Life, which, considering that it appeared in a Cork newspaper immediately after O'Connell's death, is a meritorious work, ends at 1838.
Huish's Life breaks off in the middle, and is almost
valueless; Græme's Life is the same. _The Centenary
Record_, published by the O'Connell Centenary Committee of 1875, contains some new information, which
the arrangement of the book makes as inaccessible as
possible. O'Neill Daunt's _Reminiscences_ deal almost
exclusively with the last ten years of O'Connell's life,
but are very valuable. Dr. William Forbes Taylor,
under the _sobriquet_ of " A Munster Farmer," published
a short and temperate review of O'Connell's career, called
A Munster Farmer's Reminiscences of O'Connell. I
have endeavoured to collect what was valuable from all
these sources, in order to construct at once a picture
of the man and a sketch of his career; and where
they disagreed I have presumed that the truth must
have been best known to John the son and Daunt
the friend. Mr. Shaw Lefevre's _Peel and O'Connell_ .
has been before me, but its scope is rather foreign to
the object of this book. I have not dissented from
the general estimate and conclusions of Mr. Lecky's
masterly essay in the _Leaders of Public Opinion in
Ireland_, which seems to me to possess all the finality
that is possible, until O'Connell's epoch has passed into

the cooler temperature of history and ceased to be steeped in the burning atmosphere of Irish controversy.

In addition to these works the authorities are Wyse's *History of the Catholic Association* and Charles Butler's *Historical Memoirs of the Roman Catholics;* Mr. W. J. Amherst's *History of Catholic Emancipation,* which is carried only to 1820, is also a useful book. For the Repeal period, Duffy's *Young Ireland* and *Four Years of Irish History* are of the first importance. For the legal part of O'Connell's life, O'Flanagan's *Munster Circuit* and *Irish Bar* are useful. I have consulted also D. O. Maddyn's *Chiefs of Parties,* Cloncurry's *Personal Reminiscences,* the lives severally of Canning, Althorp, Melbourne, Ellenborough, Sheil, Drummond, and Dr. Doyle; Peel's *Memoirs,* the *Greville Memoirs,* Lord Hatherton's *Memoir,* Lord Colchester's *Diary,* Guizot's *Embassy to St. James' in* 1840, and Barrington's *Personal Sketches.* For visits to Darrynane Catherine O'Connell's *Excursions in Ireland* and Howitt's *Journal,* vol. i. p. 328 are useful. J. Venedey, a fair-minded German, published an interesting account of what he saw in Ireland in 1843, and in a small work by M. Cavrois, published at Arras, called *O'Connell et le Collège Anglais à St. Omer,* there are several interesting particulars about O'Connell's early and his last days. For foreign opinion the following books may be looked at, though they do not add much to our knowledge of him: an *Elogio, recitato nei solenni funerali celebratigli nei giorni* 25 *e* 30 *Guigno* 1847, by Father Gioacchino Ventura, Napoli 1848 ; Leopold Schipper's *Irland's verhältniss zu England;* Moriarty's *Leben und Werken O'Connell's*, and two pamphlets by J. M. de Gaulle and by Jules Gondon. Among Magazines, the *New Monthly Magazine* from 1821 to 1832 contains articles by Sheil and others, and *Macmillan's Magazine*, vol. xxviii., a valuable article by Mr. Ball. I have also made use of various pamphlets, and for general history have followed Mr. Spencer Walpole's excellent book.

J. A. H.

CONTENTS.

CHAPTER I.

EARLY AND PROFESSIONAL LIFE.

CHAPTER II.

THE SECURITIES CONTROVERSY.

1800-1813.

CONTENTS.

CHAPTER III.

CATHOLIC DESPONDENCY.

1814-1823.

CHAPTER IV.

THE CATHOLIC ASSOCIATION.

1823-1828.

CHAPTER V.

EMANCIPATION.

1828-1842.

CHAPTER IX.

LAST DAYS.

1843-1847.

CHAPTER X.

DOMESTIC LIFE AND CHARACTER.

30 July 67.

LIFE OF
DANIEL O'CONNELL.

CHAPTER I.

EARLY AND PROFESSIONAL LIFE.

Family, birth, education, and call to the bar—A United Irishman—
Professional success—Anecdotes of professional life.

In a house called Carhen House, long since dis-
mantled, which stood in the farthest extremity of Kerry,
between the Kenmare River and Dingle Bay, about a
mile to the north of the little town of Cahirciveen,
there was born, on the 6th of August 1775, Daniel
O'Connell. In the wild districts of south-western Ireland, the family of O'Connell, or, as they were originally called O'Conal, had long been established, at one
time in Limerick, at another in Kerry, and at another in
Clare. So remote was this part of Ireland, that through
the most rigorous period of the Penal Code, when the
law was so strictly administered that Roman Catholics
were constrained to resort, and not in vain, to the good
faith of Protestant neighbours, and to avoid confisca-

tion by conveying to those good friends, as unavowed
trustees, the lands, which the laws forbade persons of
their faith to hold themselves, the O'Connells had
kept unconfiscated and undisturbed a small mountain estate called Glencara, simply because its inacces-
sibility and seclusion had saved it from the notice and
the grasp of the law. At the end of the eighteenth
century they were country gentry of easy circumstances
and good standing in their neighbourhood. Darrynane
Abbey, the family seat, an old farmhouse increased to a
considerable size by picturesque but irregular additions,
was in the possession of Maurice, the head of the family.
It stands near the shore of Cahirdonnel Bay in a very
lovely situation, and has close by the remains of an
abbey founded by the monks of St. Finbar in the
seventh century. Another brother, Morgan, kept a
shop in Cahirciveen and dealt in silks, laces, and wines
smuggled over from France. He accumulated money
and invested it in land in the names of Protestant
trustees. He married Catherine, a sister of John, The
O'Mullane, of White Church, county Cork, and lived
at Carhen. Of his numerous family, no less than ten
survived their childhood. The eldest was Daniel.

Maurice O'Connell was childless, and soon adopted
Daniel, who was his natural heir, and another of Morgan's
children, also called Maurice, and a great part of their
boyhood was spent at Darrynane. Daniel was a bright,
intelligent child. To the end of his life, his tenacious
memory retained the recollection of having been carried in his nurse's arms to the seashore, to see two of
her boats towing Paul Jones's ship out of shallow water
to a deeper anchorage. This was in 1778. While still
but four years old he received his first teaching from an
old hedge schoolmaster, named David Mahoney, one of

that class of poor scholars, particularly numerous in
Kerry, and produced by the repressive Penal Laws, who
wandered, half-beggar, half-scholar, from house to house,
claiming, and never failing to receive, the hospitality of
the country-side. The old man took the child upon his
knee, and so won his heart and fixed his attention, that
the whole alphabet was learnt in an hour and a half.
Daniel proved a ready scholar. He would turn over the
portraits of the celebrities in the *Dublin Magazine*, saying, " I wonder will my visage ever appear in the *Dublin
Magazine*"; he composed a drama on the fortunes of
the House of Stuart at ten years old ; and so fond was
he of reading, that he would desert his play-fellows to
sit cross-legged in the window-seat, devouring *Cook's
Voyages*, and crying over its pages of adventure.

The policy of the Penal Laws had been to render the
education of their children as difficult as might be to
the Roman Catholics, if not wholly impossible. At the
beginning of the eighteenth century, they were forbidden
to establish schools of their own, to be teachers in
Protestant schools, to teach in a private house any but
the children of their own family, or to send their children abroad to receive the education, which was denied
them at home. The Catholic gentry were obliged to
smuggle their sons over seas by stealth, and many a
lugger, which had run a contraband cargo successfully
on the west coast, took back to France a few new
scholars for St. Omer or Salamanca, Louvain or Liége.
It was not until 1792 that the restrictions were removed which prevented them from setting up schools
of their own. The first school publicly opened by a
priest was kept by a Mr. Harrington at Redington in
Long Island, some two miles from the Cove of Cork,
and to this, when Daniel was thirteen years old, and

1 *

had been for some time taught at home by a tutor
named John Burke, he and his brother were sent.
Without showing particular precocity, he was indus-
trious and obedient, and enjoyed the unique distinction
of being the only boy in the school who never was
flogged. Here he remained for a year, but higher
education was still hardly to be attained by a Roman
Catholic in Ireland. Trinity College, Dublin, was practically closed to him, as were its endowments by law,
and in the usual course of the education of lads of
family, the two O'Connells were sent to the Continent.
They went first to Liége, only to find that they were too
old to be admitted there. They then went to Louvain,
among whose fifty colleges several were Irish, and
waited there for instructions from home. During the
interval Daniel attended some of the University lec-
tures. At length, in January 1791, they were placed at
the college at St. Omer. It has often been said that
Daniel was at this time destined by his uncle for the
calling of a priest, but he was himself at the pains to
deny the statement in a letter to the *Dublin Evening
Post*, 17th July 1828. He proved himself a ready and
quick-witted pupil, and, being placed in the classes of
grammar and poetry, was easily first in both of them.
Doctor Gregory Stapylton, the fortieth and last President of the College, wrote of him in January 1792,
" With respect to the elder, Daniel, I have but one sentence to write about him, and that is, that I never was
so much mistaken in my life as I shall be, unless he be
destined to make a remarkable figure in society."

On the 20th of August 1792, he went to the College
at Douai, where he was placed in the class of rhetoric,
and remained there until the 21st January 1793. At
the end of 1792, the Douai College was suppressed, and

the boys were obliged to wait some weeks before they could communicate with their uncle in Kerry. They then returned home, but it was not without danger that they reached the coast. The soldiers assaulted their conveyance, and abused them as "little priests" and "aristocrats." For safety's sake they were compelled on the journey to wear the tricolor, which they tore in disgust from their hats when they found themselves securely on board the packet at Calais. His education in France left enduring marks upon O'Connell's character. What he heard, and to some extent what he himself saw, of the French Revolution, made upon his susceptible mind an impression which influenced his whole life. He imbibed strong Bourbon opinions and an intense hatred of the Revolution and the Revolutionaries, who were the persecutors of his Church. "I was always in terror," he said, "lest the scoundrels should cut our throats ; on one occasion a waggoner of Dumouriez's* army scared me and a set of my fellow collegians who had walked out from Douai, crying '*Voila les jeunes Jesuites ! les Capucins !*' So we ran back to our college as fast as we could, and luckily the vagabond did not follow us." He was by nature devoted to his Church, and his training deepened this disposition of his mind. He was often accused, and not without truth, of Jesuitry in his policy, and the French accent which hung about his English pronunciation on his return home never entirely left him. To the end of his days he pronounced "Empire" "Empeer," and accented the word "charity" as if it were "*charité.*"

---

* Dumouriez won the battle of Jemappes in the Austrian Netherlands, about thirty-six miles from Douai, on November 6, 1792.

After spending the remainder of the year, 1793, at home in Kerry, moving among the peasantry whom he learnt to know so well, and enjoying with the ardour of a keen sportsman the hare-hunting of the Kerry mountains, O'Connell went to London to begin the period of studentship at an English inn of court, which was necessary before he could be called to the Irish bar. He entered himself at Lincoln's Inn* in 1794, and took lodgings in a court on the north side of Coventry Street, but in 1795 he removed to a boarding-house at Chiswick. That his years of studentship were spent in no merely nominal attention to the law, is proved by the fact that his learning in his profession was at all times unquestionable and profound, and that after he had been a few years at the bar, his practice and his political work were so engrossing, that he could have had little time left for further study and research. The first five years of a successful lawyer's life are those during which not the foundations only but much of the superstructure of his learning must be created. O'Connell's mind was ceaselessly active, with a natural bent for law, but he must from the first have vigorously exercised it upon text-books and case-law to have attained the knowledge which he indubitably possessed. The recollections of his life in France had made him by antipathy a strong Tory, and when Hardy was put upon his trial in October 1794, O'Connell attended at the Old Bailey day after day to see the man brought to justice, whom he

---

* O'Connell's biographers do not agree as to what inn he studied at; his son John says Lincoln's Inn, Daunt says Gray's Inn, and Shiel the Middle Temple. All of these may be presumed to have had means of knowing the truth. Fagan follows Daunt and Huish Shiel; Mr. Shaw-Lefevre puts him at the Inner Temple. There are no other Inns of Court.

regarded as the advocate and accomplice of the French Revolution. But day by day the bigotry of Scott the Attorney-General, the eloquence of Erskine, Hardy's counsel, the weakness of the case for the Crown, and the justification which appeared for Hardy's speeches, themselves effected a revolution in O'Connell's mind, and he left the court at the end of the trial cured for life of his brief fit of Toryism.

At length his studentship was over, and returning to Ireland, he was called to the Irish Bar on May 19th, 1798. Whatever may have been the intentions with which Maurice O'Connell of Darrynane had sent his nephew to St. Omer, it was clear at that time, and to a young man of his temperament, that the bar offered the only career in Ireland that could satisfy his aspirations. As a boy, O'Connell had his ambition. Once, when he was about ten years old, they were discussing Flood, Charlemont, and Grattan, then at the height of their reputation, round the fire at Darrynane. The usually vivacious child was observed to be sitting silent and abstracted. "Daniel," said his aunt, "what are you thinking of?" "Why, let me tell you," he replied, "I'm thinking I'll make a stir in the world yet." It is said that he had been particularly excited by the career of his uncle Daniel. This officer, the youngest brother of Maurice O'Connell, had entered the French service in 1759, as a sub-lieutenant in Clare's regiment, when still only a lad of fourteen. By 1787 he had risen to the rank of a major-general, and was colonel in command of the German regiment of Salm-Salm in the French army. In 1788, he invented a system of infantry tactics, which was soon adopted by all the armies of Europe. Subsequently he was made Count O'Connell, and when, about 1794, several regiments of the Irish Brigade were drafted into the British service, he became a colonel in the British army. But apart from his uncle's brilliant reputation, there was enough in the career of a barrister to tempt O'Connell to climb that way to eminence. He had, as strongly as ever any Irishman has had it, the legal turn of the Irish mind ; he was subtle, ready, disputatious, astute. In a country where the aristocracy and the landlord class were always prone to absenteeism, and if resident pinned their hopes on the favour of the Government ; where the body of merchants, though well-to-do, indeed, and enterprising, was small and almost confined to Dublin and Belfast, the bar became the only body in Ireland capable of taking a prominent position before the public eye. The warfare of the law courts fascinated the Irish as it never has done the English. The English have been content to regard the proceedings of the law as a matter of art and even of mystery, to be respected perhaps, to be tolerated certainly, to be admired never. But to the Irish, and especially to the Irish peasantry, a trial was an arena, in which wit and craft, eloquence and cunning, performed a drama which they fully understood and followed with enthusiasm. A smart and shifty witness, a clever though unscrupulous attorney, a neat quibble, an impassioned appeal to a jury, a bold address to a judge, and a sharp passage of arms between counsel, delighted the spectators, and passed from mouth to mouth in a thousand good stories. Nor did the bar exist for law and lawyers only. Instead of an antagonism between letters and law, such as the English have always known, the best of Irish wit and Irish letters was to be found among the practitioners of the Irish bar.

The Four Courts, then just completed, have long been

a classic ground for Irish stories: every circuit in Ireland had similar traditions, and its leaders enjoyed a reputation and popularity over the counties whose assizes they attended, which was of itself a kind of fame. But not only was the profession as a profession attractive to a young man; its connection with Irish politics, and especially with Irish popular politics, was of the closest. A great number of the Irish Parliamentary leaders were members of the Irish bar, and the public had an access to the courts, which they had not to the House of Commons. Under the strict system of government which had so long prevailed in Ireland, the barrister was almost the only person who had the opportunity of making a figure before the people, while espousing the popular cause. There was no one else whose interest and duty combined to bring him on occasions into conflict with the Government *coram populo*. The gown which in England clothed some passed-master in the mysteries of replevin or contingent remainders, of ouster or trespass upon the case, was in Ireland the robe of the hero and the patriot. Political and professional success reacted upon one another. Ninety years ago, still more even than to-day, to be a popular champion in politics was no bad way of obtaining briefs in court; and to have the tongue of a ready advocate was an excellent recommendation for a young man ambitious of a public career.

When O'Connell joined the Irish bar, a new day had recently dawned for the Roman Catholic lawyer. During the earlier part of the century, Roman Catholics, who, whether in hopes of pension, place, or practice, were minded to come to the bar, had been obliged to take the oaths against Popery, which the Penal Laws imposed, and to conform outwardly to the Established religion.

Their object once attained, they had often relapsed into a suspected state, half-way between conformity and Catholicism, in which many of them were content, as the price of toleration, to become the disreputable tools of the Government. From this unhappy temptation an Act of the Irish Parliament had recently relieved the Catholics, and, although labouring under great educational and some social disadvantages, Catholic barristers had now a fair field for their talents. Into this field O'Connell was among the first to step.

For two or three years after his return to Dublin, though he frequented a debating society in Eustace Street, he occupied himself but little with politics. He lodged in Trinity Place, and having no relations and few friends in Dublin, he was thrown very much on his own resources. He became a Freemason, and even master of his lodge, No. 189, and continued to be one till 1801. That he had some connection with the conspiracy of 1798 is probable. He was sworn in as a United Irishman and attended at least one meeting at which John Shears was present, but he took no part in the proceedings. His most intimate friend in London had been a young Irishman, of good family, Richard Newton Bennett, and Bennett was a member of the Directory of United Irishmen. An accident gave him a hint of the danger of going farther. He was at this time living a convivial and dissolute life. Though no drunkard, and indeed one of the first to set his face sternly against the extravagance of compulsory wine-bibbing, which then prevailed among the Irish gentry, he occasionally got drunk. Coming home emboldened with good liquor, from a party at the house of his friend Murray, a cheesemonger of 3, Great George Street, one evening in the month of March, 1798, he found a knot

of miscreants persecuting a poor street-walker. With
generous courage he interfered to protect the girl, and
was at once attacked himself. Being a finely-built
athletic young fellow, he knocked three of his assailants
down, but was then pinioned from behind and hit
savagely about the face. For some days his bruises
compelled him to keep his room. His landlord, a respectable fruiterer named Ryan, took the opportunity of
giving him some good advice. He warned his lodger
to have nothing to do with the conspirators and their
plans, as from what he had heard at the Castle in the
course of his business, he knew that the Government was
quite alive to all the details of the plot.

Such is the story told by O'Connell's son ; but a son
of Murray's used to declare that his father only prevented the arrest of O'Connell, who was desirous of
going to swear in members at a neighbouring meeting of
United Irishmen, by prevailing on him to go down to
the quay and quit Dublin that night in a turf-boat.
Scarcely was he gone when Major Sirr reached Murray's
house, which he had just left. A few months afterwards his life was very nearly cut short by a violent
illness. While staying at Darrynane, and before his
first circuit, in August, he got wet through on the
hills in following his favourite sport, and heedlessly
slept in his wet clothes in a peasant's hut. Next day
he was taken ill, and for many days lay at death's
door with typhus. His brother John came to see him.
The insurrection had then broken out. He recovered
consciousness, and cried out, " What news from the
disturbed districts ? I am to be a delegate." But
his vigorous constitution stood him in good stead, and
his life was saved.

From whatever source his lesson came, O'Connell

accepted it, and, from the disastrous results of the rising of 1798, contracted a life-long horror of all armed rebellion, and of secret societies, whose members are always so much at the mercy of a spy. He never forgave the men of '98, and used to speak of them in terms of harsh and almost unjust censure. " It was they," he said, "who helped Pitt to carry the Union." During Emmett's rising, he served in the Lawyer's Artillery Corps, and was called out on various services, in the course of which, at considerable risk to himself, he restrained his comrades from the commission of gross illegalities. What he then saw strongly impressed him with the inferiority for the maintenance of civil order of a volunteer body to a regular military force. Its want of discipline and professional self-restraint hurry it into the commission of excesses just when forbearance is most needed. He saw the tendency, as he put it, " when a man has arms in his hands to be a ruffian."

He made by his profession in his first year £58. In his second he made £150, in his third £200, in his fourth £315, and thereafter his income rose rapidly. He joined the Munster Circuit, which included the counties of Cork, Kerry, Limerick, and Clare, where his family connection was strong. In the autumn of 1813 there were twenty-six cases at the Limerick Assizes, and he was briefed in every one of them. He continued to go circuit for two or three and twenty years, and after that only went for a special fee, when his visits were made the occasion of public rejoicings. In his last year of practice, though he lost a whole term, he made nine thousand pounds. " The last hour of my practice at the bar," he said of himself, " I kept the court alternately in tears and in roars of laughter." As Shiel says of him, " from some of the witnesses he

extracted that they were unworthy of all credit, being
notorious knaves or process-servers ; others he inveigled
into a metaphysical puzzle touching the prisoner's
identity ; others he stunned by repeated blows with the
butt-end of an Irish joke : for minutes together the
court and jury, galleries and dock, were in a roar." For
a long time his practice lay very largely in criminal
courts, but his opportunities of making speeches were
for some time very limited. Counsel for the prisoner
in those days was not allowed to address the jury, and
O'Connell's skill lay in his knack of insinuating half-a-
dozen speeches to the jury while pretending to argue a
point of law to the judge. The rank of King's Counsel
was conferred only on Protestants, and Roman Catholic
juniors were obliged to apply themselves to the exa-
mination and cross-examination of witnesses. For
this, O'Connell's intimate knowledge of the Irish
peasant's mind peculiarly fitted him, and as a cross-
examiner he was unrivalled. Once, in 1822, he
cross-examined a witness with such severity that the
man made a rush at him from the table, but fortunately
fell to the ground. Numberless are the stories of his
astuteness in dealing with witnesses, whose evasions and
shifts, though paltry in their design, were ingenious and
clever with a wholly Irish cleverness. In one case the
issue was whether a purported will had been duly exe-
cuted by the testator or was a forgery. O'Connell was
struck by the fact that one witness reiterated several
times in one set phrase, that he saw the testator's hand
sign the will " while life was in him." He turned suddenly on the man. " By virtue of your oath ! " he
cried, " did not someone write with the dead man's hand,
while a live fly was placed in his mouth ? " The witness, crestfallen, admitted it, and the case was won.

To another witness, who denied that he was drunk, because "he had only had his share of a quart," O'Connell quietly said, "Come, wasn't your share all but the pewter?" and the man owned that it was. A prisoner whom he had successfully defended upon some charge thanked him with topsy-turvy goodwill. "Och! Counsellor," he said, "I've no way here to show your Honour my gratitude, but I wish I saw you knocked down in my own parish, and wouldn't I bring a faction to the rescue!"

His indefatigable energy and great physique enabled him to carry on a gigantic practice hand in hand with the labours of agitation and the pleasures of society. The anecdotes of what are really feats of strength are many. On his first circuit he left Darrynane at four in the morning, reluctantly leaving his brother to go coursing, while he rode for the assizes and covered sixty Irish miles that day. He went to a ball and danced, danced with Irish energy, until the small hours, and, rising again at half-past eight, rode on his way all day. In 1829, a Mr. George Bond Low, a Cork gentleman, was fired at, and a conspiracy, called the "Doneraile conspiracy," to murder him and some other gentlemen of Doneraile, county Cork, was supposed to have been discovered. In October a first batch of prisoners was tried by a special commission at Cork, consisting of Baron Pennefather and Mr. Justice Torrens. Dogherty, the Solicitor-General, was for the prosecution. O'Connell, then fifty-four years old, was resting at Darrynane, after the year of incessant conflict which won the Emancipation battle, and he had declined to defend the prisoners. The first four were convicted. Their friends were filled with panic: in such a result they had been unable to believe. O'Connell and O'Connell alone could save the rest. A farmer named William Burke was despatched post-haste to Darrynane, ninety miles away. Travelling in Kerry was still slow and difficult. The first four-horse mail from Cork into Kerry had only been run in August 1810 ; the Limerick mail-coach was a thing of but four years' standing. About thirty years before, O'Connell had been four days in getting from Darrynane to Limerick, and, until 1839, there was a portion of the road to Darrynane, five miles long, so insecure, that the horses had always to be taken out, and the chaises, the rough conveyances of the country, dragged with ropes by men. Burke arrived early on a Sunday morning, and told O'Connell his tale. The counsellor said he would come to the rescue. With only two hours' rest, Burke set out again for Cork, to prepare relays of horses along the road, and raise the spirits of the prisoners and their friends. O'Connell set off and drove himself in a chaise all that day and all the night. At Macroom he snatched three or four hours' sleep, and at daybreak he pushed on. The court was to sit at nine ; the judges had refused to delay the trial for O'Connell's arrival. All Cork was quiver-ing with anxiety ; would the counsellor be there in time ? At length the watchers descried him dashing along the Kerry road and lashing his horse as he came. The cheer that went up from thousands of throats broke in upon the Solicitor-General's opening speech.· Pushing through the crowd, O'Connell pulled up at the court ; his horse fell dead in the shafts. As he entered the court Dogherty turned white, and the prisoners dared to hope. Apologising to the bench, O'Connell took his seat, and, snatching a hasty breakfast of milk and bread as he sat in his place, plunged into the case. The Crown witnesses were not prepared to face him.

He browbeat the Solicitor-General, mimicked his pronunciation, and sneered at his law. Though the evidence was the same as that which had convicted the
first batch, the jury, under the influence of O'Connell's
ascendancy, disagreed as to the second, and acquitted
the third. No wonder that he lived in the hearts of
the Munster men, who had so often seen their friends
and relatives saved by his skill. The Irish peasantry,
who gave to O'Connell through a quarter of a century an affection and obedience which they have never
given to any other leader, always loved better than all
his titles the name of "the Counsellor."

Yet some of O'Connell's popularity in his profession
was won by discreditable arts. Ireland is a country in
which it has never been particularly unpopular to attack
a judge for his conduct on the bench, either in court or
in the press, and there were many occasions upon which
O'Connell, without censure or loss of reputation, assailed the court or his opponents in language which
cannot be justified, and which darkens the splendour of
his great forensic career. It is one of the commonplaces
of Irish history to say that at the beginning of this
century the Irish bench was bigoted, intemperate, and
corrupt, the law-officers unscrupulous and ungenerous,
that juries were packed, and the well of justice poi-
soned at the spring. It is true that none but Protestants
received Crown appointments, and that promotion from
Government posts at the bar to a seat on the bench,
was the natural ambition of a Crown lawyer. It is
unfortunately true that persons of inferior capacity,
defective temper, and insufficient learning were placed
upon the bench. Such judges often delivered themselves with harshness and prejudice; but it is to be
remembered that in England too at that time public

opinion was perfectly tolerant of judicial severity and of a strong leaning in favour of Government, when questions of law and order were concerned; and it has chiefly been in political trials that the conduct of the Irish bench has been impugned. That the lists of jurors were often tampered with is probably but too true, and the two cases of the trial of Magee and of O'Connell himself are, unhappily, notorious examples of it; but this appears to have been done by over-zealous and unscrupulous underlings in the various sheriffs' offices. The Crown, too, made an habitual use of its right to order jurors to stand aside so as to exclude Roman Catholics from juries. Now it is easy to see that the practice is indefensible; yet there were often grounds then for fearing that in particular cases and seasons of excitement a Roman Catholic might not be an impartial juror; nor is branding a Dublin Protestant by the term of "Castle tradesman" enough of itself to place him beyond the pale of justice and fair dealing. O'Connell himself said, before a Parliamentary Com- mittee in 1825, "In the Court of King's Bench every- thing is done that one can wish. I cannot say that of the Court of Common Pleas or of the Exchequer, though there are individual judges in both, of whom I think highly. The Court of Chancery is not so well, indeed it gives no satisfaction at all. The apprehension of partiality is more occasioned by the kind of instru- ments that are used to bring questions to trial than in the superior judges themselves."

His conduct in court was at times deplorably violent; at times improperly crafty. He was accustomed to defend himself by saying that he found extravagant language necessary to awaken the self-respect of the down-trodden Roman Catholics, and to persuade them

2

that they too had rights, and a champion who was not afraid to assert them. But the plea is unavailing. Once he was defending a prisoner, who was being tried upon a capital charge. He saw that there was upon the merits no defence at all; but it happened that, in the absence of the regular judge through illness, Serjeant Lefroy sat as commissioner and tried the case. O'Connell determined to practise upon the fears and conscientiousness of an untried and inexperienced judge. He began to ask the witnesses questions which were wholly irregular and inadmissible. To these Serjeant Gould, who appeared for the Crown, made objection, as he was in duty bound to do. Serjeant Lefroy, of course, allowed the objection. It was for this O'Connell had been playing. He affected righteous wrath, threw away his brief, and crying, "If you won't let me defend him, his blood be on your head," flung out of court. Lefroy lost his nerve, began to act as counsel for the prisoner, summed up in his favour, and the man was acquitted. " I knew," said O'Connell afterwards, "the only way was to throw the responsibility on the judge!" "Good God, my Lord!" he once cried at Cork Assizes to a judge, who had employed his evening after his day's work in refreshing his memory upon some point of law, and on coming into court gave him a favourable decision, "If your lordship had known as much law yesterday morning as you do this, what an idle sacrifice of time and trouble would you not have saved me, and an injury and injustice to my client!"

On another occasion, during a motion for a new trial, counsel called on a young Kerry lawyer, who was attorney on the other side, to produce some document or make some admission. O'Connell, who chanced to be in court, but, for aught that appears, knew nothing whatever of the rights and wrongs of the case, and had nothing to do with it, stood up in court and told the attorney to refuse. Baron McClellan, one of the judges on the bench, asked him if he had a brief in the case. "No, my Lord," said O'Connell, "I have not, but I will have when the case goes down to the assizes." "When I was at the bar," said the judge, "it was not my habit to anticipate briefs." "When you were at the bar," cried O'Connell, "I never chose you for a model, and now that you are on the bench I shall not submit to your dictation." "Leaving his lordship to digest this retort," says O'Connell's admiring biographer, "he took the attorney by the arm and walked him out of court. In this way he dealt with hostile judges." It is to be hoped that this vigorous effort was rewarded with the expected brief, but the tone employed to the judge was one which, as the story has it, "would be offensive from its Maker to a black beetle."

Saurin, the Attorney-General, one of the most distinguished of lawyers, was the object of O'Connell's peculiar animosity, and what took place between them upon the trial of Magee in 1813 is remarkable. Some time after the verdict, on November 27th, the Attorney-General moved the King's Bench in aggravation of the sentence upon Magee, upon the grounds of the line of defence adopted by O'Connell at the trial, and of the subsequent proceedings of the defendant. O'Connell chose to take umbrage at one of Saurin's expressions, and proceeded thus :—   .

Even here do I yield in nothing to the Attorney-General. I deny in the strongest terms his unfounded and absurd claim to superiority. I am his equal at least in birth, his equal in fortune, his equal certainly in education, and as to talent I should not add that, but there is little vanity in claiming equality. . . . I do most sincerely rejoice that the

Attorney-General has prudently treasured up his resentment since July last, and ventured to address me in this court in the unhandsome language he has used, because my profound respect for this temple of the law enables me here to overcome the infirmity of my nature and to listen with patience to an attack which, had it been made else-where, would have met merited chastisement.

*   *   *   *   *

Mr. Justice Osborne.—I will take the opinion of the court whether you shall not be committed.

The Chief Justice.—If you pursue that line of language we must call upon some other counsel upon the same side to proceed.

Mr. Justice Day.—Now, Mr. O'Connell, do you not perceive that while you talk of suppressing those feelings you are actually indulg-ing them. The Attorney-General could not mean you offence in the line of argument he pursued to enhance the punishment in every way of your client. It is unnecessary for you to throw off or to repel as-persions that are not made on you.

Mr. O'Connell.— . . . What did he mean when he imputed to the advocate participation in the crime of the client? This he distinctly charged me with.

Mr. Justice Day.—You shall have the same liberty that he had, but the Court did not understand him to have made any personal attack upon you.

Mr. Justice Osborne.—We did not understand that the Attorney-General meant you, when he talked of a participator in the crime of your client.

The Attorney-General.—I did not, my lords; I certainly did not mean the gentleman.

Mr. O'Connell.—Well, my lords, be it so. . . . I am therefore enabled at once to go into the merits of my client's case.

It may be that during the whole course of this case the air was so electric, that O'Connell really had sup-posed that something had passed which he ought to resent, but the affair had very much the air of a piece of factitious indignation. The end of O'Connell's speech rather confirms this impression. As Curran had once done to Lord Clare, he attacked both the Attorney-General and the Bench by drawing his own portraits of them to their faces in the blackest colours, and speculating what his course would have been, had those been his opponents and judges, and not the admirable persons he saw before him. Of Saurin he spoke in this hypothetical way as " some creature, narrow-minded, mean, calumnious, of inveterate bigotry and dastard disposition . . . whose virulence will explode by the force of the fermentation of its own putrefaction, and throw forth its filthy and disgusting stores to blacken those whom he would not venture directly to attack." Having regard to the nature of the motion before the court and to the grounds of it, one does not wonder that at the close of this speech, O'Connell's own junior rose, and on behalf of his client Magee, repudiated his leader's language.

CHAPTER II.

THE SECURITIES CONTROVERSY.

1800-1813.

Position of the Catholic movement—Leadership of John Keogh—The
period of " dignified silence "—The Veto—The Catholic Board—
Grattan's Bill of 1813—Quarantotti's rescript—Collapse of the
Catholic party.

In 1800, the movement for Catholic Relief, which had
begun about 1760 and culminated in 1793, was in a
state of profound quiescence, almost of torpor. The
Catholic party, thankful for what it had won and fearful
of collision with the Government, was without policy or
organization and almost without leaders. In that condition it remained for several years, and when it again
became active it had new leaders, new methods, and a
goal so different as to be hardly any longer the same. This
comprehensive change was the work of O'Connell. From
the fall of Limerick to the Declaration of American
Independence the Irish Roman Catholics had groaned
under a penal code of terrible rigour. Enacted for the
most part in the reigns of William III. and of Anne,
something had been added to its severity under every
succeeding Sovereign. For nearly a hundred years Ire-

land caused England neither anxiety nor solicitude. The Cromwellian policy had been to exterminate the Roman Catholics, and had failed. The Penal Code sought by heaping up disabilities to reduce them to political insignificance and impotence, and to such justification as success can give that policy was entitled. It was not until England found herself surrounded by imminent perils from without, that the first part of the Code was abrogated, nor until the best public opinion of England could no longer tolerate such laws that the second part was swept away. The aim of the penal laws was to make and keep the Roman Catholics weak, disunited, ignorant, and fearful, and so long as those laws were enforced in their entirety they succeeded in that dark endeavour. Long after their worst severities had been relaxed O'Connell was accustomed to say, that you could tell a Roman Catholic in the street by his hesitating gait, his timid carriage, and his demeanour of conscious inferiority. The evil effects of the disabilities long survived their repeal.

Still, during the latter half of the eighteenth century the lot of the Irish Roman Catholic had been greatly improved, until indeed in 1800 it was better than that of his English co-religionist. The movement first began among the Catholic aristocracy and gentry. In 1760 the first General Association of Catholics of Ireland was formed, and in 1776 their position was enormously changed for the better by the repeal of several Acts, which disabled Roman Catholics from being owners of land.

But the Catholic gentry were jealous of the Catholic merchants, and when the outbreak of the French Revolution was greeted by the latter with enthusiasm and hope, the leaders of the former seceded in a body from the organization. The blow to the Catholic cause seemed paralysing, but it was in fact a fortunate event. It threw the leadership into the hands of a man of talent and force, John Keogh of Mount Jerome. Keogh, without any gifts of oratory or grace of manner, was typical of his class, a merchant of rough force and direct insight, who combined daring with caution, and possessed an instinctive comprehension of the means at his disposal, the goal to which they could carry him, and the right tactics for success. For twenty years he remained the leader of the movement. In 1791 he went to London, alone and at his own charges, saw Burke, was by him introduced to Henry Dundas, and by his plain but adroit diplomacy, persuaded the Minister of the wisdom of listening to the prayer of the Irish Catholics. By direction of the English Ministry a Bill was introduced into the Irish Parliament and passed, which opened to the Catholics the bar, removed the remaining restrictions on education, and repealed the Intermarriage Act. Returning to Ireland, Keogh undertook, with the assistance of Wolfe Tone, a personal propaganda throughout the country, and procured the appointment of upwards of two hundred delegates, who assembled in Dublin in a convention, which was nicknamed from its place of meeting the "Back Lane Parliament." The Convention appointed a deputation of five, of whom Keogh was one, to wait upon the King and present their petition. They crossed the Channel, were graciously received by His Majesty, and had an interview with Pitt. O'Connell, who had but scant respect for Keogh, long afterwards charged him with having on this occasion, in effect, ruined the Catholic cause, for he was sent to demand equality with Protestants and allowed Pitt to cajole him into accepting the municipalities and the franchise. But having regard to Keogh's character, to the circumstances of the time, and to the magnitude of his achievement, it may be well doubted if more could have been hoped for than Keogh got. At the instance of the English Ministry, a bill was introduced into the Irish House of Commons, and ultimately passed, which in point of legislative change did more for the Roman Catholics than Kenmare did in 1776 or O'Connell in 1829. It opened to them the magistracy, the grand juries, the military forces, and the municipalities; it relieved them from most of the remaining private disabilities, penalties, and forfeitures, and, much against the wish of the Protestant members and even of the Catholic nobility, it admitted them to the electoral franchise. They remained excluded only from Parliament, and a few of the highest military and civil posts. The qualification for the franchise was fixed at a freehold interest of the nominal value of 40s., and, as a leasehold interest for life was held to confer the franchise, vast multitudes of Roman Catholic peasants obtained it. But the vote of the tenant was regarded as the landlord's property by unquestioned right. It was a common thing for the tenants to be driven up in flocks to the poll like sheep, to vote as their landlord directed; and the gentry and nobility of Ireland, purely to increase their own political importance, set themselves to manufacture freeholders upon a gigantic scale. Innumerable small holdings were created, no matter at what cost of sub-division of tenancies and increase of a pauper population, and leases for lives were granted of the requisite annual value, but determinable on non-payment of rent, which, to preserve the landlord's control, was deliberately kept in arrear far beyond the peasant's ability to pay on demand. This class of voters had neither education nor independence. A tenant who disregarded his landlord's direction at the poll, was promptly called upon to pay his arrears of rent, and on his inevitable failure to perform that impossible task, he forfeited his lease, his holding, and his vote. Both socially and economically the system did irreparable harm to the tenantry, and unhappily it endured long enough to effect the whole of its mischief. It was not for thirty-five years that the revolt of the peasant against his landlord came, and when it came, O'Connell was the author of it.

From 1793 to 1800, the Catholics attempted little and effected nothing. They saw that from Grattan's Parliament they had little to hope; it was to the English Parliament that they had to look. In the negotiations for the incorporating union, distinct promises of emancipation were made to the Roman Catholics, and distinct support was given in return. But when the Act of Union passed, and the time came for satisfying the hopes that had been excited, Pitt, in whose scheme Catholic Emancipation was an integral part, found that he had not sufficiently reckoned with the opposing force of the King's crazy conscientiousness, and the intriguing resistance of the high Tory lords. The Roman Catholics were left with the feeling that they had been baulked of their hopes, and even defrauded of their rights. For peaceful persuasion and influence the Imperial Parliament seemed both too distant and too ignorant; rebellion after rebellion, begun in folly and quenched in blood, had proved that there was no hope for them in force, and the time was still a generation distant when O'Connell could shew them that it was possible for the English legislature to be terrorised without insurrection, and for the unarmed

Irish to extort by threats what persuasion could not obtain.

For some years their leaders, alike Keogh for the merchant middle class, and Lord Fingal for the aristocracy, were content to advise an attitude of " dignified silence." Much had been gained in the previous twenty years. The legal position of the Irish Catholics compared favourably with that of Catholics or of Protestant Dissenters in England. Among them the franchise was so profusely distributed, that with less than one-fiftieth of the real estate of Ireland they had a clear majority of votes in the counties. The magistracy, the grand juries, and the bar, though not the bench, were open to them. With the exception of some thirty of the highest posts, they could enter both the civil and military services of the Crown. They were eligible for university degrees, and for admission to corporations. In England, on the other hand, the Test and Corporation Acts were still unrepealed. A Catholic could neither take a degree nor be an alderman. In the army he could rise no higher than the grade of a lieutenant ; he was ineligible for civil office, and was excluded from the franchise. It is true that these privileges, which were theirs in law, were but little, if at all, open to the Irish Catholics in fact; but their inferiority to the Protestants was nothing in comparison with their superiority to the position which their own fathers had held, and for a time they were disposed to be passive, and to acquiesce in the policy of Keogh. O'Connell, occupied in founding his practice at the bar, accepted this state of things; but presently the Catholics began to move, and he was among the earliest of the band of barristers who attended all the meetings, and took a lively interest in the course pursued. In 1805 a meeting

assembled, but timorously rejected a proposal to petition for the admission of Catholics to Parliament by
336 to 124, and although Keogh talked of forming
another General Committee, nothing came of it. In
February 1806 the Talents Administration came in, and
in April the new Lord Lieutenant, the Duke of Bedford,
arrived in Ireland. On the 8th of the month a meeting
was held, at which a vague association was formed, which,
through fear of the Convention Act of 1793, took no definite shape. The Duke of Bedford promised, on behalf of
the Prince of Wales, that he would admit the Roman
Catholic claims whenever he should be in a position to
do so, and the same promise seems to have been given
personally by the Prince to Lords Fingal, Petre, and
Clifden at Carlton House. Keogh, however, was not
entirely satisfied, and a speech of his at a meeting on
24th January 1807 expressed such a determined attitude
that it was reported to the King, and was not without its
influence in inducing him to refuse his assent to Lord
Howick's Relief Bill. The Catholics saw their Whig
friends, Grenville and Howick, fall in 1807, as they had
seen their Tory allies, Pitt and Canning, fall in 1801, in
a vain effort for the Catholic cause. From this time
O'Connell became convinced that it was not by soft
words, or by deferentially forbearing to advance inconvenient claims, that these claims would meet with a just
recognition.

To the "natural leaders," however, of the Catholics,
the nobility and the old-fashioned merchants, O'Connell
seemed a turbulent and importunate young man, and
their movement continued to follow the same timorous
course. Their business was managed by committees
appointed by aggregate meetings, cautiously summoned
for that purpose and immediately dissolved. A kind of

representative organization was attempted in 1807, when
delegates were summoned from several Dublin parishes ;
but on April 18th of that year a meeting was held at
which the Catholic petition was withdrawn, and the
association dissolved. Nor did any definite result follow
from the meeting held in January 1808. At last, largely
at the instance of O'Connell, a numerous meeting was
held on the 24th May 1809 at the Exhibition Room in
William Street, Dublin, and a permanent organization
was adopted. It was formed from the remaining
members of the delegation of 1792, and of the " thirty-
six addressers," and was really, if not in form, a representative body. This Committee met on November the
8th, decided to present a petition to Parliament, and
appointed a sub-committee to prepare it. The move-
ment had now a $\pi o\hat{v} \, \sigma \tau \hat{\omega}$, and proceeded continuously,
and meetings of the General Committee were held from
time to time during 1809 and 1810. In 1810 its scope
was extended by a resolution to form local boards or
committees in connection with it, but nothing more
was done than to hold occasional local meetings,
chiefly in the southern counties, during the Munster
Assizes. These meetings mark the growing influence
of O'Connell and the other Catholic barristers, men
who brought to the cause the prestige of their profession, with easy eloquence, business-like habits of
speaking, and the art of presenting a case in a broad
and telling way, but also its disadvantages, a tendency
to quibbles and to chicane, and a proneness to debate
trifles till the main object was lost sight of. At the
various meetings O'Connell was an indefatigable attendant and speaker. Two of the resolutions of the
meeting of May 1809 were proposed by him. To him
fell most of the work of drafting resolutions ; and the

Report on the Penal Code, a work of much elaboration
and research, which was principally prepared by Scully
for the Catholic Committee, was in part O'Connell's
work. Keogh was now living in a retired but respectable old age at Mount Jerome. The principal peers
who led the Catholics were Lord Fingal, Lord French,
Lord Trimleston, and Lord Gormanstown. But the
business of the organization was done in committees,
and there the leadership naturally fell into the hands of
the barristers. For a time the chief of these was James
Scully, nicknamed the Abbé Siéyes, a man of a sardonic
and scheming turn, without any gift of oratory, who
preferred to gain his ends by Machiavellian diplomacy
rather than by open agitation. While keeping himself
studiously in the background, he was, in fact, for a time
the most influential man in the body. Prominent men
also were Hussey and Clinch, members of the bar, and
Dr. Dromgoole, " the Duigenan of the Catholic cause,"
an implacable and impracticable bigot, saturated with
mediæval theology, and unable to perceive that he was
living in the nineteenth, and not in the fourteenth
century. But gradually the untiring energy, the self-
devotion, the legal acumen, and the eloquence of
O'Connell, brought him more and more to the front, till
by the beginning of 1811 his leadership was virtually
established. He would stand on the Carlisle Bridge
accosting Roman Catholic passers-by, and pressing
them to come into the meeting at the adjacent Exchange
Rooms, which were taken for the purpose in his name.

For more than twenty years before Emancipation [says his Letter to
Lord Shrewsbury] the burthen of the cause was thrown on me. I had
to arrange the meetings, to prepare the resolutions, to furnish replies to
the correspondence, to examine the case of each person complaining of
practical grievances. . . . At a period when my minutes counted by the

guinea, when my emoluments were limited only by the extent of my physical and waking powers, when my meals were shortened to the narrowest
space, and my sleep restricted to the earliest hours before dawn, at that
period, and for more than twenty years, there was no day that I did not
devote from one to two hours, often much more, to the working out
of the Catholic cause, and that without receiving or allowing the offer
of any remuneration, even for the personal expenditure incurred in
the agitation of the cause itself. For four years I bore the entire
expenses of Catholic agitation without receiving the contributions of
others to a greater amount than £74 in the whole.

A man of this calibre could not have been passed
over, but O'Connell, who was never tolerant of a rival,
forced his way to the front in a way that showed little
respect or reverence for the age and services of the
leader whom he was ousting. Long afterwards, when
he was himself ripe in age and service, and in his turn
had young men about him impatient of his cautious
policy, he told Daunt—

Keogh saw that I was calculated to become a leader. . . . The
course he then recommended was a sullen quiescence. He urged that
the Catholics should abstain altogether from agitation, and he
laboured hard to bring me to his views. But I saw that agitation was
our only available weapon. . . . I saw that by incessantly keeping
our demands and our grievances before the public and the Government, we must sooner or later succeed. Moreover, that period above
all others was not one at which our legitimate weapon, agitation, could
have been prudently let to rust. It was during the war, and while
Napoleon, that splendid madman, made the Catholics of Ireland so
essential to the military defence of the Empire, the time seemed
peculiarly appropriate to press our claims. About that period a great
Catholic meeting was held. . . . Keogh drew up a resolution, which
denounced the continued agitation of the Catholic question at that
time. This resolution, proceeding as it did from a tried old leader,
was carried. I then rose and proposed a counter-resolution, pledging
us all to incessant, unrelaxing agitation ; and such were the wiseacres
with whom I had to deal, that they passed my resolution in the
midst of enthusiastic acclamations. . . . Thenceforward, I may say, *I
was the* leader.

In O'Connell's hands, and conducted upon these principles, the agitation became so considerable that the Government was no longer able to ignore it. The Catholics were shrewdly advised, but at last they made a false step. Till the summer of 1809 the meetings had cautiously passed formal resolutions disclaiming any representative or delegated character. Then, growing bolder, they dropped them. In the beginning of 1811, upon the advice of O'Connell that such a proceeding was legal, Hay, their secretary, issued a circular calling on every county to elect delegates to the association in Dublin. Clare's Convention Act of 1793 was ready to the Lord Lieutenant's hand. On February 12th the Chief Secretary issued a letter to all magistrates, calling on them to arrest all persons advocating or taking part in any such election. On February 23rd, Darby, a police magistrate, appeared at a meeting of the Committee, and called on those present to disperse, but after a quibbling discussion he withdrew. Another attempt of the same kind was made on July 9th. On August 12th two leading delegates, Taafe, a banker, and Kirwan, a merchant, were arrested, and a warrant was issued against Dr. Sheridan. On October 19th a new Catholic committee met, composed, in defiance of the Government, of elected delegates, ten from every county, and was required to disperse by a police magistrate named Hare. On November 23rd its meeting was actually broken up, and the Catholics thought it wise to dissolve their committee. On December 26th they met and elected a non-representative Catholic Board. This was an admission of defeat. The first of the prisoners, Dr. Sheridan, had already been tried and acquitted on November 22nd, but on January 30th 1812, Kirwan was found guilty, though no sentence was passed upon him; and the

action for false imprisonment, which on Sheridan's
acquittal had been brought against Chief Justice
Downes, who had issued the warrants, resulted in the
defendant's favour. The Government was master of the
field. The Catholics had to content themselves with
holding occasional meetings in the country to protest
against the blow.

To O'Connell and the Catholics no statesman was so
hateful as Mr. Perceval. In October 1810 George III.
relapsed into insanity, and in February 1811 the Prince
of Wales became Prince Regent, but under considerable
restrictions. These expired in February 1812, and it
was thought that the Prince would indulge his Whig
proclivities by dismissing his Tory Ministers. To the
Catholics he had made many promises, and they looked
now with painful anxiety for their fulfilment. The
Prince made no sign ; Perceval remained in office. On
the 11th May, Perceval was shot in the lobby of the
House of Commons, by a crazy tradesman named Bel-
lingham. Again the Prince forgot his promises. The
influence of the Hertford family in the royal closet was
a fatal obstacle to the assumption of office by Grenville and Grey, and Perceval's colleagues continued
to carry out Perceval's policy. The mortified Catholics, with O'Connell at their head, fell into a childish
pet of rage. Perceval had hardly been in his grave a
month when O'Connell was saying of him :—

For my part, I feel unaffected horror at his fate, and all trace of
resentment for his crimes is obliterated ; but I do not forget that he
was a narrow-minded bigot, a paltry statesman, and a bad minister ;
that every species of public corruption and profligacy had in him a
flippant and pert advocate ; that every advance towards reform or
economy had in him a decided enemy ; and that the liberties of the
people were the object of his derision.

At this meeting, 18th June 1812, the Catholics passed these impolitic and impotent resolutions :—

That from authentic documents now before us we learn with deep disappointment and anguish how cruelly the promised boon of Catholic freedom has been intercepted by the fatal witchery of an unworthy secret influence, hostile to our fairest hopes, spurning alike the sanctions of public and private virtue, the demands of personal gratitude, and the sacred obligations of plighted honour.

That to this impure source we trace but too distinctly our afflicted hopes and protracted servitude, the arrogant invasion of the undoubted right of petitioning, the acrimony of illegal State prosecutions, the surrender of Ireland to prolonged oppression and insult, and the many experiments equally pitiful and perilous, recently practised upon the habitual passiveness of an ill-treated but high-spirited people.

The Catholics must have been simple indeed, and ignorant of the movements of the parties of their times, if they thought that it needed any " secret influence " but that of his own convenience to make the Prince break his word, or that nothing prevented instant Emancipation but the religious scruples of a royal favourite.

But while the Catholics conducted their agitation thus openly in Ireland, they had left the conduct of their interest in Parliament in the hands of Lord Grenville and Mr. Grattan. To Keogh, and afterwards to Lord Fingal, it was left to keep up such communication as they thought fit between the parliamentary advocates of Emancipation and the Irish party; and this method of procedure by semi-secret diplomacy led to dissension and disaster. Pitt's intention had been to deal with the Irish Catholics in a liberal spirit. His plan seems to have been first generally made known by Castlereagh in a speech in the House of Commons on 25th May 1810. " He had been authorised," he said, "to communicate with the Catholic clergy. It was then distinctly understood that the political claims of the Catholics must remain for the consideration of the Imperial Parliament, but the expediency of making without delay some provision for their clergy under proper regulations was fully recognised. The result of their deliberations was laid before Government in certain resolutions signed by ten of their bishops, including the four metropolitans, in January 1799." The bishops had met in Dublin on January 17th, 18th, and 19th, 1799, and their resolutions were:—

That a provision, through Government, for the Roman Catholic clergy of this kingdom, competent and secured, ought to be thankfully accepted; [and that] in the appointment of prelates of the Roman Catholic religion to vacant sees within the kingdom, such interference of the Government as may enable it to be satisfied of the loyalty of the persons appointed, is just and ought to be agreed to.

They went on to suggest that this interference might be provided for by sending to the Government the names of those persons whom the Catholic clergy had selected for submission to the Pope, which the Government, if satisfied with them, might thereupon forward to Rome, or, if not, return to Ireland.

For several years this idea had been at rest, but in 1808 Grattan and Ponsonby, anxious in bringing on again the question of the Catholic claims to be able to allay if possible the jealousy of English Protestantism, inquired of Fingal, who was spokesman for the Irish Catholic laity, and Dr. Milner, Vicar-General of the Midlands, who acted as agent in London for the Irish prelates, whether there was no pledge or guarantee which could be offered by the Catholics. Fingal and Milner then mentioned the check on the nomination of bishops to which the Irish prelates had been willing to con-

3 *

sent in 1799, and Milner said that the bishops,
while immovably opposed to a positive interference of
Government in their affairs, would accept such nega-
tive interference as would give the Government additional means of satisfying themselves of the loyalty of
episcopal candidates.

Accordingly, Grattan in the House of Commons,
and Lord Grenville in the House of Lords, announced
that they were empowered on the part of the Roman
Catholics to offer such an arrangement as part of
the general emancipation. Ponsonby said that the
Catholic bishops authorised him to say that they
would consent to their appointment by the Crown.
In fact, however, the Roman Catholics proved to be
divided upon the question, and, not without disin-
genuousness, Milner hastened next day to withdraw
from his pledge. The Irish bishops thought that
whatever they might have been willing to agree to nine
years before, when endowment was offered to them,
to consent to a veto now was to give up their Church's
exclusive control over her own discipline. A synod
was held of all the bishops of Ireland, which condemned it with but three dissentients; and on 14th
September they formally resolved that it was inexpe-
dient to make any alteration in the mode of appointing
bishops. An address of thanks to them for this course
was signed by forty thousand laymen. Among the
Catholic laity, however, there was a party, who on this
point were in close agreement with Charles Butler and
the English Catholics, with whom the idea of this
Crown veto seems to have originated about 1791.
Lord Southwell and Sir Edward Bellew requested an
explanation of the meaning of this episcopal resolution.
Archbishop O'Reilly cautiously replied that, without de-

finitively pronouncing a Crown veto contrary to the doctrine and discipline of the Church, the bishops saw danger, for the present at least, in such interference by Ministers in Church affairs. Their opposition, however, became steadily more uncompromising, and the majority of the laity applauded their action.

In 1810, on February 25th, the bishops voted their unconditional adherence to the resolutions of September 1808, and declared "that it is the undoubted and exclusive right of Roman Catholic bishops to discuss all matters appertaining to the doctrines and discipline of the Roman Catholic Church," and that they knew of no stronger pledge of their loyalty than the oath then in force. Grattan, in presenting the Catholic petition in that year, was obliged to announce that he could no longer offer any securities on the part of the Catholics. On the other hand, the nobility, almost without exception, and no inconsiderable part of the middle class members of the committee, were for the veto. Lord Fingal, Sir Edward Bellew, and Woulfe, afterwards Chief Baron, seceded from the Board. Sheil, then a very young but rising man, opposed a motion of Dromgoole's against securities in any form, with a declaration that the agitation about securities had deplorably thrown back the cause of Emancipation, and that if restrictions not more severe than those borne by the Church of England would satisfy the invincible prejudices of the English, the English ought to be humoured. O'Connell took him sharply to task. He pronounced this view a "doctrine of slavery," a "base and vile traffic," and "a peddling and huxtering speculation." He said that to accept the restrictions was to plead guilty to all the charges that the English made against Papists; that no Protestant

Minister could act honestly in the appointment of
Roman Catholic bishops; that ministerial bishops
would be a means of uncatholicising Ireland, and
bishoprics the reward of the political services of ministerial toadies; and he laid down in the most explicit
terms the absolute discretion of the bishops themselves in the matter. "If the revered and venerable
prelates of our Church, exercising their discretion as to
that which belongs to them exclusively, the details of
discipline, shall deem it right to establish a domestic
nomination purely and exclusively Irish . . . the Board
will not interfere with such arrangement."

Meantime, to the English Emancipationists the course
of Irish Catholic opinion was of no moment, except in
so far as its violence might endanger the cause, by disgusting the English public. It was the episcopate of
the English not of the Irish Catholic Church, the House
of Commons and not the Catholic Committee, which had
to be persuaded. From the time when Castlereagh joined
the Government in 1812, Emancipation was an open
question. Napoleon's invasion of Russia, as yet pros-
perous, was filling the nation with alarm, and bringing
it into a conciliatory frame of mind; and on June 22nd,
1812, Canning moved a resolution, which pledged the
House of Commons " early in the next session to take
into their consideration the laws affecting the Roman
Catholics, with a view to their final and conciliatory ad-
justment." It was carried by a majority of 129, the
largest majority in favour of the Roman Catholics in
Canning's lifetime. Charles Butler thereupon began to
draft a bill, and, largely upon Canning's advice, inserted elaborate " securities " clauses. One provided
for an oath to be taken by every Catholic clergyman,
that he would not assent to or concur in the appoint-

ment of any Catholic prelate in Ireland, unless he should consider such prelate to be of unimpeachable loyalty and peaceful conduct, and the oath proceeded, " I have not and will not have any communication with the Pope tending directly or indirectly to overthrow or disturb the Protestant Government or the Protestant Church of Great Britain and Ireland, or the Church of Scotland as by law established, or on any matter or thing not purely spiritual or ecclesiastical." To further ensure the safety of Protestantism, a Board of Commissioners, partly Protestant and partly Roman Catholic, was to be appointed to inquire into the character of nominees for vacant sees or deaneries, in order to ascertain whether there was any shadow on their loyalty or conduct. Subject to these restrictions, the House of Commons and all offices except those of Lord Chancellor or Lord Keeper and Lord Lieutenant or Lord Deputy, were to be thrown open to the Roman Catholics. On March 2nd, 1813, Grattan carried a motion in the House of Commons in favour of Emancipation by 264 to 224, and in April he introduced this bill. The majority rose to 42 on the second reading, but in committee, on the motion of Abbott, the Speaker, the admission of Catholics to Parliament was thrown out by 251 to 247 on May 24th, and the bill was withdrawn. It never was reintroduced, for on the very verge of victory the friends of the Catholics found their cause compromised by the conduct of the leaders and people in Ireland. When the rumour of the proposals got abroad, they provoked not gratitude for the boon, but fury at the safeguards. Before the result of the Speaker's motion was known in Ireland the prelates had met on May 27th, and unanimously resolved " that the ecclesiastical securities are absolutely incompatible with

the discipline of the Roman Catholic Church and with
the free exercise of our religion; without incurring the
guilt of schism we cannot accede to such regulations,
neither can we dissemble our dismay and consternation
at the consequences which such regulations, if enforced,
must necessarily produce." The Catholic Board hotly
debated whether the laity were to be excluded from a
boon because the prelates objected to its attendant
securities as uncanonical. O'Connell warmly defended
the bishops, and attacked Grattan violently for ever
consenting to such clauses. During the autumn, meetings in various parts of Ireland denounced Grattan's
" securities." In November a correspondence took place
between the Board and Grattan and Lord Donoughmore, in which both the latter refused further communica-
tions if the policy was to be that no securities were to be
inserted in any Relief Bill, except such as might please
the Roman Catholic bishops; such a demand, said they,
was to dictate to Parliament and leave it a bare choice
between Aye and No. Personal relations grew strained.
Scully declined to meet Plunket; Plunket talked of not
attending Parliament at all; and Lord Donoughmore was
with difficulty restrained from challenging his opponents
on the Catholic Board. In the following spring O'Connell moved at the Board to take the petition out of
the veteran Grattan's hands, and to send over a deputation to select some English member to whom it might
be entrusted. He withdrew his motion, but though
Grattan consented to present the petition, neither the
demand of the Board nor an aggregate meeting could
prevail upon him to move its discussion.

Meantime, both parties naturally had their eyes
turned to Rome. Wyse and others were in Rome on
behalf of the Vetoists; a friar named Richard Hayes, a

nominee of O'Connell's, represented, but without tact or discretion, the Domestic Nomination party. Since the annexation of the States of the Church in 1809, the Pope had been the pensioned prisoner of Napoleon in France. Quarantotti, the Vice-Prefect of the Propaganda, was in charge of the Holy See. In the beginning of 1814, it appeared that the Holy See itself had none of those fears of schism which agitated the Irish prelates. On February 16th, Quarantotti wrote from Rome to Dr. Poynter, the English Vicar Apostolic :—

Nos, qui summo absente pastore sacris missionibus præfecti sumus et Pontificiis omnibus facultatibus ad id communiti, muneris nostri partes esse putavimus omnem ambiguitatem atque objectionem removere, quæ optatæ conciliationi possit obsistere. Habito igitur dóctissimorum præsulum ac theologorum consilio, perspectis litteris tum ab Amplitate tua, tum ab Archiepiscopo Dubliniensi huc missis, ac re in peculiari congregationi mature perpensa, decretum est, ut Catholici legem, quæ superiore anno rogata fuit pro illorum emancipatione juxta formam, quæ ab Amplitate tua relata est, aequo gratoque animo excipiant et amplectantur.

The letter fell on the Irish Catholics like a bombshell. From the highest to the lowest they were in dismay. "What shall we do," said a servant-maid, "is it, can it be true the Pope has turned Orangeman?" But the clergy soon rallied. They pronounced the letter of Quarantotti a nullity and a usurpation. Dr. Coppinger, Bishop of Cloyne, called it "a very mischievous document." O'Shaughnessy, Bishop of Dromore, pronounced it "pernicious." The priests of the Archdiocese of Dublin resolved that it was non-obligatory, for want of the signature of the Pope, and expressed an opinion that nothing less august than an Œcumenical Council was competent to deal with the relations between an Irish bishop and an English Secretary of State. The bishops assembled at Maynooth and voted

the letter not to be mandatory.   An aggregate meeting
of the laity, held at Dublin on May 19th, was even
more sturdy.   Though throughout the controversy the
securities question had been treated as a matter peculiarly of a canonical and ecclesiastical nature, the meeting resolved " that we deem it a duty to ourselves and
our country solemnly and distinctly to declare that any
decree, mandate, rescript, or decision whatsoever of any
foreign power or authority, religious or civil, ought not
and can not of right assume any dominion or control
over the political concerns of the Catholics of Ireland."
In July they even procured of the Pope the dismissal of
the luckless Vice-Prefect and a repudiation of his
letter.   But the Catholics of Ireland had resisted too
long.   Grattan abandoned the Catholic claims for the
session.   The Allies entered Paris; the war was over;
the pressure of twenty years of danger was removed.
Irish discontent no longer put the English in any jeo-
pardy.   On the 3rd of June the Catholic Board was
proclaimed.

    This stubborn objection to securities in any shape or
form cost the Catholics fourteen years of waiting for
Emancipation, and cost both England and Ireland no
one can say how much strife and ill-feeling, agitation
and bigotry.   It is difficult to suppose that the large
majority in the House of Commons, which voted for
Catholic Relief in 1813, was much actuated by fear
of Catholic discontent during the continuance of the
war or by anything but a sense of the injustice under
which the Catholics laboured.   The effect of unanimity
among the Catholics and of moderation in their language would, it can hardly be doubted, have turned the
scale in their favour within a very short time.   In 1812,
the Marquis Wellesley, who had every opportunity of

forming a just forecast, was standing with Charles Butler behind the throne during the Catholic debate in the House of Lords. "Sir," said he to Butler, "if the Catholics conduct their cause with propriety, I insure you success in three years, perhaps in one." That the success which was then so close at hand was not achieved until 1829 was the doing of the priests and O'Connell.

A change had come over the priesthood since the last generation, which had profoundly altered its character. The priests then were necessarily educated abroad, and naturally, therefore, were drawn from families of means and position. Many of them were Englishmen. Thus they were ready enough to acquiesce in a control which, in its intention at least, was nothing but a legitimate assurance by the State of its own safety. But the alteration in the Catholic laws had given the clergy the means of education at home, and their body had become more insular and isolated, more professional and more Irish. A few prelates breathed secret fears that domestic nomination pure and simple might vulgarise the episcopate, but, practically without exception, the priesthood would accept no State supervision of their conduct in ecclesiastical affairs. In this they were supported by O'Connell with ardour and even intemperate heat.

There was something of the ecclesiastic in O'Connell's temperament; he had been educated by priests, and his deep personal piety attached him to the priesthood so unhesitatingly, that even in politics, where most men, however religious, feel a lurking doubt of ecclesiastics, however disinterested, no mistrust came between him and them. There was, indeed, much to be said against the veto, though perhaps not enough to outweigh the advantage of a settlement of the question forthwith.

Hitherto the Church of Rome had been subject to no State control in ecclesiastical matters. It was subject to prohibitions, which were disregarded, and to penalties which were not enforced, but in its spiritual affairs as such the State did not interfere. The veto required the priests to make a sacrifice of spiritual freedom ; the freedom which was to be thereby purchased was a temporal one, to be enjoyed by the laity. Pitt's veto was to have been in consideration of an endowment to Roman Catholics, but there was now no suggestion of any endowment. The clergy resolved to wait for better terms. With its past and its principles, the Church of Rome has a corporate pride, which it prefers to maintain at the price of a moderate martyrdom.

O'Connell, however, had a political object in resisting any such compromise. Though the Imperial Parliament had done nothing for Ireland since the Union but pass Coercion Acts, which, it must be admitted, intermittent rebellion and chronic disturbance during a time of national struggle with foreign foes did much to justify, there was no specific reform, except Catholic Relief, which any unanimous or influential party then demanded. Although perhaps no part of the law was beyond need of a radical change, the most immediate cause of Irish discontent was the corrupt state and constant maladministration of the unpaid magistracy. But behind all questions and grievances there remained a deep, though voiceless, yearning for Repeal, and it was his desire for Repeal that determined O'Connell for the present to keep open the grievance of the Catholic Disabilities. Ardent as he was for the relief of his co-religionists, his first aim in politics, as it was his last, was to restore their Parliament to his countrymen. " It was the Union," he said, " which first stirred me

up to come forward in politics. I was maddened when
I heard the bells of St. Patrick's ringing out a joyful
peal for Ireland's degradation, as if it were a glorious
national festival. My blood boiled, and I vowed on
that morning that the dishonour should not last if I
could put an end to it." The meeting at which he made
his first public appearance had been one held by the Catholics in the Royal Exchange Hall on 13th January 1800,
to protest against the Union. He had risen, an unknown lawyer, to make his speech, when the tramp of
yeomanry was heard outside, and the clank of musket-
butts grounded on the stones of the portico. Major
Sirr appeared in the midst of the affrighted Catholics
and demanded to see the resolutions. They had been
originally drafted by Curran in very fiery terms, but in
deference to the timidity of some of the Catholics, they
had been toned down, and were found unexceptionable.
Sirr threw them back on the table saying "There is no
harm in these," and retired, and the meeting was
allowed to proceed. But as time went on, O'Connell
saw that to weld the people of Ireland into a compact
united mass, resolutely demanding Repeal, was at once
indispensable and almost hopeless. Faction had been
the bane of Irish politics. Even on the Emancipation
question he found the clergy timid, the aristocracy
jealous of the merchants, the merchants jealous of the
aristocracy, the barristers jealous of one another, and
the masses ignorant, utterly unused to political deliberation or action, willing to throw up their hats and
cheer if a favourite of the hour appeared upon the
street, but fickle and untrustworthy, and politically
powerless. A resort to arms was a madness and a
crime. Nothing but a generation of agitation could
educate and unite the Irish people into a political force,

and no question but Catholic Relief could be agitated through a generation. In the thick of the veto conflict he said, at a meeting in Dublin on 29th June 1813 :—

> Your enemies say that I wish for a separation between England and Ireland. The charge is false, to use a modern quotation, " false as hell." Next, your enemies accuse me of a desire for the indepen- dence of Ireland. I admit the charge, and let them make the most of it. I have seen Ireland a kingdom. I reproach myself with having lived to behold her a province. Yes, I confess it—I will ever be candid upon the subject—I have an ulterior object, the Repeal of the Union, and the restoration to Ireland of her old independence. . . . Desiring as I do the Repeal of the Union, I rejoice to see how our enemies promote that great object. Yes, they promote its inevitable success by their very hostility to Ireland; they delay the liberties of the Catholic, but they compensate us most amply, because they advance the restoration of Ireland. By leaving one cause of agitation they have created, and they will embody and give shape and form to a public mind and a public spirit. I repeat it, the delay of Emancipa- tion I hear with pleasure, because in that delay is included the only prospect of obtaining my great, my ultimate object, the legislative independence of my native land.

Whether O'Connell was wise or unwise in his strategy must depend on the view which is taken of the prospect, and the value of Repeal. But of his disinterestedness he gave the best of proofs. As yet, outside of Dublin, agitation had not won him the adoration of the populace. The course that he took did win for him the dislike of the nobility and the gentry of his party. It is true that on December 16th, 1813, the Catholics presented him with a service of plate of the value of a thousand guineas, but year by year agitation cost him much in money and more in time, which was more precious to him than money. He had a large practice, but he had also a large family,* large expenses, and as yet little or no patrimony. The " good behaviour" of the Irish Catholics could hardly

---

* O'Connell married his cousin, Mary O'Connell, in 1802.

have failed, on the passing of Grattan's Bill, to have been rewarded with professional promotion. O'Connell, not yet obnoxious to any English person or party, would have been one of the first recipients of a silk gown, and must have risen inevitably at a stride to the highest position and emoluments of his profession ; and if he wished for more, who so likely to be among the first Roman Catholic members of Parliament as the great King's Counsel, the eloquent orator, the champion of the Catholic cause, in the sense in which the gentry understood the term ? All this was within his grasp, and he threw it all away. He preferred to fight the battle of the priests and of Repeal, at the cost of the disapproval of equals and of professional sacrifices. Of the wisdom of this policy the course of events has raised, and still sustains, a doubt ; but of the courage, foresight, and disinterestedness of O'Connell there can be none.

CHAPTER III.

CATHOLIC DESPONDENCY.

1814-1823.

State of Affairs after the Dissolution of the Board—O'Connell's Duel
with D'Esterre—Affair with Peel—Trial of Magee for libel on the
Duke of Richmond—Visit of George IV. to Dublin.

THE suppression of the Board was a terrible blow to
the Catholics.   Except his last days, the next seven
years were the darkest of O'Connell's life.   A meeting
was held at his house, which resolved upon submission; indeed, there was nothing else to be done.
For the time being the back of the agitation was
broken.   In vain he endeavoured to rally his followers.
Next year, with characteristic hopefulness he declared
that after much deliberation he was sure during that
session they would get at least a portion of emancipation.   He was wrong in his forecast, and his hopefulness effected nothing.   The Vetoists, too, were
powerless.   Small and timid meetings were held at Lord
Fingal's house, which merely resolved to leave the
Catholic petition in the hands of Grattan and Lord
Donoughmore, and to found an association to take the

place of the Board. The split between the two parties, the "securities" men and the "bold measure" men, was too deep to be remedied. The controversy had degenerated into a personal struggle, in which each party imputed to the other every baseness. It was long before this animosity was appeased, and the misfortune was the greater because English public opinion never was more favourable to Emancipation than then. The two parties endeavoured, but in vain, to support separate organizations. The Vetoists held meetings at Lord Trimleston's house; the Catholic Association, which succeeded the Board in February 1815, met at Fitzpatrick's in Capel Street. The former left their petition in Grattan's hands; the latter entrusted theirs to Sir Henry Parnell. Both were represented by Lord Donoughmore in the House of Lords. O'Connell boldly denied that a small body of seceders, meeting in private, had any right to speak for the Catholics at large. In February 1817 the Vetoists advertised a meeting to be held in Dublin at No. 50 Eccles Street. O'Connell and a few others decided to invade it. They were confronted at the door with an order, signed by Lord Southwell and Sir Edward Bellew, that no one was to be admitted who was not a party to the Catholic petition committed to Grattan the year before. They put the footboy and his orders aside, and, to the consternation of the decorous meeting upstairs, appeared in the drawingroom. They were requested to withdraw, and declined. The outraged Vetoists took refuge in a motion for an immediate adjournment. O'Connell challenged it, and delivered a long and vigorous speech against the "securities." But nothing practical resulted. Such a course might inspire his own shrinking followers with temporary courage, but it failed to conciliate the Veto party. By this time the politics of the see of Rome had changed with the restoration of the Pope to the Vatican. The Association had adopted an address of remonstrance to His Holiness on the 16th September 1815, but the Pope evaded their reproaches by treating it as a lay intervention in matters ecclesiastical, and declined to receive it officially. The parish priests and a majority of the prelates were in O'Connell's favour, but so exclusively moral was their support, that they could not even raise the rent of the rooms in Capel Street which the Association occupied. For a time he paid the rent himself, and then, finding that he had to bear the whole working expenses of the Association, removed it to smaller rooms in Cross Street. In January 1817 he made an attempt to found a society of "Friends of Reform in Parliament," of which both Catholics and Protestants were to be members, but after a few meetings it collapsed. A lethargy fell on the Catholics; it was the winter of their discontent, the low-water mark of their activity. A man of only common courage must have given up the fight in despair.

In such a state of affairs as this, O'Connell, who rarely restrained his language, did not mince matters, but spoke of his opponents with asperity. He called the Dublin Corporation, then a stronghold of Protestantism, a "beggarly corporation." One of its members was a Mr. J. N. D'Esterre, a native of Limerick, who was nominally a merchant, but was said to be in indigent circumstances, though of unimpeachable respectability. In his youth he had served in the marines, and, being seized by the mutineers in 1797, during the mutiny at the Nore, was placed with the noose round his neck ready to be swung up to the yard-arm.

At the last moment they offered him life if he would join them. "No, never!" cried the intrepid officer. "Hang away, and be damned to you!" The answer so enchanted the tars that he was immediately set at liberty. He now, egged on perhaps by others, who saw a chance of getting rid of O'Connell, decided to take up the cause of his outraged corporation. The duel was at this time a recognised instrument of party warfare. Even in England statesmen and ministers stood to receive each other's fire. Pitt and Tierney, Canning and Castlereagh, the Duke of Wellington and the Earl of Winchelsea, Fitzgibbon and Curran, had fought, and even Peel was bellicose and a sender of hostile messages. Among English statesmen, it is true, these encounters were generally bloodless, but the Irish took the matter more seriously, and the chance that a political opponent might be removed in a political duel was considerable. To drink sparingly of your host's best claret, to decide at petty sessions for a tenant against his landlord, or to seduce a forty-shilling freeholder's allegiance in a county election, touched the point of honour, and the personal affront could only be atoned for with bloodshed. It was the first time that O'Connell, who was reported a good marksman, had had a serious affair. In August 1813, during the Limerick Assizes, he went out with Counsellor Magrath, with whom he had come to blows in open court, but when the combatants met in the usual battle-place, the old court-mill field, their friends adjusted the matter. On the 26th January 1815 D'Esterre wrote to O'Connell to demand explanations. Next day O'Connell undauntedly replied, that while individually esteeming many of its members, he despised the corporation generally for its bigotry. After this he prepared himself in due course to receive

4 *

D'Esterre's friends, but no friends came. D'Esterre wrote again on the 28th, but did not take the final step. At length, on Tuesday, January 31st, a rumour got about that D'Esterre, though but a little man, proposed to cane his burly antagonist in the Hall of the Four Courts, and a crowd gathered to see it done. O'Connell, determined not to baulk him, showed himself in the streets all the afternoon, and public attention being excited, a party of five hundred gentlemen followed him about to enjoy the fun or to prevent an assault. O'Connell had to take refuge from their importunity in a tavern. This scene of braggadocio was closed in the evening by the arrival of Mr. Justice Day at O'Connell's house to arrest him and prevent a breach of the peace. His lordship went away pacified with O'Connell's pledge not to be the challenger. At length next day Sir Edward Stanley, then barrack-master in Dublin, waited with D'Esterre's challenge on Major Macnamara, a Protestant gentleman, who was acting for O'Connell. A meeting was arranged for half-past three o'clock that afternoon, in a meadow in Lord Ponsonby's demesne, about twelve miles from the city. The days were short, and the snow was lying on the ground. All Dublin knew what was going on, and was in wild anxiety for the fate of O'Connell. A large number of gentlemen rode out to the field to see the fighting. Punctually at half-past three O'Connell arrived; D'Esterre was nearly an hour late. The combatants were placed opposite each other, each with a pistol in either hand, and about twenty minutes to five the word was given. They fired almost simultaneously, D'Esterre slightly the first. O'Connell aimed low, and D'Esterre, struck in the hip, fell, bleeding profusely. The party separated. As O'Connell quitted the field, there dashed up a troop of horse sent by the Executive to protect D'Esterre, in case of his victory, from the fury of the mob. The people lined the roads, and when they saw their favourite returning in safety, raised shouts of joy. Bonfires blazed till midnight in the streets of Dublin. Meantime, poor D'Esterre was carried to his house, but the ball could not be found, and, after much suffering, he expired next day. The dead man's family disclaimed any intention of prosecuting; but O'Connell was filled with remorse at this untoward event. He settled a pension on the widow, and never afterwards passed D'Esterre's house without baring his head and breathing a prayer.

At some time after D'Esterre's death, he registered a vow that he would never fight again, and upon this ground refused the many challenges which his vehement invective subsequently brought upon him. The vow, however, was not made in the first keenness of remorse for D'Esterre's loss. Peel, who as Chief Secretary was alive to the formidable power of O'Connell, took care to quote to the House of Commons passages from his more violent speeches. At an aggregate meeting on August 29th, 1815, O'Connell retaliated by saying :—

I am told he has in my absence, and in a place where he was privileged from any account, grossly traduced me. I said at the last meeting, in the presence of the note-takers of the police, who are paid by him, that he was too prudent to attack me in my presence. I see the same police informers here now, and I authorise them carefully to report these my words, that Mr. Peel would not dare, in my presence and in any place where he was liable to personal account, use a single expression derogatory to my interest or my honour.

Peel had been attacked by O'Connell fiercely enough before. He had been spoken of as "that ludicrous

enemy of ours, who has got in jest the name he de-
serves in good earnest of Orange Peel, a raw youth
squeezed out of the workings of I know not what factory in England, who . . . was sent over here before
he had got rid of the foppery of perfumed handkerchiefs
and thin shoes." But this was too direct an attack to
be passed over. On the 31st Sir Charles Saxton waited
on O'Connell on Peel's behalf, and offered him the
usual satisfaction if he felt aggrieved. O'Connell replied that Peel's conduct was "handsome and gentle-
manlike," but he must consult his friends, though for
his own part he hoped they might advise fighting.
The advice of the friends was that, in effect, the speech
made O'Connell the aggressor, and the challenge therefore could not come from him. Saxton, who seems
to have thought that O'Connell wished to evade a
meeting, published a version of the affair in the
papers, which O'Connell answered by regretting that
his opponents should have preferred "a paper war,"
and calling the publication "a dirty trick." On September the 4th, Peel replied by sending a challenge
to O'Connell by Colonel Browne. The affair was,
of course, public property, and in her alarm poor
Mrs. O'Connell sent to the Sheriff to prevent a
breach of the peace. Late at night that functionary
arrived, took O'Connell in bed, and caused him to be
bound over in a considerable sum to keep the peace;
but when he went to the Chief Secretary's house to
take Peel also, he found that Peel with Browne and
Saxton had quitted it for England. Next day O'Connell sent Mr. Bennett to Colonel Browne with an offer
to meet Peel at any place on the Continent that might
suit his convenience. Browne proposed that the parties
should proceed, separately and as soon as possible, to

Ostend, binding themselves to secrecy, and should leave their addresses at the post office there. To this Peel agreed: he set off and reached Ostend on the 14th. O'Connell was to elude observation by sailing for the Continent from Waterford. But the police were on the alert; they had received orders to transmit to the Foreign Secretary the names of all passengers by the packets from the southern and western ports of Ireland, and were watching the coast of Essex. O'Connell changed his plans, and contrived to get over to England from the south of Ireland. But the authorities in London, too, were on the watch. Peel's father, not less anxious than O'Connell's wife, is said to have offered a reward of fifty guineas for O'Connell's capture. Being detained by the necessity of getting passports at the Dutch Embassy, he concealed himself as well as he could, changed his lodging from the British Hotel to Holyland's Coffee House in the Strand, and ordered a postchaise for Brighton at 4 A.M. one Monday morning. But the police were hanging about at 8 A.M. As he was stepping into his carriage he was arrested by Lavender, a Bow Street runner, armed with the warrant of Lord Chief Justice Ellenborough. He was taken before Mr. Justice Le Blanc and bound over in his own recognizances of £1,000 and two others of £500 each, to keep the peace and not to quit London till the first day of the following term. The duel was thus finally prevented: nor did O'Connell ever fight again. Some short time afterwards O'Connell was arguing an obscure legal point before Lord Norbury. "My Lord!" said he, "I fear I do not make myself understood." "Oh! Mr. O'Connell," said his lordship, "I am sure no one is more easily *apprehended.*"

Later in life O'Connell's bitter tongue brought on

him other challenges.   In 1825, being challenged by
Leyne, a Kerry barrister, he lodged an information
against him.   A year or two later Sheehy, an outraged
newspaper proprietor of Cork, cuffed him in the streets
of Dublin with the same result.   In 1830 the Chief
Secretary, Sir Henry Hardinge sent him a message,
Lord Alvanley sent him one in 1835, and in the same
year Mr. Disraeli challenged his son.   He incurred
the severest censure for running riot with his tongue
while denying to his wounded opponents the satisfaction
of falling by his pistol ; but although it is impossible
to approve his conduct in using the strongest language and declining to take the consequences, his
action certainly did a great deal to discredit the
practice.

Meantime he was pursuing his practice at the bar,
and his professional fame was at its height.   Unlike
Curran, whose bitter enemy, Lord Clare, practically ex-
pelled him from practice in the Court of Chancery,
O'Connell could not be ousted from any court, however
grievously he offended the judges.   His practice lay
equally in equity and at common law.   In July
1813 the trial of John Magee, the proprietor of the
Dublin Evening Post, for a libel on the Duke of
Richmond, gave him the opportunity of his greatest
forensic effort.   The libel in question had been written
by James Scully, though some of Magee's friends even
suggested that it came from O'Connell's hand.   As
Peel wrote to the Speaker Abbott, the prosecution was
intended to wrest from the Catholic Committee its most
formidable weapon, the Press.   If Magee gave up the
writer's name he would become the enemy of the Committee ; if the Committee left him to take the punishment himself, it would become the enemy of Magee.

The trial took place in the hottest hour of the "securities" controversy. After innumerable wrangles about challenges, and charges of misconduct in striking the panel, an Orange jury was sworn. There was but too good a reason to fear that the jury panel had been tampered with. John Gifford, a bitter and bigoted partisan, whom Lord Hardwick, when Lord Lieutenant, had dismissed from the Registrarship of the Dublin Custom House for his violent attacks on the Catholics, and the Duke of Richmond, during his term of office, had reinstated as Accountant-General of Customs, had said of such a jury, with profane glee, in the previous year, " If Our Saviour himself were in the dock they would find him guilty if it served their party." To such a jury O'Connell thought it useless to appeal, and, abandoning any attempt to secure an acquittal, he devoted himself to a full and brilliant exposition and defence of the Catholic policy. The Chief Justice checked him and said it was irrelevant. "You heard the Attorney-General traduce and calumniate us," cried O'Connell, fiercely ; "you heard him with patience and with temper— listen now to our vindication." Such a course was not likely to help Magee's cause much, whatever it might do for the Catholics. He was convicted, and sentenced to two years' imprisonment and a fine of £500.

But through these years O'Connell was chafing impatiently at the apathy of his party and the helplessness of his political condition. The Parliamentary position of Emancipation had suffered severely by the loss of the Relief Bill of 1813. It was not mentioned in the session of 1814 ; and Parnell's motion on presenting the Catholic petition was lost in 1815 by 228 to 147, in the very Parliament which had been in its favour two years before. In 1816 Grattan's motion on presenting the petition of the Vetoists was rejected by 31. In 1817 the hostile majority was 24; in 1819 he made his last effort on behalf of the Catholics and was defeated in the House of Commons by 2 only (243 to 241); but the Lords remained staunch and rejected a similar motion by 147 to 106. In 1820 Grattan died and Plunket succeeded to the conduct of the question. On the 28th February 1821, in the greatest of all his speeches, he moved that the House should go into Committee on the Catholic claims, and he carried his motion by 6 (227 to 221). On March 7th he introduced two Bills, one of which opened to Catholics the House of Commons and all offices except the Lord Chancellorship and the Lord Lieutenancy, and the other gave the Crown a veto on the appointment of bishops and required of Catholic priests an oath similar to that of 1813. The two Bills were consolidated, and carried by 216 to 197 in April. But the Lords were immovable; the Duke of York denounced it, and it was lost by 39.

O'Connell, however, concerned himself more with Irish than with English feeling. Willing to clutch at any straw for help, he proposed, on January 1st, 1821, in one of the public letters that since 1819 he had periodically addressed through the Press to the Irish people, that the Catholics should ally themselves with the English working-class democracy, and postpone Emancipation to Reform. Sheil, who knew better the strength, which their friends proved in Parliament six weeks afterwards, at once issued a strong letter against the proposal, denouncing it as "pernicious." O'Connell replied on January 12th with a caustic epistle, which left the honours of controversy with him, though in judgment and common sense Sheil had the best of of it.

In the autumn George IV. paid the first Royal visit
to Ireland since the reign of William III. He landed
on the 12th August, and was received with acclamations of applause. The Catholics founded great
political hopes on so rare an event. O'Connell and
the Ascendency champion, Bradley King, ex-Lord-
Mayor, were reconciled. A political banquet was
arranged, at which Catholics chose the Protestant
stewards and Protestants the Catholics. O'Connell, who
less than a year before had solicited and obtained
the Queen's Attorney-Generalship in Ireland, in order,
as he said, "to annoy some of the greatest scoundrels
in society, and, of course, the bitterest enemies of Ireland," now declared that "in sorrow and in bitterness
he had for the last fifteen years laboured for his unhappy country. One bright day had realised all his
fond expectations. . . . It was said of St. Patrick that
he had the power to banish venomous reptiles from the
isle, but His Majesty had performed a greater moral
miracle. The sound of his approach had allayed the
dissensions of centuries"; and the Catholics presented
an address, which assured the King that "you are hailed
with the benedictions of an enthusiastic and undis-
sembling people." When His Majesty departed,
O'Connell knelt and presented him with a laurel wreath,
which his sovereign was graciously pleased to accept.
To tempt His Majesty to return, he started a subscription to build him a royal palace; but could only raise
funds sufficient to build a bridge. He founded a Royal
Georgean Club to perpetuate the sentiments of amity
which the royal visit had awakened. But the bright
hopes of 1821 were doomed to the bitterest disappointment. The winter was disgraced by outrage and disorder and rendered lamentable by famine. In 1822

Plunket did not venture to raise the Catholic question.
In Dublin, Catholic and Protestant fell to their quarrels
as before, and dissension broke out among the Catholics
themselves.   Their temporary unanimity only made
their perennial dissension more painful.

  At the beginning of 1823 [said Sheil in 1827] an entire cessation of Catholic meetings had taken place.   We had virtually abandoned the question; not only was it not debated in Parliament, but in Ireland there was neither Committee, Board, nor Association.   The result was that a total stagnation of public feeling took place, and I do not exaggerate, when I say that the Catholic question was nearly forgotten . . . we sat down like galley-slaves in a calm.   A general stagnation diffused itself over the the national feelings. . . . What was the result?   It was two-fold.   The question receded in England, and fell back from the general notice.   There it was utterly forgotten, while in Ireland the spirit and energy of the people underwent an utter relaxation, and the most vigorous efforts were necessary to repair all the moral deterioration which the whole body of the Irish Catholics had sustained.

CHAPTER IV.

THE CATHOLIC ASSOCIATION.

1823-1828.

The germ of the Catholic Association—The Catholic Rent—The Act
of 1825—The Relief Bill and Wings of 1825—The New Catholic
Association—The Waterford and Clare Elections.

In April 1823 O'Connell was staying at Glencullen, in
the Wicklow Mountains, at the house of his friend
Thomas O'Mara. Sheil, with whom he had been in
not unfrequent conflict during the previous ten years,
and a few other friends were there. To them, one
evening after dinner, he broached the scheme out
of which grew the Catholic Association and the Catholic Relief Act. He had long seen that the disunion
of the upper and educated classes was the bane
of Catholic politics. Two forces there were which had
never been awakened and unchained—the Priest and the
Peasant. The failure of the hopes which the King's
visit excited determined him to look to the upper classes
no longer : from thenceforth he would go to the people.
   He conceived the plan of enlisting the enthusiasm of
the whole agricultural population of Ireland, while
keeping the leadership in the hands of the educated

classes, by means of a gigantic system of local and central organizations, officered by the priesthood and controlled from Dublin. The funds, which an agitation on so great a scale would demand, were more than the donations of the opulent could raise; he determined that the main source of the riches of his new Association should be the poor. All classes were to be admitted to it. It was to be divided into two kinds of members, those who paid a guinea per annum and those who paid a shilling. It shows how miserably poor the Irish were, that a contribution of a farthing per week should have been enough to make each member feel that he had a share in the great Association. Yet two years later it was proved in evidence that wages in Ireland were but fourpence a day, and that out of a population estimated at seven millions, one million lived by mendicancy or plunder.

The moment seemed one of the very darkest for the hopes of Ireland that O'Connell, at least, had ever seen. The Irish, whom legislation had deprived of their manufactures, and want of coal had prevented from regaining them, were a purely agricultural community. The fall of prices upon the termination of the long war had produced grave distress among the farmers. This had been intensified by commercial panics and the depreciation of commercial credit. The winter of 1822 had been marked by famine, which was followed by pestilence. One-third of Clare was starving, nor was the rest of the south and west better off. In Cork 120,000 persons were living on charity. Crime, too, was rife; 366 persons were tried by special commission at Cork alone, and thirty-five of them were sentenced to death. The tentative measure of Catholic Relief which, in default of the reintroduction of Plunket's

Bill of 1821, Canning had brought in and carried through the House of Commons, was ruthlessly rejected by the House of Lords, and the Lord-Lieutenancy of Lord Wellesley, which was to have been a period of reconciliation, was marked by fierce outbreaks of sectarian animosity, culminating in the ludicrous but discreditable "Bottle Riot" of December 1822.

A preliminary meeting, which a few gentlemen were induced to attend, was held at Dempsey's Tavern, Sackville Street, on April 25th, 1823. From May 12th the meetings were held at Coyne's, the bookseller's, at 4, Capel Street, in a mean room on the second floor. Rules were framed for holding public debates upon a Parliamentary model, to which reporters and the public were to be admitted. By now the old bitterness of the veto controversy had had nearly ten years in which to die out. Some of those who had shared it were dead, others had forgotten the issue which, though not openly mentioned, had been really in dispute, whether layman or ecclesiastic was to control party politics. The way for united action was open. Slowly peers, prelates, priests, and peasants gathered round the young Association. Lord Gormanstown sacrificed his early views to join it. Lord Killeen, Lord Fingal's eldest son, and Lord Kenmare, became members of it. But it was no aristocratic movement; it was in truth a revolt of the democracy against the aristocracy. The peasants found that their complaints and grievances were listened to, and that redress was always promised and sometimes obtained. The Association offered them legal assistance against the law. Emancipation was no longer a movement which was only to benefit and did only touch the upper classes; it offered to the poorest a bright and indefinite vista of relief and reformation. The priests

who had hitherto held aloof from politics, began,
under the guidance of their bishops, to take part in
the work of the Association, of which they were all *ex
officio* members. By the end of 1823 O'Connell's hopes
of a union of Catholic feeling began to be justified.

But the most successful of all the devices of the new
organization was one which at first met with ridicule
and almost failure. In the days of the old Catholic
Committee, O'Connell had seen the need of a more
steady and more abundant revenue, and had endeavoured, without much success, to organize a parochial
subscription. He now proposed, by the methodical
collection of the smallest subscriptions from the poorest
contributors, at the same time to enlist the enthusiasm
of multitudes, and to raise an otherwise unapproachably
large fund. This was the " Catholic Rent."

Yet broad as was this scheme, so languid was the interest that the new association at first excited, that even
at the meeting on February 4th, 1824, at which he was
to introduce his proposal for establishing the Rent, no
quorum appeared for five-and-twenty minutes, and by
the rules the meeting stood adjourned if none appeared in half-an-hour. O'Connell rushed out, met
an eighth man on the stairs, and, darting into the street,
found two young priests from Galway gaping in at
Coyne's shop windows. *Ex-officio* they were members.
To seize them by the arms, to overbear their diffidence
partly by force and partly by persuasion, and to pull them
into the meeting was the work of a minute ; the quorum
was completed, but not one second too soon. The proposal was made and duly carried, but outside the
association people laughed at it. His schoolfellows
taunted O'Connell's son, John, with his father's " penny-
a-month plan for liberating Ireland."

By the end of the year, however, matters wore a different aspect. The rent came in at £350 a week in October, at £550 a week in November, and at £700 a week in December. The Association hired the Corn Exchange Rooms at £150 per annum, and appointed Æneas M'Donnell its parliamentary agent in London at a salary of £300 a year. The incessant activity of O'Connell was rapidly making the Catholic agitation, so long dormant, once more troublesome to the Government. He knew that he was treading on thin ice at every step. To hold language at once passionate enough to inflame a people, who had never known any alternatives but those of torpor or outrage, and also constitutional enough to baulk the Government upon an indictment for sedition, to do this day after day in a multitude of meetings and harangues, for which he had not an instant's leisure to prepare, and to keep in check impulsive and unguarded satellites, and tone down their indiscretions, was no light task. Rare as was O'Connell's self-mastery even in the wild excitement of triumphant oratory, even he made slips sometimes. At that time the nascent republics of South America were in revolt against Spain, and Bolivar was one of the heroes of that revolution. On December 16th 1824, after a hard day's work in Court, O'Connell went out to address a meeting in the Corn Exchange, and referred to the various wars of liberty then in progress in the world. "The Greeks," he said, "were engaged in warfare for the defence of their rights. The Roman Catholics trusted that their ends would be procured through more peaceable means. He hoped that Ireland would be restored to her rights; but if Ireland were driven mad by persecution, he hoped a new Bolivar might arise to defend her." This occurred on

5

Friday. Late on Monday afternoon, as he was sitting
at home with his family, Alderman Darby entered
his house with a constable, and required him to enter
into recognizances to appear at the next sessions,
and answer a charge of seditious libel. What the words
imputed were, or who the informer was, he declined,
under superior instructions, to say. The bill was
duly preferred, but to prove the words used was
not so easy. O'Connell was a rapid speaker. The
papers complained of the difficulty of reporting a man
who could utter two hundred words a minute for three
or four hours together. The Government had to appeal
to the press-reporters, and the reporters refused assistance. On December 21st, Vousden of the *Dublin
Morning Post*, and Leech of the *Freeman*, were summoned by the police, but declined to produce their
notes, or to depose to any words without them. Haydn,
editor of the *Star*, declared that such an office should
not be put upon a journalist. The reporter of *Saun-
ders' News Letter* was called, and ingeniously swore that
just at that part of O'Connell's speech he fell asleep.
To this comedy there was but one issue. The Grand
Jury threw out the bill.

On February 3rd 1825 the session of Parliament
opened. The King's speech, echoing the fears of many
respectable persons, "regretted that Associations should
exist in Ireland which have adopted proceedings irre-
concilable with the spirit of the Constitution"; and
this was followed up on the 10th by Goulburn, who introduced a bill to suppress both the Catholic Association
and the Orange Lodges. In less than a month it was
law. By O'Connell's advice the Association at once
dissolved. It held its last meeting on March 18th, and
the Government breathed again.

But in the meantime the cause of Emancipation was making progress in England. A deputation consisting of O'Connell, O'Gorman, Sheil, and others, had been appointed on 10th February 1825 to go to London and press the Catholic claims. O'Connell was heard at the Bar of the Commons as counsel for the Catholics, and was examined before a Parliamentary Committee on March 9th. " His whole deportment," says Lord Colchester, "was affectedly respectful, except in a few answers, when he displayed a fierceness of tone and aspect." The deputation was entertained at dinner by Brougham, and by the Duke of Norfolk, and they addressed a Catholic meeting at the Freemason's Hall. O'Connell, who on this visit first became known to the English public, remained some months in London, and on May 21st argued a case before Lord Eldon in the House of Lords, who found him " not so shining in argument as he expected." Meantime, Parliament had seen that it was impossible to suppress the Catholics' organization and to do nothing for their claims. Burdett carried a motion in their favour in March by 247 to 234. He introduced a Bill, and it was passed on the second reading by 268 to 241. A great impression was created when Brownlow, M.P. for Armagh, and afterwards Lord Lurgan, Maxwell, M.P. for Downpatrick, and Forde, M.P. for Downshire, hitherto stout Protestant Ascendency men, spoke and voted in its favour. As the liberation of the Catholics seemed now to be close at hand, a demand arose for " securities," and two Bills for that purpose, called " the Wings," were introduced, one by Littleton, the other by Lord Francis Leveson Gower. Littleton's Bill, which proposed to raise the qualification for the franchise to £10, was carried on the second reading by 233 to 185 ; Leveson Gower's, which provided for an endowment of £250,000 per annum for the Catholics, by 205 to 162. Burdett's Bill passed the Commons on May 10th. It was thought the Lords must yield. To facilitate matters Peel offered to resign, but Liverpool refused his resignation. But the Lords proved immovable. The Duke of York, who was next in succession to the Crown, declared, in presenting a petition from the Dean and Canons of Windsor, that " to the latest moment of his existence, whatever might be his station in life, he would oppose Catholic Emancipation, so help him God !" It was known that the King pardoned the anticipation of his demise in consideration of the piety of the sentiment. The Duke instantly became the most popular man in England, and the eponymous founder of countless public-houses ; his words were blazoned by the No Popery party in letters of gold. The Lords rallied to such influences, and threw out the Bill by 178 to 130.

To the hopes of the Catholics this double disappointment was a terrible blow. Nothing less than O'Connell's resourcefulness, energy, and buoyancy, could have restored them to composure. The Suppression Act, which he instantly dubbed the " Algerine Act," had been the work of a divided Cabinet, and was but loosely drafted. He proceeded to found a New Catholic Association, whose existence was a standing insult to the statute. The Act rendered any society illegal if " constituted for redress of grievances in Church or State, renewing its meetings for more than fourteen days, or collecting or receiving money." In July the New Catholic Association was founded exclusively for purposes of public and private charity and " for all purposes not forbidden by the Act." It disclaimed any action for the redress of grievances, the alteration of the law, or the prosecution of suits, civil or criminal. It was to have neither separate parts nor separate branches, neither elected delegates nor local secretaries. Christians of all denominations were admissible and were to pay an annual subscription of £1. Its objects were to promote public peace and private harmony, to encourage religious education, to provide Catholic churches and graveyards, to promote agriculture and manufactures, and to defend the Catholics from untrue aspersions cast on their faith or conduct. For the purposes of agitation, aggregate meetings were held entirely apart from this benevolent association, some for one day only, some for fourteen days, " pursuant to the Act of Parliament," each of which severally arranged for the preparation of a petition and dispersed. The New Association took over the £14,000 which the old one had in hand when it was dissolved. The rent was collected as before ; most persons paid in their money " for the relief of distressed Catholics " ; O'Connell his " for all purposes allowable by law."

The Government allowed itself to be trifled with by this flimsy evasion of the Act. It cannot be that they never desired to put their new powers in force. One thing seems clear : if to pack juries and to dictate sentences to a subservient judiciary had really been the customary procedure of the Irish Government, it is inconceivable that they should not have suppressed this agitation and trusted to their partisan judges and packed juries to declare their conduct within the Act. The New Catholic Association was admittedly and notoriously the Old Catholic Association. The guise of charity was a mere colourable evasion of the Act. That Manners, the Chancellor, and Goulburn, the Chief Secretary, would not gladly have enforced the Act, can hardly be doubted; but it is equally clear that they were prevented from doing so and obliged to be content with a posture of ridiculous impotence, by their respect for the letter of the law, and by their inability to secure either such a verdict upon the facts from a jury, or such a construction of the statute from the bench, as would have been necessary to give effect to the indubitable but ill-expressed will of the Legislature. Their conduct at this time acquits both themselves of jury-packing and the judges of servility.

The Irish had borne the suppression of the Catholic Association with comparative composure; but the rejection of the Relief Bill and the adjurations of the Duke of York filled them with rage. O'Connell, while in London, had been in close league with Burdett and his friends, and indeed went so far as to write to the newspapers claiming the authorship of the Relief Bill, a claim which Tierney repudiated with mortifying explicitness in the House of Commons. Following the unfortunate precedent of 1808 of secretly negotiating with the Parliamentary party without any communication with the party in Ireland, he had assented to the Wings, both the one which disfranchised the forty-shilling freeholders, and that which provided for the payment of the clergy. For this abandonment of principle, the Irish priests on his return to Ireland took him severely to task. It was only by prompt and even abject renunciation and contrition, that he recovered his lost ground. He disavowed the Wings and threw himself actively into the agitation. The great thing to be aimed at was to keep alive the interest of the Catholics, to arrest their attention, to keep them in motion; a precise goal and definite achievement was of less importance. Even at the risk of provoking hostility, O'Connell was anxious to keep up the heat of his followers' enthusiasm : " An enemy," says Wyse, " is nearer to conversion than a neutral." The Protestants began to appear on Catholic platforms ; there was too much condescending patronage on their side, too much fulsome adulation on O'Connell's, but the fact was important. More and more strongly the priests became identified with the Association; they collected the rent; the meetings were held in their chapels and the platforms set up before their altars. A series of provincial aggregate meetings was held, at Limerick in 1825, at Cork and Waterford in 1826, at Clonmel in 1828. To keep constantly before the public mind the vast disparity in the numbers of Catholics and Protestants, Shiel suggested a religious census, to be taken, parish by parish, by the clergy. An affiliated Catholic Association was formed in New York, and American subscriptions began to come in. Foreign opinion was appealed to and the proceedings of the Association were sent to foreign Governments. The Catholics aspired to have a foreign policy ; and they gratified their taste for splendour by adopting a uniform or costume, of blue, gold, and white, of velvet and of silk. The English were surprised at this awakening of Irish feeling and universal activity ; but a greater surprise was to come.

Of the Protestant territorial magnates, whose wide possessions and family influence seemed to give them a prescriptive and indefeasible title to direct the issue of Irish elections, none were so powerful as the Beresfords in county Waterford. They had controlled the county time out of mind ; they had held the seat for the city for seventy years. Upon the register they had an immense

majority of votes at their beck and call. The Marquis
of Waterford lived on his estates and had done much
to earn Catholic good-will. He had introduced the
Catholic Relief Bill in the Irish House of Lords in
1793, and had been conspicuous for his humanity when
in command of the Waterford Regiment of Yeomanry
during the rebellion of 1798. A trivial circumstance,
arising out of a proposed address to the Lord Lieutenant after the " Bottle Riot " had made him for the time
unpopular with some of the Protestant gentry.

The general election of 1826 was at hand, and it was
decided to oppose his candidate, the sitting member,
Lord George Beresford. Villiers Stuart, afterwards
Lord Stuart of the Decies, a young squire of good
family but moderate means, was asked to stand. He
posted home from the Tyrol and issued his address. The
Beresfords replied with indiscreet and irritating counter-
addresses, denouncing clerical influence. The priests
in turn became the most active and most successful of
canvassers for Stuart. They menaced with the guilt of
perjury those who voted against their consciences to
please their landlords. Every chapel became a centre of
agitation. Four thousand troops were poured into the
county and had nothing to do ; in vast orderly processions the forty-shilling freeholders moved about the
country or attended Stuart's meetings, without disorder
or crime. Chiefly to give him a *locus standi* for a
speech, O'Connell, who was Stuart's counsel, was put
in nomination for the county, and after speaking two
hours retired in his client's favour. It was the first
nomination of a Catholic ever known, and the precedent
was significant. The people of Kilmacthomas had
drummed Lord George out of the village ; the people of
Portlaw, which lay at the gates of the Marquis' castle,

claimed the privilege of going first to the poll to vote against their landlord. There was a majority against the Marquis on the first day, mainly composed of his own freeholders; on the fifth Lord George retired. The contest had begun as a forlorn hope ; it had passed into a determined battle ; it ended in a complete victory. The effect was immense. But that the Wexford election had been decided before that in Waterford, the Catholics would have carried that county. An obscure barrister named Alexander Dawson, without effort and with but three days' notice, carried Louth, and the dismayed Orange candidates were left to struggle for the second place. Westmeath was won ; two Emancipators were returned for Armagh, and Monaghan was wrested from its hereditary representatives, the Leslies, the Blayneys, and the Shirleys. It was the revolt of the forty-shilling freeholders against their masters. The landlords had created them to increase their own importance, and now found the creature rising against the creator. For thirty years Frankenstein's monster had been a submissive slave ; but now he had turned on his master and had rent him.

The landlords thus defeated began to threaten and in some cases to carry out ejectments for non-payment of the long arrears, which were kept for this purpose hanging over the heads of the forty-shilling freeholders. The Catholic Association interfered to protect its clients. It threatened to buy up outstanding judgments and to procure the foreclosure of mortgages against landlords, who acted in this way. It carried on an active registration of votes in the Catholic interest and looked, at another election, to carry three-fourths of the Irish seats. It established Protecting Committees in the counties which had been recently contested, and collected a " New Rent " for the relief of evicted tenants. The old rent reached vast proportions, £16,000 to March 1825, £6,260 more to December 1826, and £3,000 for 1827. In 1828 it was £21,400 ; in two months of 1829, £5,300. But it was imperfectly collected, and having been left too much to casual and volunteer effort, often to busy priests, had never approached the desired £50,000 per annum. O'Connell proposed a strict parochial organization. Two churchwardens were to be appointed in every parish, one by the priest and the other by the people, to collect the rent. They were to send up to Dublin monthly reports in a prescribed form, giving particulars as to the Catholic rent and census, the Church cess and tithes, evictions of tenants and attempts at proselytism. That too much might not be left to the initiative of the churchwardens, local associations were, on Wyse's proposal, formed in each parish, to look after the wardens ; an association in each county controlled the parish clubs, and all were subject to the central association. The Weekly Register of the Association's proceedings circulated to the number of 6,000, and was read aloud by the wardens at chapel after mass. The central association supplied journals to the country branches. In nine years the circulation of newspapers in Ireland increased 25 per cent. These clubs were founded in every county in Munster, and in most of those in Leinster and Connaught, and enforced a strict maintenance of the peace and observance of the law. By this means, on 21st January 1828, simultaneous meetings were held in no less than fifteen hundred parishes ; and the meetings were held without the slightest disorder.

When Canning took office in 1827, he sent a private message to the Catholic Association, begging them for the

sake of English opinion to be temperate, and promising in
that case to do his best for their claims. The Catholic Association refused to moderate its tone. The accession to office of the Duke of Wellington, on Goderich's
resignation, was regarded as the accession of a Catholic
foe. The Association passed a resolution binding itself to
oppose with all its force any Irish member who took office
under him. The Catholics, in spite of the stubborn resistance to Emancipation of the bulk of the English Dissenters, had always supported their cause, and 800,000
signatures were procured by O'Connell to a petition for
the repeal of the Test and Corporation Acts. In 1828,
when this had been carried, Lord John Russell wrote
to the Association, desiring it, now that the principle of
Emancipation had thus triumphed, to withdraw the
anti-Wellington pledge. O'Connell urged, as he had
urged the year before, that the advice should be taken.
Again he was overruled. For the Association saw now
that not to go forward was to go back, and the pledge
was insisted on.

An opportunity for acting on the resolution soon
arrived. The East Retford dispute led to the resignation of Huskisson, and among the Ministerial changes
which followed was the appointment to the Board of
Trade of Vesey Fitzgerald, M.P. for Clare. His re-
election seemed certain. He belonged to an old and
popular family. His father, Prime Serjeant Fitzgerald,
had voted against the Act of Union. He himself had
consistently voted in favour of Emancipation. Both
father and son were excellent landlords. He had behind
him the Ministerial influence and the whole body of the
landlords of Clare. The resolution of the Catholic
Association bound them to oppose him, but they
despaired of success. Steele, however, and Tho O'Gor-

man Mahon, who were magistrates for the county, posted down to see what could be done. Arriving at Limerick on a Sunday morning, they found that personal obligations to the Fitzgeralds prevented Major Macnamara, who was to have been their candidate, from opposing the new minister. They hurried on into Clare, holding hasty meetings at the chapels, and by night joined Lawless at Ennis. Everywhere they found a general enthusiasm for a contest among the peasantry. To the contemptuous amazement of Fitzgerald's party, Steele remained to urge that if no gentleman would come forward some grave-digger should be put up. O'Gorman, half-dead with fatigue, posted back to Dublin to beat up a candidate. Lord William Paget was applied to, and refused. On the 21st of June, Sheil declared at the meeting of the Association that someone absolutely must stand. O'Connell was inclined to dread the effect of a defeat. Next day, in the early morning, Sir David Roose, ex-High Sheriff of Dublin and a Tory, met Fitzpatrick in the street by chance, and suggested that a Catholic, O'Connell himself, should be the candidate. Fitzpatrick remembered that years before he had heard Keogh suggest a similar thing; he caught at the idea, rushed to the Association Rooms and made the proposal. Then followed two hours of hesitation. They saw the advantage of getting on their side the innate English respect for the formal result of an election, even though the elected person be ineligible, and they decided to take the chance. The die was cast. By the end of the week Steele, in Clare, knew that he would have no need to put up any grave-digger; the candidate would be the most popular Catholic in Ireland. O'Connell issued his address on the 24th. It was marked by a pledge " to bring the question of the Repeal of the Union at the earliest possible period before the consideration of the legislature." It was foreseen that the cost of the election would be heavy, but £2,000 was collected in Dublin in one day, and £14,000 in ten. O'Connell himself could not leave Dublin till the last moment, but Sheil and O'Gorman went down to Clare at once. Then followed one of the most singular scenes in the history of Ireland. O'Gorman announced his willingness to fight any squire, who felt aggrieved at seeing his tenants canvassed, and proceeded to canvass the tenants. Shiel went from chapel to chapel, and "made every altar a tribune." The priests exerted themselves for O'Connell almost to a man. One, indeed, sided with Fitzgerald, and the people stopped his stipend. On the other hand, every Whig and Tory landlord supported Fitzgerald. He was nominated by Sir Edward O'Brien, and O'Connell only by Steele. The candidates addressed the freeholders. Fitzgerald wept before them, and his tears touched their emotional hearts. O'Connell replied with a virulent attack, calling him the "friend of the base and bloody Perceval," who, though he had been fourteen years in his grave, and had died by an assassin's hand, was still not safe from abuse. The polling days arrived. Vandeleur of Kilrush drove into Ennis at the head of his three hundred tenants, and under their landlord's eye they cheered O'Connell and broke away to poll for him. Sir Edward O'Brien was bringing up his men, when Father Murphy of Corofin met them, and with a few words gathered the sheep into O'Connell's fold. One look of a priest converted the tenants of Augustine Butler. At the close of one day's voting a vast crowd was waiting anxiously to hear the state of the poll. Up rose a gaunt

priest, who announced that a Catholic had voted for
Fitzgerald. The crowd set up a yell of hatred.
"Silence," cried the priest; "the hand of God has
struck him; he has just died of apoplexy. Pray for
his soul!" The awe-stricken multitude fell on its
knees in silent prayer. During those July nights
thirty thousand men bivouacked in the meadows about
Ennis, and no case of disorder occurred. The only
man who got drunk was O'Connell's English coach-
man. Clare had been pre-eminent among Irish counties for faction-fighting; in that county hereditary foes
espied one another only to commence a violent riot.
During the whole election not the slightest affray took
place. Lord Anglesey had massed troops upon the
place. There were three hundred police in Ennis; upwards of two thousand troops were within call, and
thirteen hundred more only thirty-six hours distant.
Not a corporal's guard was required. From the first
the contest was hopeless. As Fitzgerald wrote to Peel,
he had polled " all the gentry and all the £50 freeholders—the gentry to a man," but out of 8,000
electors all but 200 were forty-shilling freeholders. On
the first day O'Connell was six votes ahead, on the
third almost a thousand. On the fifth Fitzgerald withdrew, and O'Connell was member for Clare.

CHAPTER V.

EMANCIPATION.

1828–1842.

Result of the Clare Election—Dissolution of the Catholic Association—
Catholic Relief—Refusal of O'Connell's claim to take his seat—
Second Clare Election—Repeal Agitation—Conflict with the Mar-
quis of Anglesey—Reform.

THE first question which had presented itself to the
Wellington Administration in 1828, had been the renewal of the Coercion Act of 1825. It expired with
the session of 1828, and must either be renewed, or
allowed quietly to lapse. It had been a failure. Neither
the Catholic agitation nor the Orange processions, at
which it was aimed, had been touched by it. The
Marquis of Anglesey advised the Ministry not to stir;
there were dissensions, he said, among the Catholics of
Ireland, who were not unanimous in supporting the
Association, and there were jealousies within its ranks.
The prelates looked askance at its influence with the
parochial clergy, and the landlords at its sway over
their tenants. The country was quiet. A new Act
would be difficult to frame, and could only be passed at
the cost of new conflicts. Upon this advice they decided to take the risk of dropping the Act, and to let
sleeping dogs lie.

But the Clare election changed the whole face of affairs. O'Connell returned to Dublin amid the triumphant acclamations of the whole country through which he passed. As soon as the Act lapsed, the old Catholic Association was instantly re-established, and at the same time the Orange lodges, which it had suppressed, also formed themselves again. The Catholics were active in agitation, but so were the Protestants. They established, up and down the country, Brunswick Clubs, which held language as violent as that of the Association, and by their proceedings drove many of the Protestant Liberals, who had hitherto held aloof from politics, into the arms of the Catholics. The Association, in return, decided to extend its operations into Ulster, and despatched "honest Jack Lawless" as its emissary to the North. Meetings were still an attractive novelty in Ulster, and agitation was still fresh there, and in the neighbourhood of Dundalk he was highly successful; but when he announced his intention of entering the "black north" at Ballybay, co. Monaghan, with 140,000 enthusiasts in his train, some fifteen thousand* Orangemen mustered to resist him. This was on the 22nd of September. The magistrates of the locality called on General Thornton, the officer in command of the district, to interpose between the two hosts, and Lawless, finding his senses or losing his nerve, took to his heels. Never was Ireland nearer to a conflagration. The peasantry of Tipperary had abandoned their faction-fights to prepare for more serious work. In August a great provincial meeting had been held at Clonmel. A disciplined levy of the peasants

---

* So Wyse, but the Chief Secretary wrote to Peel, on Oct. 6, that the Protestants numbered 1,700.

en masse marched into the town, 50,000 strong, wearing green cockades and green uniforms, preceded by bands, and commanded by officers. Uniforms were so common, that one Cork firm alone sold £600 worth of green calico for the purpose. In addressing this meeting, O'Connell had used language of the most unwise violence. The Orangemen had talked of armed suppression of the Catholic movement. "Would to God," cried O'Connell, "our excellent Viceroy, Lord Anglesey, would only give me a commission; and if those men of blood should attempt to attack the property and persons of His Majesty's loyal subjects, with a hundred thousand of my brave Tipperary boys, I would soon drive them into the sea before me." The fierce yell of applause which followed his words showed how his hearers hungered for the fray. It was known that there were stores of arms hidden in the mountains, and all through September the marching and counter-marching of these strange armies went on. Had Lawless provoked bloodshed at Ballybay, it is the opinion of Wyse, the historian of the Catholic Association, writing at the time, that there would have followed in the south of Ireland " another Sicilian Vespers."

The Lord Lieutenant was neither an alarmist nor a tyrant; he was a cool soldier, and a friend of Emancipation, but he foreboded insurrection. He filled the district with troops, but he knew that his troops were wavering in their loyalty. English regiments had been largely recruited with Irishmen, and Protestant ones with Catholics. The contagion of popular enthusiasm had seized upon the soldiers. The priests had been at work among them, and they were becoming divided into religious factions. As early as July he had asked for the removal of Irish soldiers and the despatch of Scotch regiments to Ireland. Without the concession of Catholic Relief, he said, he could not answer for the peace of the country for longer than until Parliament met. The leaders "could lead on the people to rebellion at a moment's notice," and "the probability of present tranquillity rests upon the forbearance of O'Connell."

O'Connell himself saw that an outbreak meant absolute ruin to the Catholic cause on the very eve of its final triumph. As yet there had been no disturbance; but a spark might kindle a civil war, which the Government might be unable to quell. He recalled Lawless from the North; he issued a manifesto to the people of Tipperary commanding peace, and directing the formation of companies of one hundred and twenty men, each to be under a " pacificator," who was required to be a communicant, and two "regulators" appointed by him, all three to be jointly responsible for the conduct of their men. The effect was magical; almost without a struggle the agitation disappeared. "Divisions of 1,000 or 1,500 marching in uniform to the place of rendezvous in ignorance of what had happened, were met on their way by a copy of the address, and instantly retraced their steps in peace. Others who had actually assembled, separated, and departed quietly to their homes."

But in spite of this obedience, Catholic feeling continued to be intensely embittered. In November, one of the directors of the Wexford Provincial Bank, a highly respectable institution managed jointly by Catholics and Protestants, had attended a meeting of a Brunswick Club. In revenge for this the Catholics secretly concerted a run on the bank. Immense numbers of its notes were simultaneously presented for payment. The bank had to obtain in a single week £1,500,000 in gold. The movement threatened to spread to Clonmel and Kilkenny, but fortunately it was stayed. About the same time, Ford, a Catholic solicitor, proposed a resolution in the Catholic Association in favour of exclusive dealing with Catholic tradesmen, and it was with difficulty that his motion was shelved in December. At such a moment proceedings like these would have been suicidal. As it was, such uneasiness was awakened among commercial men, that in the following March, though the banks of issue were highly solvent concerns, they felt obliged to hold very nearly £5,000,000 in specie to protect a note circulation of but £7,000,000 in all.

Meantime the Ministry had been undergoing deep searchings of heart. It was supposed to have been constituted upon an anti-Catholic basis. Peel had long been the ablest and best exponent of the argument against Emancipation. To his logical mind it followed that Emancipation must lead to the overthrow of Protestant ascendency. To relieve the Catholics from disabilities in law, and to enforce them in fact, by refusing to appoint persons of that religion to office under the Crown, was to him irrational. But his experience at the Irish Office had led him to believe that the appointment of Catholics was incompatible with national security. At the same time, his was a highly constitutional mind, and the Clare election showed him that his position was fast becoming constitutionally indefensible. The parliament of 1826 had been elected upon an express "No Popery" cry; but when the question came for the first time before it in 1827, they rejected Burdett's motion for a committee on the Catholic claims by but four votes in 540, and, after the success of Rus-

sell's proposals in 1828, Burdett obtained in May a
majority of six in its favour. Even its opponents no
longer ventured to say that things could remain as they
were. Dawson, Peel's brother-in-law, M.P. for Derry,
and one of the leaders of the Ulster Protestants, in a
speech afterwards called " Peel's pilot balloon," owned,
after O'Connell's election, that the time for concession
had arrived. Left to itself, the House of Commons
would probably have passed a Catholic Relief Act at
any time during the last fifteen years, and although the
stiff Protestant party was very strong in the country,
especially in the Midlands and West, the true centre of
resistance was in the House of Lords and the Royal
Family. For a generation past all the most distinguished men in the House of Commons, except Peel
himself, had been against the disabilities. A majority of
the representatives in each of the great counties of
Yorkshire, Lancashire, Middlesex, Kent, Surrey, and
Devon, a moiety of those of London, Liverpool, Leicester, Coventry, and Norwich, and the whole of those of
Westminster, Southwark, Newcastle, Chester, Derby,
and Preston, were Emancipationists. But the Clare
election produced a still greater effect. With their
eyes open the electors had chosen a man whose right to
take his seat was highly doubtful, and would certainly
be denied. They had known their strength too well to
be violent. At a moment of wild excitement, in a
county that had never been orderly before, complete
order had prevailed. Above all, the election marked a
silent but constitutional revolution, a complete trans-
ference of power from the class on whom the whole
fabric of Protestant exclusiveness had rested, to the
class which Protestantism had trampled under foot. The
landlord was dethroned, and the priest reigned in his

stead. Peel had to ask himself what was to be done. Civil government was paralysed and brought into contempt by the existing state of things. The authority which kept the peace of Ireland, such as it was, was that of the Catholic Association, and not the king's. During the autumn of 1828 England was at peace with all the world; her regular infantry force in the United Kingdom was some 30,000 men; 25,000 of them had to be devoted to the maintenance of tranquillity in Ireland. Civil war seemed so imminent that it appalled even the stout heart of the Duke of Wellington. The existing situation was intolerable. Yet there seemed to be no issue from this *impasse.* To suppress the agitation by force of arms was hopeless, for neither troops nor police could any longer be trusted. To ask coercive powers of a House of Commons which had declared in favour of Emancipation was idle. To dissolve was to provoke an insurrection, and to bring about another Clare election in every constituency in Ireland. One thing could be done, and one only, and that a thing which none but a Tory anti-Catholic government could have had weight enough to do. It was to yield; to yield without any conversion of English opinion, to force the stubborn bigotry of the British to submit to the pressure put upon it by a portion of the people of the United Kingdom, their inferior in numbers, wealth, education, and strength. There was something heroic in such a self-effacement.

Parliament met on February 5th 1829. The speech from the Throne said that "His Majesty recommends that . . . you should take into your deliberate consideration the whole condition of Ireland; and that you should review the laws which impose civil disabilities on His Majesty's Roman Catholic subjects." But the same speech contained a request for a grant of further powers for maintaining the law, as a preliminary to Catholic Relief, and Peel introduced a Bill for the suppression of the Catholic Association on February 10th. The Whigs, relying on the near prospect of a Relief Bill, offered it little opposition. They thought that with the passing of a Relief Bill the use and occasion of the Suppression Act would disappear. It was carried in the Commons by 348 to 160, and finally passed the House of Lords on February 24th, and received the royal assent on March 5th. The more moderate friends of Emancipation urged obedience to the new Act without waiting for it to be put in force. The Marquis of Anglesey wrote to Dublin urging its leaders to dissolve the Association forthwith. O'Connell, indeed, who was now on his way to London, and had less faith in the intentions of the Tory Ministry, wrote from Shrewsbury, and wrote again on reaching London, urging them to do nothing of the kind. But by far the most influential of its leaders, after O'Connell himself, was Sheil, and Sheil was in Dublin, and was for moderation. He moved and carried a resolution on February 12th, that the Catholic Association, now 14,000 strong, should dissolve. At the same time the collateral " Association of Friends of Civil and Religious Freedom " was dissolved also. Yet even at this moment, when harmonious action was so necessary, and victory was won, dissension broke out. A few weeks afterwards O'Connell was in conflict with MacDonnell, the London agent, about his exorbitant claims to remuneration for services in London, and with the secretary, O'Gorman, about his claim to appropriate, as his private property, the minute books and records of the Association.

Peel introduced the Relief Bill on the 5th March.

The King had given to it a reluctant assent. At the last hour, the intrigues of Eldon and the Duke of Cumberland had so far influenced his weak and disingenuous mind, that he withdrew his assent to his ministers' policy, on the pretence that he had not expected, and could not sanction, any modification of the Oath of Supremacy. He parted from his ministers with kisses and courtesy, and for a few hours their resignations were in his hands. But with night his discretion waxed as his courage waned; his ministers were recalled, and their measure proceeded. In its main provisions it was thorough and far-reaching. It admitted the Roman Catholic to Parliament, and to all lay offices under the Crown, except those of Regent, Lord Chancellor, whether of England or of Ireland, and Lord Lieutenant. It repealed the oath of abjuration, it modified the oath of supremacy. It was attended, as all Catholic Relief Bills had been attended, by a "securities" Bill. It approximated the Irish to the English county franchise by abolishing the forty-shilling freeholder, and raising the voter's qualification to £10. All monasteries and institutions of Jesuits were suppressed; and Roman Catholic bishops were forbidden to assume titles of sees already held by Bishops of the Church of Ireland. Municipal and other officials were forbidden to wear the insignia of their office at Roman Catholic ceremonies. Lastly, the new Oath of Supremacy was available only for persons thereafter to be elected to Parliament. Introduced by Peel, almost the only person of first-rate capacity in the party which had uniformly opposed all previous measures of Emancipation, the Bill met with but little opposition of a formidable character. After some violent debate it passed the House of Commons by 353 votes to 180, the House of Lords by 217 to 112, and finally on April 13th received the Royal assent. After sixty-nine years of agitation, Catholic disabilities were removed, and the victory was won.

The true significance of the Relief lay in the disfranchisement of the forty-shilling freeholder, a unique and sweeping measure of electoral restriction. It was a counter-revolution to that of which the Clare election had been the visible sign. Although to the last moment of the struggle the "No Popery" feeling in England was very strong, although the House of Commons had been elected on a "No Popery" cry, and was importuned with numberless petitions against Emancipation, there can be no doubt that the Opposition to it among thinking men was in the main political. The Irish members were the choice of the landlord interest, for in Ireland, as in Great Britain, the representation rested on a territorial basis. The Tories saw that to emancipate the Catholics was to alter this state of things in Ireland; it was to pass an indirect Reform Bill by anticipation. The question in Ireland was complicated by the state of the franchise, which was in an artificial and unnatural condition. It was vastly more democratic in law than that of England, for the electoral qualification was absurdly low; it was in practice much more aristocratic. In truth, the state of the Irish franchise was very analogous to the representation of the Slave States in the United States Congress in 1860. For the purpose of enhancing his master's political power, the peasant counted as a freeman; for the purpose of exercising power of his own he was to be only a slave.

The Irish landlords of the beginning of this century were a class, which the modern imagination can comprehend only as figures in farces or caricatures in fiction. They were violent and dissolute, spendthrift and irresponsible. To vie with one another in tasteless splendour and grotesque profusion, they burdened their estates with mortgages and their tenantry with high rents. They lived in a labyrinth of charges and encumbrances, and protected themselves by doing violence to the officials of the law, who sought to bring them within reach of its process. With them to be sober was to be a nincompoop, to observe common prudence to be a niggard. The duel was a sacred institution; smuggling a reputable calling; the abduction of heiresses a common mode of repairing broken fortunes; and the impartial administration of the duties of a county magistrate, an incomprehensible pedantry when it affected others, an unpardonable insult when it affected oneself. Much as the Roman Catholics had suffered from the system of the Penal Code, its worst victims were the landlords themselves. The constitution as it stood made them the guardians of the country, the administrators of its daily concerns and the possessors of its political power. Against their incapacity or their prejudices, a Government, however well-meaning, struggled in vain. Brought up as despots and surrounded by an ignorant and degraded population, recruited from the ranks of Roman Catholic renegades, and corrupted by innumerable exchanges with the Government of votes and seats in return for pensions or places, they had become in three or four generations unfit for power. Yet there was an affection and sympathy between them and their subjects, which mitigated the worst evils of the situation. The Irish peasantry, perhaps more than any other agricultural population, looked up to their natural leaders, the possessors of the soil. The landlords were

Irish like themselves, Irish to the core. Their reckless gallantry, their careless profusion, their wit and their weakness, endeared them to peasants whose nature was the same, and whose habits in their sphere were not dissimilar. It was O'Connell who destroyed this allegiance. He made the priest and not the landlord the leader of the people. This Peel saw. He knew that the forty-shilling freeholders were a class too ignorant, too excitable, too little accustomed to political deliberation and action, to be anything but a dangerous force as soon as they got out of passive control. By his very success the forty-shilling freeholder was doomed to extinction. The Act which completed his victory annihilated him. It was the first good deed he had ever done, the first free political step he had ever taken, and it was his last. Like Samson, he was greater in his death than in his life.

But although the main provisions of the Act were excellent, it was attended by two of those miserable restrictions which, to the sensitive Irish people, often seem to outweigh a solid boon. The provision that Roman Catholic prelates were not to seize upon titles already appropriated to Protestant bishops, would seem a trumpery punctilio without a parallel, were it not for Lord John Russell's Ecclesiastical Titles Act. It was inserted as a sop to the English bishops. The exclusion of O'Connell from Parliament, unless he either took the oath of abjuration or underwent a second election, was a mere fatuity. It was done against the will of the Cabinet to gratify the spite of the King.

It must be remembered that, so far as Emancipation was due to Irish effort, it was due to O'Connell. The Irish had had great political combinations before, though hardly peaceable ones; they had had the Volun-

teers and the United Irishmen. But the one was a
military body officered by the aristocracy and gentry;
the other was a traitorous conspiracy. O'Connell had
had few persons of weight, either intellectual or social,
to aid him in his task, and he had been faced by the
most powerful opposition. Except Sheil, he had hardly
counted a supporter. of real strength. And yet he, all
but single-handed, had combined the Irish into an agitation, which though potent was peaceable, and in crea-
ting a revolution he had kept within the Constitution.
Single-handed he had vanquished the Duke of Wellington and all the forces of Evangelicalism at his back. Yet
this was the man who was selected for a flout of the
most ungenerous kind. At the time of the Clare election he had hazarded the opinion, and Charles Butler
had taken the same view, that it was possible to sit and
vote in Parliament without ever taking the oaths. At
any rate, it was possible to elect him, and the question
of his taking his seat might be indefinitely postponed.
He had at once begun to exercise his privileges as a
member of Parliament by franking letters, and the Post
Office admitted his right to frank. The moment the
Sheriff signed the return, a friend asked him to frank
a letter, which was sent to London. It was delivered
to the correspondent while he was arguing a case in
the House of Lords, and was almost the first announcement of the news of the election. The frank
was handed round and excited curiosity, alarm, and
rage. But for eight months O'Connell made no attempt
to take his seat. To obviate the necessity of a second
election in Clare in case the House should deny his
claim to take the new oath, he offered Sir Edward
Denny £3,000 for one of his pocket boroughs, but the
offer was refused. The Sheriff of Clare had made a

special return to the writ. A petition had been presented against O'Connell's return, and a committee of
the House, appointed under Grenville's Act, unanimously
reported him duly elected. He arrived in London on
February 9th 1829, and put up at Batt's Hotel. Ellice,
Burdett, and Hume called upon him to urge the immediate dissolution of the Association. The Whigs proposed to amend the Relief Bill so as to admit him as soon
as it had become law, but he knew the advantage it would
give him to be treated unhandsomely by the Government,
and begged them not to imperil Catholic Relief for
the sake of a personal matter affecting only himself.
Rumours of a coming disfranchisement had been rife
for months, and on December 16th, 1828, the Catholic
Association had resolved that " they would deem any
attempt to deprive the forty-shilling freeholders of their
franchise a direct violation of the Constitution." In
speaking to this resolution, O'Connell said :—

> If any man dare to bring in a Bill for disfranchisement of the forty-
> shilling freeholders, the people ought to rebel, if they cannot other-
> wise succeed ; [and having expressed his contrition for giving his
> consent to the " Wings " in 1825, he proceeded], " sooner than give
> up the forty-shilling freeholders, I would rather go back to the
> Penal Code. . . . I am loyal to the Throne, and my disposition and
> my interest combine to produce in my mind an attachment to the
> ruling powers ; but if an attempt were made to take from the forty-
> shilling freeholders the privileges vested in them by the Constitution,
> I would conceive it just to resist that attempt with force, and in such
> resistance I would be ready to perish in the field or on the
> scaffold.

Now, however, possibly lest it might endanger the
passing of the Relief Act, possibly because it seemed
hopeless, he made no attempt to avert the disfranchisement of the forty-shilling freeholders. He comported
himself with moderation, and showed himself a well-

bred man of the world. He dined with Ponsonby to meet Stanley and Greville. Like a loyal subject, he waited upon his Sovereign at the Levée. The King's eye fell upon him. "There's O'Connell," His Majesty was pleased to say, " God damn the scoundrel."

At length, on the 15th of May, about three in the afternoon, O'Connell presented himself to take his seat. Multitudes stood in the streets about the House and within it the gallery was crowded. He was introduced by Lord Duncannon, M.P. for Kilkenny, and by Lord Ebrington, M.P. for Tavistock. His demeanour was quiet and courteous, and he advanced to the table with the customary bows. There was a dead silence. The oaths which had been long in use were those of allegiance, of supremacy, and of abjuration. The first two he was willing to take, but not the last. They were printed on cards, and Ley, the Clerk of the House, tendered them to him. He was seen to raise some objection, and Ley went to refer to the Speaker. The Speaker decided that the old oaths, which Ley had tendered, were those which must be taken. O'Connell was directed to withdraw. Brougham moved that he be heard at the Bar forthwith, but Peel desired delay, and an adjournment was agreed to till the 18th. O'Connell was then heard in support of his claim to take the oaths as modified by the new Relief Act. It was a striking occasion, and the keenest attention was paid by the House to one whom some of them had been taught to regard as a kind of grotesque barbarian, and others were accustomed to speak of as an adventurer and a traitor. His speech was calm and temperate ; his manner that of a polished gentleman ; his argument, if not convincing, won the encomiums of some of the ablest lawyers in the House, Tindal and Brougham, Scarlett and Sugden. He had twice set out his view in letters to the House, published on February 2nd and May 9th, in which he urged that the proper course was to allow him to take the oaths as he desired, and leave his right to do so to be tried at law, in an action against him by an informer for the penalties for sitting and voting without taking the oaths.   He claimed to be within the letter of the law in taking the new oath, for the Act of Union provided that "till Parliament shall otherwise provide every member shall take the oaths required by law."   For the period between his election and the passing of the Relief Act, no penalty was provided in respect of his non-compliance with that requirement.   Now, since the Relief Act passed, Parliament had "otherwise provided"; a new oath was prescribed, and this he claimed to take. In any case he was within the equity of the new Act. Since it had passed, six Catholic peers had taken it in the House of Lords, and one, Lord Surrey, the Duke of Norfolk's eldest son, had been elected to the House of Commons, and had taken the oath under the Act.   If he was to take the old oaths, as he was the first, so he would be the last Catholic to do so. The House heard him with attention and respect, and he was directed to withdraw.

Some Parliamentary pedants, of whom Charles Wynn, a high authority on procedure, was one, seem to have thought that a mere technical difficulty of this kind would prove an insuperable difficulty to O'Connell's admission.   Others hoped that a second election might have a different issue, and that the £10 electors might reject the chosen of the forty-shilling freeholders. By 190 to 116 his claim was refused.   He was called in, and the Speaker asked if he would take the old oath. He asked to see it.   "There is one assertion in this oath," said he, as he read it, "which I do not know to be true; there is another assertion in it which I believe not to be true. I cannot, therefore, take this oath." He was dismissed, and a new writ was ordered to issue for Clare.

He returned to Ireland vowing vengeance. He issued an address to the Clare electors, couched in violent language. It was called sarcastically the "Address of a hundred promises." Though, on Lord Anglesey's advice, it was silent as to Repeal, it pledged him to Parliamentary Reform; to demand the re-enfranchisement of the forty-shilling freeholders, the repeal of the Subletting Act, and "an equitable distribution of the revenues of the Established Church between the poor on the one side and the most meritorious of the Protestant clergy on the other," "to cleanse the Augean stable of the law," and to urge "the abolition of the accursed monopoly of the East India Company."

The Clare electors cared nothing for the East India Company but a great deal for their champion, O'Connell. When he went down to Clare from Dublin, the people received him like a conqueror. He reached Armagh late in the evening, but the town was immediately illuminated. He pushed on to Limerick through the night, and was compelled by fatigue to go to bed on his arrival in the morning. His enthusiastic admirers planted a large tree before his windows and filled its branches with musicians playing Irish airs. A triumphal car awaited him at Ennis. He addressed numberless meetings, and excited the new electorate as he had excited the old. The dissolved Catholic Association was summoned under the form of an aggregate meeting and voted the sum of £5,000, which the Association had in hand when it dissolved, towards the expenses of his election. There was no opposition and no contest, and, on July 30th, he was returned unopposed.

As if this slight to the foremost Catholic and foremost Irishman in Ireland were not deep enough, the Government put upon O'Connell a hardship in his profession also. He had now been at the bar thirty-one years ; he had been its greatest advocate for almost one half of that time, and because he was a Catholic he still wore a stuff gown. When Canning came in, his hopes of more generous treatment rose. Later on he wrote to Spring-Rice, protesting against the professional injustice which the denial of this merited promotion did him, and he was told that the matter would be made to turn on professional considerations alone. Now, in 1829, the Cabinet considered who should be made the new Catholic King's Counsel. There were six in all, Sheil, Woulfe, Perrin, O'Loghlen, and two others, but O'Connell was not among them. He had been the advocate and the law officer of Queen Caroline, and the King could neither forgive nor forget that in any man. He had compelled His Majesty, in sanctioning Emancipation, to do violence to his piety. At the cost of keeping open the breach between Great Britain and Ireland, the royal resentment was gratified.

At the beginning of the Session of 1830 O'Connell came to London and took his seat. He was fifty-five years of age, an age at which few men can adapt themselves to unfamiliar circumstances or learn new and difficult lessons. He had been rarely in England, and was unfamiliar with the temper of English society. He was intensely Irish, and the Irish were then little known in England and less liked. A large party hated him bitterly. He used to say that for the first two years the Speaker deliberately avoided seeing him when he wished to rise. Yet from the first moment he had the ear of the House, and the Doneraile discussion established his position as a formidable gladiator of debate. He was abused and he was hooted, but he was never despised, and he soon made himself feared and admired. Of all the feats of his life, there is none more remarkable than the ease with which, on the verge of old age, he imposed himself upon the attention of an audience so difficult to understand or to please as the House of Commons. In this session he spoke frequently, but without extravagance. His first speech was made on the motion of Knatchbull to amend the Government's Address to the Crown, by calling His Majesty's attention to the state of the landed interest. On May 28th, he moved for leave to bring in a Bill for triennial Parliaments, a practically universal suffrage, and vote by ballot. It was refused by 319 to 13. The King died in June and Parliament was dissolved.

The new elections told heavily against the Government. The counties in England went against them by 8 to 1, the great towns by 9 to 1. O'Connell was elected for Waterford. The Irish elections turned chiefly upon the questions of Tithe and of the Irish Church, Repeal not being made a test, and the majority against ministers was heavy. Emboldened by the revolutions of July on the Continent, during which, upon the election of a King of the Belgians, some dry Belgian wags nominated and voted for him, O'Connell raised the flag of Repeal and the cry spread fast. He had founded a society called "The Friends of Ireland of all Religious Persuasions." Its objects were twenty-five in number, but the principal was Repeal. "The society" was to "consider with the deepest solicitude

the means of procuring such a universal combination
of Irishmen as may render the Repeal of the Union
irresistible, and thus give to Ireland the blessing of a
free and domestic legislature, connected with Britain by
the golden link of the Crown, but independent of all
ministerial or undue control."

Unlike the Act of 1825, the Act for the suppression
of the Catholic Association attempted no nice legal
distinctions between lawful and unlawful associations,
but empowered the Lord Lieutenant to suppress them all
at his discretion. On April 24th, the Duke of Northumberland had proclaimed the "Friends of Ireland." O'Connell presently summoned a new society, or rather the old
one under a new name, to be called the Anti-Union Association. At a ball at the Viceregal Lodge in October,
Hardinge, the Chief Secretary, accidentally saw its ad-
vertisement in a newspaper. The Lord Lieutenant was
absent, but Hardinge, like a bold soldier, though running to the very verge of legality, proclaimed it himself. The guests as they drove home from the ball in
the morning, found his proclamation wet upon the walls.
Next day O'Connell founded an "Association of Irish
Volunteers," which shared the same fate. He denounced
Hardinge, and received a challenge, which he declined.
This was the first the English heard of his scruple
about duelling. They failed to understand it. When
he went to London next month for the opening of Parliament, men turned their backs upon him at Brooks',
and no one would speak to him at his clubs. Infu-
riated, he took advantage of the Government proposal to equalise the Irish and English stamp duties
by a letter advocating a run on the banks, and the
panic in Ireland which ensued was wild though short
lived.

· Suddenly the scene changed. Returning with weakened forces after the General Election, the Wellington Administration fell, and Lord Grey came in. It was the standing maxim of the Whig managers to " buy O'Connell at any price," and his hopes were justly excited. He was a man whose income though large had been swallowed up by still larger expenses; he was embarrassed by debt; attendance in Parliament meant the abandonment of his profession. His reputation entitled him to hope for office, or, at least, for a judgeship. The votes of the Irish members had been enough to turn the scale against Wellington and in favour of Grey. If Catholic Emancipation was not to be an insulting mockery, Catholics must no longer be excluded from professional advancement and from places in the Administration. Now was the time to see if the Whigs were grateful to their Irish supporters, or the English sincere in extending justice to the Catholics.

The Marquis of Anglesey, whose previous Lord Lieutenancy had endeared him to the Irish, was to replace the Duke of Northumberland in Ireland. Having known O'Connell personally and even acted with him politically, he sent for him in December, before leaving London for Ireland, and an interview of two hours took place between them at Uxbridge House. The Marquis announced that he did not intend to disturb the old law-officers, Joy, the Attorney-General, and Dogherty, the Solicitor-General. O'Connell replied that if Emancipation was not to be made a practical thing in the administration of Ireland and the distribution of patronage, he must agitate for Repeal. Then, said the Marquis, he must coerce the agitation.

There was worse to come. Sir Anthony Hart retired from the Irish Lord Chancellorship and Plunket
succeeded him. This left a vacancy in the Common
Pleas, which O'Connell was eager to fill. Dogherty was
appointed. This was peculiarly galling to O'Connell,
for in the previous session he had denounced Dogherty
for his conduct of the Doneraile case, and accused him
of having kept back depositions on the trial of the first
batch of prisoners, whose production on the trial of the
second and third had shown such discrepancy from the
sworn evidence as to lead to an acquittal. It was in this
debate that he branded the office of Chief Secretary
with the epithet " the shave-beggar " of the Ministry ;
but, on the whole, in the controversy, Dogherty, by
his calm and lofty sarcasm, had come off very much
the best. Still, the Solicitor-Generalship might pro-
perly have been given to O'Connell, and at the
same time, by the promotion of Joy, the Attorney-
Generalship fell vacant also. Blackburne, a Tory,
was appointed to the latter ; Crampton, a Whig, to the
former.

O'Connell declared that there was to be no justice
for the Catholics, and hastened to Ireland. He was
received in triumph ; he advised that Lord Anglesey's
arrival should be contemptuously ignored. Lord Anglesey determined to retaliate. A procession of trades
unions was to have been held on December 27th. Half-
an-hour before the notice convening it was to have been
posted on every chapel door in Dublin, a proclamation
against it appeared. The workmen asked O'Connell
if they should obey, and by way of proving that he and
not the Lord Lieutenant ruled Ireland, he advised them
to show a colourable deference to the proclamation by
holding the meeting on the 28th. He began the Repeal

struggle with the new year. He published a letter in which he said :—

Ireland will achieve one more bloodless and stainless change. Since I was born she has achieved two such glorious political revolutions. The first was in 1782, when she conquered legislative independence; the second was in 1829, when she won for her victory freedom of conscience. The third and best remains behind, the restoration of a domestic and reformed legislature by the repeal of the Union. This we will also achieve, if we persevere in a legal, constitutional, and peaceable course. Let my advice be followed, and I will venture to assert that the Union cannot last two years longer.

A few days afterwards he founded a " General Association for the Prevention of Unlawful Meetings." It met at the "Parliamentary Intelligence Office," a newspaper-room in Stephen Street, which he had established the year before. It was proclaimed. He proposed that he himself should be constituted the Repeal Association, beyond the reach of legal dissolution, and should receive subscriptions and be assisted by a club, which should hold public breakfasts and public debates. Accordingly he constituted "A Body of Persons in the habit of meeting weekly at a place called Home's Hotel." It was dispersed. Then followed "The Irish Society for Legal and Legislative Relief," and it perished. Another phœnix rose from its ashes, an " Anti-Union Association." In quick succession this Protean organization became " An Association of Irish Volunteers for the Repeal of the Union," a society of " Subscribers to the Parliamentary Intelligence Office," and, finally, a mere breakfast party at Hayes' Hotel. As fast as O'Connell created a new society, Lord Anglesey cut it down with a new proclamation. At length this farce, so humiliating to the more serious Irish, so irritating to the Administration, was abruptly closed.

As Anglesey wrote to his wife, " things are now come
to that pass that the question is whether he or I shall
govern Ireland."

On January 13th, 1831, a proclamation was issued,
which forbade an association under any name. O'Connell replied with a manifesto, threatening another run
on the banks. He assembled a breakfast party of 350,
and next day held a meeting of his committee of
thirty-one advisers in Dawson Street. It was dispersed
by two police magistrates, and on January 19th, at
ten in the morning, he was arrested in his own house.
An indictment of the usual cumbrous description
was preferred on the 24th. In fourteen counts he was
charged with offences against the Act of 1829 ; in
seventeen more with a conspiracy at Common Law.
He had made one slip in holding his breakfast in defiance of the proclamation ; he now made another in the
conduct of his case. He demurred to the fourteen
counts. But a demurrer implied an admission of the
facts charged, and an issue only as to their legal effect.
He had debarred himself from a trial on the merits.
He asked and obtained leave to withdraw his demurrer,
and enter a plea of " not guilty." The trial was fixed
for the 17th of February, and a defence fund of £7,000
was collected. But before the trial came on, seeing that
it could have but one ending, he entered into a compromise with the Government. To the amazement of the
public, the Attorney-General entered a *nolle prosequi*
on the conspiracy counts. O'Connell withdrew his plea
of " not guilty," and submitted to a verdict on those
which alleged an offence against the Statute, and the
case stood adjourned for judgment to the first day of
Easter term. He then wrote a letter intended to be
shown to the Chief Secretary, Stanley, in which he

offered to abandon Repeal if the Government would
abandon the prosecution. Stanley sternly refused.
Undoubtedly O'Connell was humiliated. He had been
defeated by the English Government, which he had so
often overcome. His matchless legal dexterity for once
had failed him. He denied in the House of Commons
that he had offered to withdraw the question of Repeal,
and gave out that he feared there would have been a
popular outbreak at his trial. But even his friends did
not believe it. Sheil said his heart had sunk at the
prospect of a gaol ; and " how," he asked, " could a
man face a battle who could not encounter Newgate ?"
The supporters of the Government were jubilant, but they
had not long much cause for exultation. It was rumoured
that O'Connell was to be treated gently, because the
Government was bidding for his vote in London. Stanley
denied the rumour. " The Crown," he said, " has procured a verdict against Mr. O'Connell, and it will undoubtedly call him up to receive judgment upon it." But
the event showed that the world knew better than the
Chief Secretary. On March 2nd the Reform Bill was introduced ; on the 9th O'Connell spoke brilliantly in its
support. The first day of term approached, but he could
not be spared from Westminster. The delivery of
judgment in his case was postponed till May. But
judgment never was pronounced at all. On April 22nd
Parliament was dissolved ; the Act of 1829 thereupon
expired. The Government gladly availed themselves of
the plea that, the Act against which he had offended
being gone, O'Connell could not now be punished for
his offence. He was a free man.

Until the close of the Reform contest, O'Connell,
who had now been returned for Kerry, spoke and voted
with the Whigs. But in spite of the most strenuous

efforts in committee on the Irish Bill, he was unable
to recover for the Irish peasants any of the ground they
had lost in 1829.   He pointed out that proportionately
to the wealth of each country, a £10 franchise in Ireland was as high as a £20 franchise would be in England.
He complained that the registration was cumbrous, the
number of members inadequate, and that Ireland, which
had 8,000,000 inhabitants, and in 1829 had had nearly
800,000 voters, had now only 26,000, while the English electorate was to be raised from 200,000 to
850,000.   Stanley sternly refused to enfranchise the
forty-shilling freeholders, and the House of Lords inserted a clause restoring the franchise to freemen in the
boroughs, who were invariably Protestants, and often
corrupt.   The pressure, however, upon the Government to do something to conciliate so useful an ally
and so formidable an opponent grew stronger.   In August,
1831, Dr. Doyle, a highly esteemed and influential
Roman Catholic bishop, urged them to confer office upon
him.   In Michaelmas term he received his patent of
precedence as a King's Counsel, and hoping to fetter
him by imposing upon him official responsibility, the
Government authorized Sir H. Parnell to sound him,
through Dr. Doyle, about taking office.   If it were certain that he would accept the offer if made, no insuperable obstacle existed to their making it.   It was a
tempting opportunity, but O'Connell felt obliged to
refuse.   He required a promise of substantial change
in the Government's Irish policy.   This Grey and
Stanley would not give.   Their view was one which
Stanley afterwards expressed in the phrase "Ireland
must be taught to fear before she could be taught to
love," and merely to conciliate a man whom they
hated, they would not abandon the principle.   But as

yet circumstances had not forced them to avow or to act upon this view. Though O'Connell could not take office with the Whigs, he conceived that he had done them good service, for which he was entitled to their gratitude, and when the last unreformed Parliament was dissolved in December 1832, he hoped that a new day was dawning for Ireland. He was doomed to a bitter disappointment.

CHAPTER VI.

THE REFORMED PARLIAMENT.

1833–1835.

Tithe War—O'Connell renews his agitation against Tithe and for Repeal—The Reform Bill—"Who is the traitor?"—Coercion Bill of 1833—O'Connell's Repeal motion—Intrigue with Littleton—Fall of the Whigs—Peel's Administration.

SCARCELY had the Irish obtained Emancipation, when they fell upon evil days again. From the year 1830, a cloud of misery and crime gathered over Ireland. Practically valueless, and economically injurious, the forty-shilling freeholders, who had lost their votes, now lost their holdings, and were freely evicted. Prices were low; employment was ill-paid and difficult to obtain; in the South wages were 5s. a week, and even less, and even at that rate work was scarce. In the autumn of 1830 the potato crop failed; in the winter famine made its appearance in the South and West, and unfortunately there was no poor law, as there was in England, to relieve the distress. Hundreds and thousands were literally reduced to beggary. The people suffered from two imposts peculiarly offensive to Irish Catholic feeling. They were liable to Church tithes for the support of a clergy whose ministrations it was schism to enjoy,

and to Church cess for the erection and repair of build-
ings, where heretical ceremonies were performed which
they believed could lead only to perdition. Gross abuses
and gross hardships were but too often connected with
these taxes. The burden of the tithes had been thrown
deliberately upon the Roman Catholics. The tithe was
in many cases let for a fixed sum to tithe farmers, who
collected it with little regard to anything but their
own profit; and being often due in almost incredibly
minute sums, it was, even when collected from cot-
tiers by the ministers of religion themselves, a tax
hateful for its past injustice and its present hardship. The disproportion between the numbers of
the Protestant parishioners and of the Protestant
parishes was glaring. There were no less than 151 incumbents of parishes who had not a single parishioner.
Between the incomes of the bishops and those of the
clergy of the Established Church the inequality was
no less preposterous. While there were many poor
incumbents, the number of bishoprics was indefensibly
great, and their incomes exorbitantly high. The
Church cess was levied by a Protestant vestry upon a
Catholic peasantry for the repair of Protestant churches;
instances were known in which costly churches were
erected for non-existent congregations, and others, in
which funds raised to build churches had been spent
upon dwelling-houses for Protestants. The spirit of
the Irish had been awakened during the struggle for
Emancipation, and their hopes raised by its issue.
They now resolved in their distress to submit to these
burdens no longer, and the Tithe War began.

The agitation, which O'Connell carried on, quick-
ened this spirit. The Executive forbade it; but suppressed though it was by authority, it did not remain

barren of results. Repeal was the object at which he
ultimately aimed, but he directed his efforts towards
ends far more attainable than Repeal. On the 7th
January 1830 he had published a manifesto to the
people of Ireland, in which he set forth his programme. This included the repeal of the Sub-letting
Act and of the Vestry Act, an elaborate plan for the
reform of grand juries, various proposals for the reform
of legal procedure, as to which he called himself
" a thorough Benthamite," reform of corporations and
radical parliamentary reform, and finally the abolition
of Tithes and of Church cess. On July 14th 1832
he wrote a letter to the National Political Union, in
which he formulated his plan for dealing with tithe. It
was to be ultimately extinguished, but compensation
was to be given to existing interests in possession; and
he followed this proposal with another more sweeping,
to disendow the Church of Ireland beyond such sums as
were required for its actual ministry and congregations,
and to devote the funds so liberated to charity and to
the provision of parish houses and glebes for the
parochial Catholic clergy and Presbyterian ministers.
A few months later, as the conflict became more bitter,
he wrote again to the same body a long letter, which he
concluded by solemnly declaring, " First, I am determined never again voluntarily to pay tithes; second, I
am determined never again voluntarily to pay vestry
cess; third, I am determined never to buy one single
article sold for tithes or vestry cess."

The Irish profited by his teaching. The refusal to
pay tithe or cess was general. As early as the end
of 1831 the arrears of tithe were very large, and the
clergy found themselves powerless to get them in. But
tithes were the chief support of hundreds of the clergy,

and by hundreds they were reduced to destitution. Their lamentable condition attracted, as that of the tithe-payers did not, the attention of Parliament. Committees of both Houses sat to examine the question. O'Connell indignantly pointed out that not a single Catholic sat on either. "It seems," said he, "Roman Catholics have nothing to do with tithe but to pay it." Committees so composed contented themselves with a proposal for collecting the tithes, not for abolishing them, and, in spite of O'Connell's opposition, a measure was carried, by which the Government advanced £60,000 for the immediate relief of the clergy, and itself undertook the collection of the tithe. But the efforts of the Government were as fruitless as those of rectors or tithe-farmers. After many struggles and some bloodshed, they collected £12,000 of tithes in arrear; the effort cost £14,000. When the people refused to pay, the Government proceeded to distrain. The sheriff, assisted by a military force, seized a cottier's cow. Escorted by a troop of horse, the cow was solemnly driven across country to market. Its appearance was the signal for a universal cessation of business. As if it had been plague-smitten, everyone held aloof; not a buyer could be found, and nothing remained to be done but for the sheriff of the county to drive the cow away again, escorted by a troop of His Majesty's dragoons. The vindication of justice was degenerating into a farce.

Unhappily it too often terminated in a tragedy. Never had crime and disorder been more rife than in the winter of 1832. Multitudes of secret societies sprang up, cattle were mutilated, tithe-proctors and process-servers were murdered. There were in 1832 9,000 crimes connected with political disturbances, and of these 200 were homicides. The record of certain counties was peculiarly black. In Kilkenny, during the twelve months, 34 houses were burnt, 519 burglaries were committed, and the murders and attempts to murder were 32. Queen's County was even worse. The burglaries were 626, the homicides 60. Evidence was not to be obtained, and juries would not convict. It became plain that a more stringent law was needed.

The Government possessed an overwhelming majority in the first reformed Parliament. The necessity of concentrating every effort upon the return of Reform candidates had induced O'Connell to sink the question of Repeal at the General Election in the summer of 1831. But Reform once carried, he insisted upon the general imposition of a Repeal pledge at the General Election in the winter of 1832, and published a series of thirty letters, instructing the constituencies in the clearest detail, what persons were entitled to vote, and how votes should be claimed. He had himself been returned for Kerry without a contest, and would have preferred to sit for his native county, but it became clear that no one but he could defeat the Tories in Dublin, and for Dublin he was constrained to stand. He was elected, and his followers won almost all along the line. He nominated about half the candidates who were returned. Three of his sons and two of his sons-in-law formed his "household brigade." Repealers came in for the cities and boroughs of Dublin, Cork, Waterford, Wexford, Clonmel, Ennis, Tralee, Kilkenny, Athlone, Roscommon, and Galway; and for the counties of Cork, Dublin, Limerick, Waterford, Mayo, Tipperary, Kilkenny, Kerry, Wexford, Westmeath, King's County, Galway, Sligo, Wicklow, and Meath. Of 105 Irish members, but 23 were Tories; of 82 Liberal members, 45 were pledged Repealers. The support of 52 Irish members had carried the Whig Reform Bill against a majority of the members from England and Scotland ; the Whigs had now a majority which would enable them to pass anything, and the Irish looked for their reward.

The first Irish measure which the Ministry brought forward was a Coercion Act, more severe than any of its predecessors since the Act of Union. The fiery Stanley's influence with Lord Grey had prevailed over the conciliatory advice of Melbourne, Althorp, and Grant. Seeing what was coming, O'Connell began the battle early, and fought the Government policy with courage, tenacity, brilliance, and vituperation almost unparallelled. He initiated a four nights debate upon the Address on February 5th, in a speech in which he denounced the Government as " bloody and brutal " with a reiteration that compelled the Speaker to expostulate with him, and, with more damaging effect, declared that the policy of the Executive had made the Catholic Relief Act a dead letter. Since it passed, four years had gone by. There was still not a Catholic judge upon the bench ; there was but one Catholic high sheriff and a handful of Catholic magistrates. Of 34 stipendiary magistrates, all nominated by Lord Anglesey except 8, 82 sub-inspectors of police, and 5 inspectors-general of police, for the most part appointed since the Whigs came in, not one was a Catholic, and now, he said, came a Royal Speech which was to Ireland a " declaration of civil war." The Government, however, carried the Address by a huge majority.

On the 11th of February O'Connell renewed the conflict by a speech on the Report of the Address, in which he pronounced enthusiastically for Repeal, and

on February 18th, by another on the Estimates, denouncing coercion, and declaring that "this projected
measure of His Majesty's Government is more condu-
cive to a Repeal of the Union than all my agitation."
On the 27th, Althorp rose to move the first reading
of the Bill for the Suppression of Disturbances in Ireland. To him it was, indeed, an uncongenial task.
He plodded drearily through pages bristling with the
statistics of crime and the records of misery and discontent, and produced even on his supporters so adverse an
impression, that the Coercion Bill was all but still-born.
Graham, who saw how ill matters were going, despatched
Le Marchant to Earl Grey for reinforcements. Althorp's
box of papers was taken to Stanley, and he shut himself up in a room upstairs. In two hours he was master
of the case ; and at midnight he rose to deliver almost
the only speech in the annals of the House of Commons that has won votes as well as changed opinions.
He marshalled the facts of Irish crime with brilliant
effect ; he directed upon O'Connell an onslaught so
fiery and overwhelming that O'Connell "looked like a
convicted felon." He declared, without mincing matters,
that for her crimes, and their inevitable punishment,
Ireland had to thank the agitation of O'Connell. He
charged him with writing, on February 10th, to the
Society of Volunteers, to tell them, contrary to the
then usage of secrecy on such matters, that the member
for Armagh and the two members for Limerick had
voted against Ireland on the Address, and begging their
constituents not to forget it. This O'Connell did not
seek to deny. He quoted from reports of a speech of
O'Connell's delivered at a Trades Union banquet, in
which he was said to have called the House of
Commons a body of "six hundred and fifty-eight

scoundrels "; and although O'Connell followed with
a short explanation and denial of the words, his
speech at the conclusion of the debate made no impression. But O'Connell was not a man to be long
or easily put down. It was his policy to make himself, in the opinion of the whole House, what Cobbett
had called him, "the member for Ireland." His
imperturbable assurance, not less than his abilities
and the air of authority, with which he expressed his
opinion on all Irish matters, gradually gave him an
influence on the new members most prejudicial to the
Government. He spared no effort to improve his position, being always ready to afford information to other
members, and most bland and courteous in his intercourse
with them. In committee Stanley found him an assiduous
and formidable opponent. But the Irish were too few
in number; only eighty-four members voted against the
second reading. The Bill passed by large majorities,
and the Government was armed with powers to proclaim
districts, to suppress associations, to confine people to
their houses after dark, to search for arms, to proclaim
martial law, to suspend the Habeas Corpus Act, and
to try prisoners by court-martial. O'Connell's Irish
Society of Volunteers did not wait to be suppressed;
it transferred its powers to its author and dissolved.

The Whigs, however, were not insincere in their
desire to alleviate the sufferings of the Irish. They
introduced a Church Temporalities Bill, to abolish
Church cess and substitute for it a tax on the incomes
of the clergy, to suppress nearly half of the bishoprics
and a crowd of livings, and to devote to non-ecclesias-
tical purposes the sum of £3,000,000 so liberated.
O'Connell approved the principle of this appropriation:
but the Tories, who could not defend the sinecure bene-

fices and profusion of bishoprics, opposed the appropriation. To conciliate them it was abandoned, and the
Bill passed ; but thus reduced to the abolition of the cess
and the internal reform of the Church, it attracted little
gratitude from the Roman Catholics. In the recess
ministerial changes took place. Stanley went to the
Colonial Office, and was succeeded by Littleton. Lord
Anglesey retired, and the Marquis of Wellesley became
Lord Lieutenant. Efforts were made to conciliate
O'Connell. The Protestant party was appalled to see
a Roman Catholic agitator positively dining with the
Chief Secretary. They were spared the further pain of
seeing him in office. O'Connell writes to a friend :
" The Ministry have made and are making more direct
offers to me . . . but all this does not make me one
whit the less immovable. If I went into office I
should be their servant—that is, their slave ; by staying out of office, I am, to a considerable extent, their
master."

For upwards of three years he had now been advocating and impressing upon the Irish by speeches,
letters, and organization, the necessity of a union of all
classes and creeds in Ireland in a determined agitation
for Repeal. He had broached the subject in his first
Clare election address. He had deeply stirred the South
of Ireland by letters and speeches in the autumn of
1830, and although his mind was not made up either as
to the exact value of Repeal or the precise form it should
take, he was characteristically sanguine of its not distant success. He wrote on December 3rd 1830, to his
constant correspondent, Dr. MacHale, Roman Catholic
Archbishop of Tuam :

The moral and political revolution is plainly on its march. . . . I
am convinced as I am of to-morrow's sun that within the space of

probably less than two years the monopolies of corporations and the still more gigantic oppressions of the Established Church will have passed away for ever. . . . There must be a law to take off the Church burden. An Irish Parliament alone can do that. There must be an end to absenteeism. An Irish Parliament alone can do that.

When he endeavoured during his prosecution in 1831 to induce Stanley to forego a trial by the offer of an abandonment of Repeal, he seems to have thought that an Irish Parliament was only machinery, a means to an end, and that if an English Parliament would endeavour to remedy Irish grievances equally effectually, Repeal became needless. In 1833, too, he said in the House of Commons: "The only reason I have for being a Repealer is the injustice of the present Government towards my country. . . . If I thought the machinery of the present Government would work well, there never lived a man more ready to facilitate its movements than I am." During the election of 1831 he allowed the question to rest, but as soon as it was over he began his agitation afresh. In October he founded his National Political Union, which met twice a week to discuss Repeal, and in 1832 he endeavoured to effect the union of it with a rival body, the Trades Political Union, " to procure that measure without which, it is my solemn, conscientious, and unalterable opinion, Ireland cannot prosper, the Repeal of the Union." He formulated a plan for an independent legislature in opposition to the subordinate assembly of Sharman Crawford's Federal scheme. At Bath the newspapers reported him, to the dismay of the Irish, to have declared himself favourable to the " union " with Great Britain. This he denied, and said that he had only declared in favour of the " connection," and had demanded " a Parliament to do our private business, leav-

8 *

ing the national business to a national assembly." He
further elaborated his plan, proposing, first, repeal of the
Act of Union, and, next, the creation of two legislatures,
each consisting of a House of Lords and a House of
Commons, each legislature to meet in October, and to
discuss private Bills, and the affairs of commerce, agriculture, and manufactures of Great Britain and of Ireland respectively, while in February a National Parliament was to meet for affairs of peace or war and foreign
policy. By the following spring the Coercion Bill had
further developed his views. He was anxious to have
Moore come forward for an Irish constituency. Moore
would neither stand as a Repealer, nor accept the position
of a "joint" in O'Connell's tail. He told O'Connell that
Separation must follow Repeal, as certainly as night
day, and therefore he could not advocate Repeal.
O'Connell said to him, "I am now convinced that
Repeal won't do, and that it must be Separation." He
was not far from the position of the peasants, who,
during the agitation of 1830, were constantly asking
O'Neill Daunt, "When do you think, Sir, the Counsellor will call us out?"

One thing, however, O'Connell saw quite clearly, that
it was useless, with the Irish agitation still only in em-
bryo, to ask the House of Commons to entertain any
proposal for Repeal, and yet in 1834 he brought the
question forward in Parliament. From the Union until
1833 the Irish members had been Whigs or Tories as
the case might be, but there had been no separate Irish
party. But with the return of a large Repeal contingent to
the first reformed parliament, there came into existence
under O'Connell's leadership that third party which
has held the balance in so many parliaments, and upset
so many ministries since then. In the brief interval

between the last election and the opening of Parliament in 1833, O'Connell had not time, although he held a meeting of his party in Dublin, to bring them into thorough discipline. But he was disposed to make an unsparing use of his strength to keep his followers in subjection. Fergus O'Connor, member for Cork, a scatter-brained squireen, was unwilling to submit. During 1833 he pressed vehemently for the immediate discussion of Repeal. O'Connell resisted while he could, and twice at the beginning of 1834 obtained majorities in the meetings of the Repeal party in favour of its postponement. But O'Connor vowed that if their leader would not bring the question forward, he would do so himself; and to avoid worse consequences O'Connell, sorely against his will, decided to introduce the question. "I felt," said he to Daunt, with a metaphor probably more forcible in those days than in these, "like a man who was going to plunge into a cold bath; but I was obliged to take the plunge."

One matter of discipline there was, in which he could interfere. Hill, M.P. for Hull, had, in a speech to his constituents during the previous autumn, said that some of the Irish members, who violently denounced the Coercion Bill in public, had in private implored Ministers not to drop it. If this were so, O'Connell's authority with his party was gone. He must either vindicate it by disproving the charge or purge his forces by unmasking the traitor. On February 5th 1834, the second night of the Session, he questioned Lord Althorp in the House as to the statement. Althorp said no such communication had been made to Ministers, but he believed that in private conversation Irish members had approved the Bill, who in debate had assailed it. Amid violent confusion, O'Connell rose, followed by the other Irish members, one by one, each asking "Is it I?" Althorp said "no" to each. The Speaker tried to pour oil on the waters, but O'Connell would not have peace, and still further troubled them. At last Sheil rose to ask if he was one of those referred to. Althorp said that he was one. Sheil, "speaking in the presence of God," passionately denied it. O'Connell thereupon ostentatiously withdrew and apologised for every harsh expression he had applied to Hill. There followed a long discussion upon the nice point of honour, which of the two, Althorp or Sheil, was to be considered the aggrieved party, who could send a challenge, and which of the two should accordingly be first required to promise to send none. The Speaker called on Sheil to undertake that the matter should go no farther. Sheil sate dumb. The Speaker turned to Althorp. Althorp said he would not follow it up outside. The Speaker was disposed to be content with this; but O'Connell was more astute, and pointed out that Althorp had said he would not send a challenge, but had not said he would not accept one. To the Speaker's demand for a full undertaking Althorp gave a refusal, and, on Burdett's motion, Sheil and Althorp were marched out of the House in the custody of the Serjeant-at-Arms.

This was a disagreeable incident for the Ministry; another was to come. On February 13th, O'Connell rose to call attention to the extraordinary nocturnal habits of Baron Smith of the Irish Court of Exchequer, who loved to come to Court at the hour when most Courts rise, and to try prisoners till the small hours of the morning. He had given notice of a motion in favour of the judge's removal. The Ministry had decided to oppose it. Suddenly he changed his

motion to one only for a select committee. Althorp
and Littleton, taken by surprise, assented. It was
carried by 167 to 74. But on reflection they saw
the ineptitude of the proceeding. A committee was
useless. The House must impeach the Baron or
address the Crown for his removal, or let him alone.
The last was the only feasible course. A week later,
on the 21st, Knatchbull, a Tory member, relieved them
from their difficulty by carrying a motion to rescind
the motion to which Althorp had assented.

After these two blows O'Connell tried the strength of
the Repeal party. The King's Speech had taken notice
of the Repeal agitation. It said of the Act of Union,
"this bond of our national strength and safety I have
already declared my fixed and unalterable resolution,
under the blessing of Divine Providence, to maintain
inviolate by all the means in my power." The Address
contained words which re-echoed this resolution;
O'Connell had moved their omission, and was defeated
by 189 to 23. The prospect was dark indeed. He
gave notice of a motion for a committee to inquire into
the working of the Act of Union. "He was one of the
most sensitive and nervous men that ever lived," says
his son. "Previous to his motion he was very unhappy
and spent several sleepless nights, which was by no
means unusual with him when any matter of importance
impended." His motion came on about 5 P.M. on
Tuesday, April 22nd. He spoke for nearly seven hours.
Beginning with a long historical retrospect, during
which he read copious extracts from Morrisson's History
of Ireland, he proceeded to argue that the Irish Parliament had no power to extinguish itself or to sell its
birthright, and therefore that the Act of Union was not
binding in law. It was not binding in morality, having

been procured by corrupt means. He even declared that for the purpose of making up a case for union the English Government had connived at the plots of the United Irishmen and deliberately fostered the rebellion of 1798. He argued that the terms of the bargain were unfair to Ireland. The English House of Lords had usurped an appellate jurisdiction so inconvenient, that this grievance of itself was sufficient to justify the demand for Repeal. Ireland had been loaded with an unfair proportion of the Imperial indebtedness. The taxation for interest on the debt and annual expenditure, to which her resources made her justly liable, was 1-17th of the whole. She had been charged with 2-17ths; and, as it was impossible for her to pay so much, it had been found necessary to amalgamate the Irish with the English exchequer. Proportionately to her population she ought to have 202 members, and on any calculation 110; she had 105. Since the Union, Ireland had decayed. From 1782 to 1800 her consumption of tea and tobacco had increased twice as fast as that of England, of coffee and wine four times as fast. But since 1800 absenteeism had become almost universal, and Ireland had fallen into poverty. In Great Britain £47,000,000 of taxation had been repealed; in Ireland £1,500,000. Taxes in England had risen 20 per cent.; in Ireland 80 per cent. The population of England had increased prodigiously in thirty-four years; in Ireland it had diminished. In that period there had been sixty select committees and one hundred and fourteen commissions on Irish affairs, and yet for all this inquiry the English had been so little able to govern Ireland that in twenty of the thirty-four years the Constitution was suspended. His case was backed up with a huge parade of quotations from various politicians by way of testimony, like proofs in a lawyer's brief, and at the end of his speech the exhausted House adjourned.

Spring-Rice was deputed to answer him, and was no less prolix and even more statistical. The Government met the motion with a proposal for an address to the Crown, pledging the House to maintain the Union and to remove all just causes of complaint in the future. The question was debated for nine nights, and O'Connell was beaten on a division by 523 to 38. In the minority but one English member voted; in the majority 57, more than half, of the Irish members were counted. The question of Repeal was at rest in Parliament for upwards of a generation.

The Whigs, however, were not unmindful of their promises to the Irish. Littleton brought in, much to the disgust of Stanley, a Tithe Bill, which commuted the tithe for a land tax. It was introduced on the 20th February, and on the 2nd May the Bill came on for second reading. But the Ministry was in a moribund state. Althorp and Littleton were for moderate reform, Grey and Stanley for ruling with a high hand; Brougham was meddlesome and treacherous, Graham vacillating and uncertain. In May came a crisis. Ward brought on his resolution in favour of the appropriation of surplus Irish Church revenues to secular objects. The feeling of a majority of the Cabinet was in its favour, and the Government proposed to meet it with a pledge for an inquiry into the Irish Church. Upon this Stanley resigned, and Graham, the Duke of Richmond, and the Earl of Ripon followed him. Thus weakened, the Government was anxious to secure the support of the Irish members for their Tithe Bill, which was obnoxious to the Tories. But the Coercion Act of the previous year had rendered the

Repealers implacable, and to add to their difficulties the Government were now met by the necessity of renewing some part of it, if not the whole. To the curfew clauses and the power of proclaiming districts, O'Connell was more or less reconciled, for the state of Ireland was still indisputably disturbed; but to the suppression of meetings he was inexorably opposed. Littleton knew that that provision and his Tithe Bill could not both pass. Hitherto Lord Wellesley had written officially to the Government pressing for a renewal of the whole Act except the court-martial clause. On June 19th Brougham sent for Littleton, and proposed to him to ask Lord Wellesley to write to Earl Grey advising that the public meetings clause should be dropped. Littleton did so, pointing out how essential to the Ministry it was to have O'Connell's support, and that if the Tithe Bill passed the clauses against mere agitation would not be required. Lord Wellesley wrote on June 23rd to Lord Grey a private letter in the sense Littleton desired. Littleton also saw Melbourne and Althorp. They were both of his opinion; the first characteristically said it would not do to exasperate Grey; the second said that sooner than assent to the clause he would resign. Convinced now that the clause would not be introduced, Littleton proposed to Althorp to send for O'Connell, hint that this was so, and beg him not to embarrass the Government. O'Connell was at that time beginning a new Irish agitation against the Coercion Bill. There was a vacancy at Wexford, and against the Whig candidate he had sent a Repealer. Althorp approved of the project, but urged reticence and caution. Littleton accordingly sent for O'Connell, who came to the Irish Office, and was told under the seal of secrecy that the Coercion Bill would be a short and limited one, aimed only at agrarian crime, and that he would do well not to agitate for the present. O'Connell accordingly withdrew his Repealer at Wexford, and declined to support a local Repeal candidate. On June 29th there was a Cabinet meeting, and Grey, though he read Lord Wellesley's letter of the 23rd to his colleagues, carried his point that the whole Act should be renewed ; but, in introducing the Bill in the House of Lords on July 1st, he suppressed the fact that Wellesley had written to advise the abandonment of the public meetings clause. Rumours had got about, no doubt due to hints dropped by O'Connell, that the Government was carrying on some negotiations with the Irish members. These were referred to during the debate, and Grey denied them. O'Connell now determined upon revenge. He thought that he had been deceived and trifled with, and he saw how Littleton had laid himself open defenceless to attack. He argued that the deceit practised upon him absolved him from his promise to hold the communication a secret, and on the 3rd he rose and in terms charged the Chief Secretary with "tricking" him in order to obtain the withdrawal of the Repeal candidate at Wexford. Littleton could not deny the substance of the conversation, which O'Connell revealed to the astonished House, though he denied the charge as regards the Wexford election. The angry combatants bandied across the table point-blank contradictions on their honour as gentlemen. Littleton was reduced to complaining that O'Connell had violated a sacred confidence. This complaint was not ill-founded, and many of O'Connell's friends and colleagues, including Hume, Warburton, O'Ferrall, O'Dwyer, and Grattan, reproached him with breach of faith. But the mischief was done. Littleton tendered his resignation, which was refused. Grey saw that it was useless to ask the House of Commons to give power to prohibit meetings, when once it knew that the Lord Lieutenant himself did not desire to possess it, and, finding the dissensions of his Cabinet now public property, himself resigned. O'Connell and Ireland had brought to the ground the great Reform Minister less than two years after the passing of his great Reform Act.

Melbourne succeeded Grey, and Littleton proceeded with his Tithe Bill. Upon the motion to go into Committee on July 20th, O'Connell pressed for delay until the Church Commission, the Commission which he had called a "wet blanket" on the tithe agitation, had reported. The motion to go into Committee was carried by 154 to 14. Next night, undeterred, he brought in an amendment to abandon the arrears of tithe and to bring the scheme, which Littleton had eventually provided for, into immediate operation. The relief to the payers of tithe was very great, and the amendment passed by a large majority. But no Bill would satisfy the Lords; they threw it out by 189 to 122, and deferred the settlement of the question for several years.

The Melbourne Ministry did not last long. The King dismissed his Ministers, and Hudson was sent post-haste to Peel at Rome. O'Connell, who, upon the rejection of the Tithe Bill, had begun a fresh agitation with a series of letters to Lord Duncannon from Darrynane, savagely exulting over Grey's fall, struck the first note of opposition to the new Government by postponing the question of Repeal and founding the Anti-Tory Association. Peel dissolved Parliament, and O'Connell exerted every nerve to defeat the Tories in Ireland. The Tories almost defeated him. He himself barely saved his seat at Dublin. His majority of 1,549 dropped to 217, and his return was immediately petitioned against. However, his three sons and a nephew obtained seats, and, although the Repeal party was less strong than in 1832, Peel, who on the English elections had a substantial majority, was in a minority of twenty upon the Irish elections. The Whigs began the Session by carrying Abercromby, their candidate for the Speakership. Meetings were held on March 12th and 23rd at Lord Lichfield's house in St. James's Square, the result of which was to secure them the co-operation of O'Connell in turning out Peel. Lord Morpeth moved an amendment to the Address condemning the dissolution, and O'Connell took the opportunity of indicating the measures in favour of which he was content to postpone Repeal, namely, the amendment of the Irish Reform Act, the appropriation of the Irish Church surplus, and the reform of the Irish Corporations. Peel introduced a Tithe Bill but little different from that which the Whigs had introduced the year before. Russell moved an amendment in favour of devoting the Irish Church surplus to education, and carried it, with O'Connell's assistance, by a majority of thirty-three. Peel resigned on April 5th, and Lord Melbourne was called upon to form an administration.

CHAPTER VII.

WHIG ALLIANCE.

1835-1840.

Disappointed of Office—Tour in Scotland—The Carlow Election
Scandal—Abandonment of Repeal—The Irish Poor Law Bill—
Accession of the Queen and O'Connell's loss of popularity in
Ireland—Reprimanded by the Speaker—The Precursor Society.

O'CONNELL'S fond hopes from his alliance with the
Whigs were doomed to disappointment. He had
grounds for believing that he was entitled to office in
the Whig Administration, and, Repeal being now laid
on one side, office would have been peculiarly grateful to
him. Rumours were afloat that he was to be Attorney-
General for Ireland, which the new Lord-Lieutenant, Lord
Mulgrave, afterwards Lord Normanby, encouraged him
to believe. He gave them credit, and, thinking that a
new era was coming for Irish officialism, was on the
look-out for a large house in Dublin in which to exercise a lavish official hospitality. The rumours reached
the King, who had little more love for O'Connell
than his brother and predecessor had had. His Majesty
so far departed from constitutional usage as to write to
Lord Melbourne that such an appointment must not be

made. Melbourne replied with spirit that it was not for the King to dictate in the matter, but that in fact he did not propose to include O'Connell in his Administration. The Whigs, indeed, saw the dangers of the position. Some alliance with O'Connell was indispensable to their existence : too close a partnership might be fatal to it. Below the gangway he could, though not without hazard, render them important service ; on the Treasury bench he could only scare away their supporters. It became necessary to communicate to O'Connell that nothing could be done for him, and Ellice, the dexterous manager of the party, with whom O'Connell had been intimately associated in founding the Reform Club the year before, was chosen for the purpose. The announcement was a blow to him, perhaps less personally than patriotically. For himself office might have been perilous: his tribute for 1833 had amounted to £13,900 ; for 1834 to not much less. Office would have risked this. As their Attorney-General he would have been the servant of the Government. Popularity was dear to him, and the Irish were little used to make an idol of an attorney-general. But he thought this, nevertheless, a serious blow to Ireland, for his appointment would have been a singular mark of conciliation, and conciliation was sorely needed.

He bore his rejection magnanimously, and took his seat below the gangway. During the next five years he rendered the Whigs a steady and invaluable support. His action and advocacy in the House of Commons during this period belongs, indeed, rather to the history of Lord Melbourne's administration than to his own personal career. Upon Irish questions he was practically a consultative member of the Cabinet, and Irish patronage was almost at his disposal ; but he was

without responsibility, and was not called upon to
originate a policy.

It was not, however, long before he found himself
engaged in the most active hostilities.   In his exaspe-
ration with the House of Lords he applied the expression "bloated buffoon " to Lord Alvanley.   Alvanley
sent Dawson Damer with a challenge, which was refused,
and Damer published the correspondence.   It was also
laid by Alvanley before the managers of Brooks' on May 2,
with a requisition signed by twenty-three members calling
for a general meeting of the Club to consider O'Connell's
conduct in the matter, but the managers decided that
they could not " take cognizance of differences of a
private nature between members of the Club." Morgan
O'Connell thereupon offered a vicarious satisfaction, and
after two shots had been fired, Alvanley was appeased.
Disraeli now thought that he too might burn some
powder.   He had sought O'Connell's recommendation
at the High Wycombe election in 1832, and had now
attacked him fiercely at the Taunton election in 1835.
O'Connell replied with still greater ferocity, in a speech
before the Dublin Franchise Association, and called him
" a miscreant," " a liar," " a disgrace to his species,"
and " heir-at-law of the blasphemous thief who died
upon the cross."   Disraeli wrote to Morgan O'Connell
on May 5th, and challenged him to fight for his father,
but the challenge was declined.

The recess was a period of greater excitement for
O'Connell than the Session had been.   The Govern-
ment was testifying its loyal intentions to Ireland.
Morpeth and Drummond, as Chief Secretary and
Under-Secretary, were carrying on the administration
with an impartiality and diligence hitherto unknown.
A Tithe Bill had been introduced, but the House of

Lords, resisted it, and the Bill was dropped. The
Municipal Corporation Bill shared the same fate.
O'Connell announced himself as the indulgent patron
of the Ministry. In a manifesto to the Irish people
he said :—

I now come before the people of Ireland to avow myself the devoted
supporter of the administration. If I see the Ministry persevere for
one year in their determination to do justice to Ireland I shall give
them another trial. If the Ministry deceive us it will demonstrate
that Repeal is our only resource.

As their powerful ally he undertook a crusade
against the Tory majority in the House of Lords. On
the rising of Parliament he went down to the North.
He visited Manchester, passed through the streets in
procession, and spoke in Stevenson Square. He went
to Newcastle, and proceeded into Scotland. Everywhere he was received with curiosity, admiration, and
enthusiasm. He addressed crowded meetings at Edinburgh. On September 21st he proceeded by Falkirk to
Glasgow, and spoke six times in a single day. "The
papers," writes Greville, "are full of nothing but
O'Connell's progress in Scotland, where he is received
with unbounded enthusiasm by enormous crowds. He
is exalted to the bad eminence at which he has arrived
more by the assaults of his enemies than by the efforts
of his friends. It is the Tories who are ever insisting
upon the immensity of his power, and whose excess of
hatred and fear make him of such vast account."

My duty [he told one of his audiences] is to propose to you as a
toast "a speedy effectual reform of the House of Lords," and that, I
confess, is the prime object of my mission through England and the
country. It is now the leading object of my political life. . . . I
disclaim occupying the principal portion of my mind with any other
topic, till I see the oligarchy mitigated and an effectual reform introduced into that House.

9

He returned to Ireland by Belfast, was received with a demonstration of trades in Dublin, and proceeded to recruit himself at Darrynane. In his retreat he formulated a plan for the reform of the House of Lords, which he published in two letters to the editor of the *Leeds Times.* His plan was, that out of the peerage, whose numbers were not to be allowed to fall below 500, 150 were to be elected by popular vote to form a second chamber. The plan was moderate and simple, but it is not easy to see how a second chamber so elected could form a very useful check upon the House of Commons.

In October he became involved in a scandal which caused him no little disquietude and some discredit. At the General Election in the spring Bruen and Kavanagh had been returned for Carlow. The return had been petitioned against, and it became plain that the seats would be vacated. O'Connell, anxious to wrest the seats from the Tories, looked round for a candidate of means to stand with the other Repealer, Mr. Vigors, who had none. A Mr. Alexander Raphael, a London tradesman, who had been Sheriff of London, had for some time solicited O'Connell's support in procuring his election to Parliament. He professed the Roman Catholic faith, and, although there was some doubt of his political sincerity, his principles appeared satisfactory to O'Connell. He had contested Pontefract and Evesham, and had thought of coming forward for Westminster. In view of a vacancy at Carlow, Raphael renewed his solicitations. On May 27th the Committee declared the seats vacant, and next day O'Connell called upon Raphael and proposed that he should contest one of them. He wrote on the 29th, " You will never again meet with so safe a speculation. I am quite sure I shall never hear of one." The parties had an interview on June 1st, and

O'Connell gave a written agreement in the following terms :—

You having acceded to the terms proposed to you for the election of the County of Carlow, viz., you are to pay before nomination £1,000 and a like sum after being returned, the first to be paid absolutely and entirely for being nominated, the second to be paid only in the event of your being returned, I hereby undertake to guarantee and save you harmless from any and every other expense whatever, whether of agents, carriages, counsel, petition against the return, or of any other description, and to make this guarantee in the fullest sense of the honourable engagement, that you should not possibly be required to pay one shilling more in any event or upon any contingency whatever.

The bargain thus closed, Raphael handed to O'Connell an old address of his to the electors of Westminster, which was to be altered to suit the taste of the electors of Carlow, and he was put in nomination on the 8th. He never went near Carlow at all. O'Connell pressed to have the £1,000 paid to his credit with Wright & Co., his bankers. Raphael would only lodge it with Hamilton, his own solicitor, from whom John O'Connell at length obtained it on June 10th. O'Connell being then in perhaps more than his normal pecuniary embarrassments, paid it into his own account at his bankers, and remitted it to Ireland by an acceptance drawn on some Irish brewers at several months' date. As, however, he offered Vigors cash if he desired it, and took no benefit to himself from the discount in settling the accounts, this course would appear to have been taken for some not very obvious but innocent reason. On the 13th O'Connell wrote to Raphael, "Our prospects of success are quite conclusive; if only one Liberal is to be returned, you are to be the man"; and on the 17th, "I send you Vigors' letter to me, just received; you see how secure we are. Return me this

9 *

letter, as it vouches £800 for me. With that you have nothing to do, as, of course, I stand between you and everybody." Raphael was accordingly elected with Vigors by a majority of fifty-six, and he at once took his seat. The return was promptly petitioned against, and it became evident that the result would turn upon a scrutiny of the register. It had been agreed that, in the event of no petition being presented, Raphael's second £1,000 should be devoted to a fund for indemnifying his voters from any loss or persecution by their land-lords. Now, however, it was required to defend the seat. O'Connell wrote on July 17th—

Send Mr. Baker (the parliamentary agent) the particulars he wants of your qualification. I will stand between you and him for all the expenses. I promised you, and repeat distinctly my promise, that upon payment of the second £1,000, to which you are at all events engaged, no demand shall be made on you for one additional sixpence. Do then at once pay the other £1,000 into Messrs. Wright's to my credit.

On the 26th Hamilton met John O'Connell, and put before him, on Raphael's behalf, the extraordinary view that the second £1,000 was not to be paid until the seat was safe. O'Connell wrote hotly next day : " Rely on it, you are mistaken if you suppose that I will submit to any deviation from our engagement." Raphael at first thought of resigning the first £1,000 and the seat, but having consulted his friends, decided to yield. The £1,000 was paid to John O'Connell on July 28th, who within an hour allowed himself to become a member of the very committee which was to try the question that the £1,000 was to be spent in arguing. O'Connell wrote to Raphael asking if he would care to be a baronet, adding that he did not ask without a reason ; but Raphael was not ambitious of the title. By the 4th of August he found that he would have to fight the petition, if at all, at his own cost. Unwilling to sacrifice his £2,000, he kept up the contest for a few days ; but by the 17th, 105 of his votes had been struck off, and being thus hopelessly behind, he withdrew, and the seat was vacated.

He took his revenge by publishing a letter to the Carlow electors, setting out the whole story. O'Connell replied on November 6th in a letter, in which he denounced Raphael as " that most incomprehensible of all imaginable vagabonds." But strong language did not mend matters. He was accused of trafficking in seats, as he might have trafficked in bacon. He was suspected of having pocketed part of the £2,000. This, added to his frequent abuse of persons whom he would not fight, induced Burdett in November to call upon the managers of Brooks' to expel him. On December 3rd O'Connell wrote to them justifying his conduct, and they affirmed the decision given to Lord Alvanley in May. Burdett, Brougham, Stanley, and Graham resigned their membership. Next session a petition from Carlow was presented by Bruen on February 11th, setting out the facts of the election. The matter looked grave. On the 16th a committee of inquiry was appointed ; it met on February 19th and 29th, heard O'Connell's explanation, which was corroborated by Vigors, and eventually on March 11th reported that although " no charge of a pecuniary character can be attached to Mr. O'Connell," and " he was only the medium between Raphael and Vigors and the political club at Carlow "; still, the letter of June 1st was " calculated to excite much suspicion and grave animadversion." It was a lenient conclusion. The whole affair shows not only how indifferent O'Connell was to the nicer particulars of public conduct, but how difficult a task it was to find Repeal candidates among Irishmen of moderate means and tolerable reputation.   Till 1829 the Irish members had been even more aristocratic than the English, and in the counties good birth and good family had been indispensable in a candidate.   O'Connell had changed all this; but a supporter, even nominally respectable, must have been hard to obtain, when Raphael could be accepted so easily.   Men of high abilities or standing were little likely to brook the complete obedience and subordination to himself which O'Connell expected of the "joints of his tail," and among those who formed his party were some who, though no doubt unsuspected by him, were generally and reasonably believed to sell to candidates for money down their promises of support in the solicitation of petty offices in the Civil Service.   The followers of O'Connell were not, indeed, inferior to the Irish Tory members, but the conduct of both classes amazed the more reserved English members of the House.   John O'Connell, not a willing witness against his countrymen, says : " Not an assertion dropped by an Irish member on one side, but it was immediately contradicted upon the other ; not a violent expression or gesture but had its counterpart with interest.   And while the Irishmen fought and blackened each other, and rose higher and higher towards boiling point, the English members looked on, as the Spartans of old at the riotings of their Helots, and asked each other with looks of pitying contempt: 'Is it not well for such men as these to have us to take care of them ?' "

The administration of Ireland, in the hands of Mulgrave and Drummond, had now been shown to be so impartial and liberal, that O'Connell felt bound to redeem his promise of abandoning the Repeal agitation. Old as he was, before Parliament met in 1836 he was incessantly active. On January 14th he was speaking at Tralee, on the 16th at Cork, on the 18th at Galway, on the 20th at Shadbally, on the 25th at Dublin. He then came to a meeting at Liverpool, spoke at Birmingham on the 28th, and appeared in Parliament when it opened on February 4th. He asked of his audiences their authority to drop the question of Repeal if he thought England was giving justice to Ireland. In Dublin, at St. Bridget's charity dinner, he said :—

When Emancipation was obtained I sought for Repeal, because I saw that the Imperial Parliament paid little attention to the affairs and condition of Ireland. Even Sir Robert Peel himself confessed that he could not get forty members together when an Irish question was to be brought forward. I, however, took up Repeal, and like the flappers we read of in *Gulliver's Travels*, I rattled it about their ears, the result of which is that the attention of the Government is almost entirely engrossed with the affairs of Ireland. . . . In looking for Repeal, both Houses of Parliament promised that if that question were given up, they would grant every other, which could be proved to be advantageous to Ireland. . . . I am now for making the experiment, whether that is a real and *bona fide* reason on their part, or a mere pretence. . . . Place us on an equality with yourselves, and then talk to me of an Union ; for then will I offer you, in the name of the Irish people, not to talk of Repeal ; but unless you do that, thank Heaven, we have seven millions of people to fall back upon the question of Repeal again. The people of Ireland are ready to become a portion of the Empire, provided they be made so in reality, and not in name alone. They are ready to become a kind of West Britons if made so in benefits and in justice ; but if not, we are Irishmen again.

A petition against his return for Dublin had been presented in the previous session. A committee had been appointed, and had delegated three barristers to conduct a local inquiry into the facts in Dublin.

O'Connell was charged with gross intimidation, with advocating exclusive dealing, and urging that every adverse voter should find a death's head and cross-bones chalked by his enemies upon his door. The register was elaborately investigated. He spent £20,000 in defending the petition, and the costs of the petitioners were £40,000, which the Carlton Club was reported to have largely taken upon itself. The commissioners sate some six months in Dublin, and after the presentation of their report the committee conducted a further inquiry for six weeks. On May 16th O'Connell was unseated, but his measures had been taken. His voice was needed in the discussion upon the Municipal Reform Bill. In anticipation of this result, Richard Sullivan, M.P. for Kilkenny, had accepted the Chiltern Hundreds, and on the 17th O'Connell was elected in his place. Meetings were held in England to raise a subscription in aid of his expenses; £3,000 was subscribed at the first, and the nett proceeds amounted to £8,489. The Duke of Bedford subscribed one hundred guineas. . The King said he might subscribe if he chose, but no supporter of O'Connell could be allowed to appear among the sculptures of Windsor, and ordered his bust to be removed from the royal gallery.

The agitation for the abolition of tithe was still going on. Sheil and O'Connell had both refused to pay it, and O'Connell had all but been outlawed in consequence by the Dublin Court of Exchequer. The Ministry reintroduced a Tithe Bill on the same lines as that of the previous year. The Municipal Corporation Bill proposed to deal with the Irish corporations, some fifty in number, in a drastic fashion. Their privileges and monopolies were numerous. They were now all to

be swept away, and an occupation franchise of £10 in
large towns and £5 in small ones, was to be fixed as the
basis of corporators' rights. Peel opposed it in the
House of Commons with a proposal for the total
abolition of these corporations. He was defeated, but
in the House of Lords he triumphed. The Bill was
thrown out by 203 to 119, and the Tithes Bill was also
lost. O'Connell resolved to " revive the Catholic Association on a broader basis " for the purpose of obtaining a full corporate reform and tithe reform. He called
his new association the General Association. It met
twice a week, and speedily became formidable enough to
excite no little outcry in England. It collected a
" justice rent," which reached £690 per week by
November. Ireland seemed again on the verge of
fresh agitation. In England the rancour of his enemies
redoubled. He had hitherto given a general support to
factory legislation, and had spoken in favour of restrict-
ing the hours of labour of children employed in factories.
In May, two Bills came before the House of Commons,
which dealt with the subject, Fielden's providing
for a working day of ten hours, and Poulett Thomson's, which regulated the conditions of factory work,
but did not adopt the ten hours day. O'Connell
was satisfied from the debate, that, in the then state of
things, to impose a limitation on the hours of work would
cause considerable loss of trade, and consequent suffering
and loss of employment to the very class it was proposed
to protect. He voted for Poulett Thomson's Bill. The
operatives, who supported the ten hours' bill, were much
disappointed, and the Tories took advantage of the
opportunity to attack him. Wilson, in an article on
" Cotton Manufacturers and the Factory System," in
the July number of *Blackwood's Magazine*, alleged that

three days before the debate O'Connell had promised
Lord Ashley the support of his party for Fielden's Bill,
and that three days after the debate he was rewarded
for his breach of faith by the admiring manufacturers
with a purse of seven hundred guineas. Bell, formerly editor of the *True Sun*, and newly appointed
editor of the *Mercury*, published in it a statement that
Mr. Potter of Manchester had promised O'Connell, who
was then much in debt, £1,000 for his support on the
question. This Potter promptly came forward to deny.
The story probably originated in the subscription to
lighten the cost of O'Connell's defence to the petition
against his return for Dublin ; but it shows with great
force how bitter and unscrupulous was the animosity
which he excited among his opponents.

For the Session of 1837 the Government measures
were the reintroduction of the Irish Municipal Reform
Bill and a Poor Law Bill. Of any application to Ireland of the English poor-law system O'Connell had
long been a steadfast opponent. He had carried on a
sharp controversy upon the subject with Dr. Doyle
in 1832, in which undoubtedly the victory rested with
the Bishop. He was now less violently hostile to
the principle, but still deeply impressed with the
difficulty of applying it. On February 13th Lord
John Russell called the attention of the House of Commons to the necessity of passing an Irish poor-law.
O'Connell expressed himself incredulous of its success,
and advised emigration as a remedy, but said that he
regarded the proposal as an experiment and would not
resist it. Upon the second reading, at the end of April,
he took a decided stand and attacked it directly. He
pointed out that there was to be no provision for out-
door relief, and the cheap workhouses which it was pro-

posed to erect for the accommodation of 80,000 poor, were wholly inadequate to the indoor relief of the two millions who were destitute. Wages, which in England were 8s. to 10s. per week, in Ireland were 2s. 6d., and even 2s. Ireland, with its smaller area and smaller population, had but 75,000 fewer agricultural labourers than England. There were no means of permanently supporting them, and it was then computed that in Ireland 585,000 heads of families were out of work for seven months in every year. Hitherto this gigantic evil had been dealt with by the spontaneous and abundant charity of the poor. Given in kind and not in coin this was felt by the giver as but a slight burden, but it sufficed to support, though on the verge of misery, many thousands of mendicants. A poor-law must abolish this. To provide a legal relief, to which every beggar was entitled, was to deprive him of that voluntary relief from his neighbours, which in default of a poor-law was never refused. The use and wont of generations had made mendicancy an honourable calling and had attracted to its wandering and unrestrained life vast crowds of beggars. The Government proposal implied as a consequence the extinction of this calling : it supplied in its stead a relief which one-tenth of the applicants would exhaust. Work for the remainder was not to be had : there remained only the sad alternative of starvation.

But the question remained undecided for the moment. In June the King died. O'Connell was full of enthusiastic loyalty to the young Queen, and at the General Election gave her Ministers all the support in his power. He put out a manifesto, in which he said : " Ireland is prepared to amalgamate with the entire Empire. We are prepared for full and perpetual conciliation. Let

Ireland and England be identified." As soon as the
election was over he dissolved the General Association,
saying that " he was still in favour of giving a fair trial
to the Union ; he would confidently entrust the fortunes
of the Irish people to the British Parliament. If the
results demonstrated the incapacity of Parliament and
Government to do full and complete justice to Ireland,
then he would unfurl the flag of Repeal and call upon
Ireland to rally round it." Upon the general result
of the elections the Ministry had a majority of twenty-
five ; without O'Connell's assistance they would have
been in a minority.

But in proportion as Lord Melbourne had sought to
govern Ireland according to Irish ideas, and O'Connell
to conduct himself according to the ideas of the English, each had lost ground with his own countrymen.
It became plain that the Whigs were kept in office
only by the Repeal vote. It was alleged that they had
sold the Irish Church for the thirty pieces of silver of
O'Connell's support. Lord John Russell was |likened
to Judas Iscariot, and the Whig Government was called
the O'Connell Cabinet. Exposed to the assaults of Peel
in front, and attacked in flank by "the Derby dilly carrying six insides," with a hostile House of Lords, a King
of erratic will and feeble health, and an heir to the throne
who was a girl in her teens, caught between the active
agitation of Exeter Hall, which opposed all countenance
to Roman Catholics, and the growing High Church cry
that the appropriation clause was a robbery of the
Church of Christ, the Ministry had found themselves
in a position in which nothing but the firmest and most
united front could bring them out of the conflict with
success or even without dishonour. But their followers
were not a united party. Some were Whigs, impracti-

cable with the pride of family, the Brahmins of politics; some were Radicals, impracticable with the pride of reason, political Pharisees; while O'Connell, in proportion as he stood loyally by the Ministry, found the Irish forgetting his fame and his services. Nor were the Ministry able to effect much for Ireland. Their administration, indeed, was admirable, but year after year, a Tithe Bill, such as Peel himself had introduced, was wrecked by the House of Lords, and the Irish were denied the Corporation Reform which their own representatives had been largely instrumental in passing for England. In the hopes of obtaining "justice for Ireland" O'Connell had supported the Whigs at the cost of his popularity, and year by year as his popularity waned, he saw the prospect of "justice for Ireland," as he conceived the term, vanishing into a more and more distant future.

In the autumn of 1836 a commercial panic occurred through the failure of the Agricultural Bank, and in the run upon the banks which followed, the National Bank, which he had founded, and to the support of which his whole fortune was pledged, was in great danger. He experienced the pressure which he had exhorted the Irish to apply to the Government five years before, and he saw that the holders of notes had no more compassion for the Liberator's bank than for the Bank of Ireland. In the beginning of 1837 he was in open conflict with Sharman Crawford upon the renewal of coercion, which he had thought justifiable, and upon the Government plan for dealing with the Tithe question, and with Smith O'Brien for his advocacy of a State endowment for the Roman Catholic clergy and his opposition to the ballot. In the autumn severe disputes occurred, especially in the shipbuilding trade, between the Dublin trades unions and the employers of labour. In a speech on November 7th at the Dublin Trades Political Union, O'Connell espoused the side of the masters, and, with great courage and devotion to his principles, denounced strikes and condemned the men. He was instantly the mark for their most violent abuse. He was hooted by his own constituents in the streets of Dublin. He had interviews for hours together with the trades union leaders, and took nothing by his arguments. He boldly challenged discussion, and held meetings in January 1838 to debate the question. The workmen forced their way in and denied him a hearing. At one meeting he was compelled to stand for nearly two hours the centre of indescribable confusion, never able to utter more than two or three sentences, and for the most part wholly inaudible. His popularity in Ireland seemed almost gone.

Scarcely had Parliament reassembled in 1838 than he found himself again in conflict with the House of Commons. It was a matter of notoriety that committees upon election petitions, though they sat as judges and were sworn to decide conscientiously, voted simply as loyal partisans. In November 1837, Buller had obtained leave to bring in a Bill to amend the practice of trying these petitions, and O'Connell, who had suffered at the hands of election committees himself, had then proposed to transfer them to the Queen's Bench. On the 21st February 1838, in a speech at the " Crown and Anchor " tavern, he reverted to the subject.

Corruption of the worst kind [he said] existed, and, above all, there was the perjury of the Tory politicians. Ireland was not safe from the English and Scotch gentry. It was horrible to think that a body of gentlemen, who ranked high in society, who were themselves administrators of the law, and who ought, therefore, to be above all suspicion, and who ought to set an example to others—was it not horrible that they should be perjuring themselves in the Committees of the House of Commons? The time was come when this should be proclaimed boldly. He was ready to be a martyr to justice and truth, but not to false swearing, and he repeated that there was foul perjury in the Tory Committees of the House of Commons.

The truth of the charge was hardly deniable, but it excited the wrath of those who suffered from the imputation. On the 23rd Lord Maidstone read the report in the House of Commons, and asked O'Connell if it was correct. "I did say every word of that," replied O'Connell, "and I believe it to be perfectly true. Is there a man who will put his hand on his heart and say upon his honour as a gentleman that he does not believe it to be substantially true?" Lord Maidstone, without going through this or any milder form of denial, gave notice that he would call the attention of the House to the speech on the 26th. The day came, and the obnoxious passage was read by the Clerk of the House. O'Connell, in a long speech, admitted and justified his words. Lord Maidstone moved "that the words were a false and scandalous imputation upon the honour of the House." A long debate followed. Ministers voted against the motion, but it was carried by 263 to 254. A motion that O'Connell should be reprimanded was carried, and on the 28th he was ordered to stand up in his place, and received from the Speaker a severe and lengthy censure. He was perfectly unabashed. Without a moment's loss of time, or so much as resuming his seat, he gave notice of a motion for a committee to investigate the whole matter, concluding with the words "I have repented of nothing; I mean not to use harsh or offensive language. I repeat what I have said, but I wish I could find terms less offensive in themselves and equally significant." '

The Ministry had made more than one attempt to reward O'Connell's staunch support. He was very near being made Irish Attorney-General in 1837. Meeting Mr. John Ball and one of the Irish members one day in that year at the corner of Downing Street, he cried, "Congratulate me; I am Attorney-General for Ireland. I have just been with Lord Melbourne, and have determined to accept the office. But nothing must be said for the present." The King, however, heard of the appointment, and put pressure upon Melbourne to revoke it.* In 1838, Joy, Chief Baron of the Irish Exchequer, died. Melbourne was anxious to promote O'Connell, but it was thought that to set him to preside over the Court, which had exclusive cognizance of those writs of rebellion, which he had so often denounced and contested, would be unwise. The post was therefore offered to O'Loghlen, who was Master of the Rolls. O'Loghlen was willing to consent to the change, but the vacancy in the Rolls thereby created was, when offered to O'Connell, refused. O'Loghlen was not transferred, and Woulfe became Chief Baron. It was not without a struggle that O'Connell refused this promotion. He told the House of Commons in 1840 that one reason for his refusal was that he feared he might not deal impartially with litigants, and that in dread of favouring Roman Catholics he might find himself unfairly hostile to them. But the principal reason was that he felt Ireland would soon have need of him again.

In 1838 Russell introduced the sixth Tithe Bill. The appropriation clause, upon which the Whigs had

---

* "O'Connell," by John Ball, *Macmillan's Magazine*, xxiii., 222.

come into power, had been abandoned the year before. Its place was taken by a tax of ten per cent. upon the incomes of the clergy for educational purposes. This, too, was given up. It was proposed that the tithe rent-charge should ultimately cease as an ecclesiastical revenue and be diverted to education. The opposition of the House of Lords was fatal to this, and the Bill ultimately passed much in the form in which Peel had introduced it three years before. O'Connell passively acquiesced, but the Bill was disappointing. By removing various glaring abuses in the Church of Ireland it strengthened her general position. Whether or not the rent-charge was generally added to the old rents by the landlords, so as to be ultimately as much a burden on the tenants as the old tithe, is much disputed, but the whole measure seemed to be of a hesitating character, and convinced O'Connell that the great Whig experiment was a failure. He betook himself to a last agitation for "justice to Ireland" as distinct from Repeal.

In August of 1838 he founded his "Precursor Society." Its name was supposed to mean, though few Irishmen divined it, that it was to be the forerunner of Repeal, but his choice of names for his societies was almost uniformly infelicitous. It was to agitate for complete corporate Reform, extension of the suffrage, total abolition of compulsory Church support, and adequate representation in Parliament. But the Irish were not united in the agitation. Many disapproved of anything less than a cry for Repeal. Connaught, which had given the last and least assistance to Emancipation, stood aloof from the Precursors altogether. "Ireland," O'Connell wrote to Dr. MacHale in January 1839, "has never acted together since the close of the Emancipation fight." The society was, however, sufficiently strong to alarm the Ministry. They wrote to O'Connell " menacingly " about it, and used every means in their power to impede its organization ; but the society was not checked. Agitation was as yet the work only of his immediate circle of associates, nor was it directed very openly to its object, but it deserved its name. Unknown, perhaps, even to O'Connell himself, Ireland was on the very eve of the struggle for Repeal.

CHAPTER VIII.

THE REPEAL ASSOCIATION.

1840-1843.

Repeal Association founded—Irish Municipal Reform—O'Connell Lord Mayor of Dublin—The founding of the *Nation*—The Repeal Debate—The Monster Meetings — The Mallow Defiance — Clontarf.

On April 15th 1840 the Repeal Association was founded. The meeting was held in the Great Room of the Corn Exchange; only a sprinkling of persons were seen in the room ; not a hundred in all were there. They waited till it became impossible to wait longer, and to that handful of people O'Connell unfolded his plan. The Association was formed at first under the title of the National Society and rules were adopted.

He was not disheartened ; he remembered the first meeting of the Catholic Association. He had himself been discouraging agitation for Repeal ; he knew that it would be a work of time to convince people of his change of policy. "As soon," he said, "as they begin to find out I am thoroughly in earnest, they will come flocking in to the Association." In truth, however, for some time Dublin was singularly indifferent to the birth of his new society. He had founded nearly a dozen in the previous ten years, beside some which were still-

10 *

born, and associations had lost their novelty. Repeal was popular, and he had set Repeal aside; the Whigs were unpopular, and he had supported them. He had offended the landlords by ousting them from their dominion in the counties; the priests by acquiescing in a Tithes Act, which only strengthened the Church of Ireland; the artisans by denouncing trades unions; the peasants by obtaining for them so little but coercion acts after six years' alliance with the Whigs. He was surrounded by henchmen of dubious respectability and deficient talent. His enemies had brought to light numbers of scandals, which, however exaggerated, were distressing to men of probity. He insisted on paying the funds of the " Precursor Society" into his own bank account instead of the Treasurer's; he had traded on the strength of his name; he had founded a bank himself; his son had founded a brewery. Another son and a son-in-law were placemen under the alien Saxon Government. Emancipation was now an old tale. Those who had fought in that agitation were aged or dead. A younger generation had grown up, to whom O'Connell's services were matter of report; who saw in him a hero indeed, but one sinking into old age after years of failure. Many of the Catholics had been educated on the English model, and prided themselves on their English ideas; many of them were suppliants for Government patronage. The merchants, the backbone of the first Catholic agitation, were impoverished, and stood aloof from politics; the priests, the backbone of the second, were satisfied with Emancipation, and had no great ardour for Repeal. To this indifferent people O'Connell appealed at the age of sixty-five with the calm confidence of middle life, and the hopeful energy of youth.

His letters to Dr. MacHale at this time set out his

reasons and the plan which he had in his mind. He was convinced that the Tories would soon be in power; the Whigs were tottering to their fall. What the Whigs had not been able to do, the Tories would not attempt to do for Ireland; much of what the Whigs had done would be undone by the Tories. Four grievances were to be remedied, first (and writing to a Roman Catholic Archbishop, he adroitly called it the greatest), was the State Church of the minority—nothing but Repeal could abolish national payments for this alien Church; second, full reform of corporations was still withheld; third, equality of political franchise was denied; fourth, the Irish parliamentary representation was insufficient. The method was to be the old one of the Catholic Association, a host of small subscriptions from a multitude of humble subscribers.

I can give Your Grace the result of thirty years and more of experience, and it is this: that once get a parish into a mood of contributing to public purposes, the more such purposes are brought before them, the more liberal will be each aggregate contribution. So many persons will not give five pounds or five shillings, but many more will give one shilling; the contributors should be individually solicited to give sums smaller than each can reasonably afford.

During the summer and autumn he addressed incessant meetings. He flew from Mullingar to Cork, from Cork to Dublin, from Dublin to Belfast, from Belfast to Leeds, from Leeds to Leicester. Towards the end of 1840 he advocated the exclusive consumption of Irish manufactures, but the expedient soon proved itself useless. The rich would not, and the poor could not buy, and to delude those whose patriotism got the better of their taste, English goods were imported into Ireland, and were marked and sold as of Irish manufacture. He carefully modelled the Repeal Association upon the Catholic Association. The Act of 1793 was still unrepealed,

and therefore a representative character was carefully
disclaimed. There were three classes, associates paying 1s. a year, members paying £1, volunteers paying
£10. All the proceedings were completely open. There
were special committees, which, during the existence of
the Association, prepared as many as sixty-five reports,
and a general committee of about eighty persons, which
conducted general business, and considered the accounts, reports, resolutions, and circulars of the Association, and there were weekly meetings of the Association itself. There were Repeal wardens, who collected
the rent, answerable to Repeal inspectors, who were
in turn controlled by provincial inspectors. The old
machinery of the Catholic Association was ready to
hand, it only needed to be furbished up again ; but
many of its old officers were dead or incapacitated, and
it was not for some time that O'Connell could find
among the younger generation men fit to take their
place and bring the whole scheme into operation.

The proximate cause of the founding of the Repeal
Association was Stanley's Irish Registration Bill of
1840. By its restrictions upon registration it practically limited the franchise. O'Connell attacked the
Bill warmly, and was warmly attacked in return. On
June 11th he was heard with so much impatience and
interruption that, losing his temper, he cried : " This is
a Bill to trample on the rights of the people of Ireland.
If you were ten times as beastly in your uproar and
bellowing I should still feel it my duty to interpose to
prevent this injustice"; and in spite of the angry
scene which followed, he would not withdraw the
phrase. The Bill, however, dropped for the session of
1840. A similar fate had befallen the Irish Municipal
Reform Bill in the previous year. Now it passed, but,

owing to the amendments of the Lords, in a form so restricted, as to make it highly unsatisfactory to O'Connell.

In 1841 the Whig Ministry was defeated ; it dissolved Parliament on June 23rd, and was utterly routed at the elections. O'Connell and his party suffered too. He lost his own seat for Dublin, and was obliged to take refuge at Cork, and many elections went against his party. He returned with a " tail " reduced to less than a dozen, of whom four were members of his own family, and two others, Dillon Browne and Somers, were his unscrupulous partisans. Nor was the Repeal movement making much headway. He prepared several reports for the Association, in the first of which, issued on May 4th 1840, he had elaborated a scheme for an Irish Parliament of 300 members, 127 borough and 173 county members, but it had not struck the popular imagination. A vast meeting had been held at Croker's Hill, Kilkenny, in October, with 20,000 mounted men, and ten times as many on foot, but nothing came of it. He journeyed to and fro all over Ireland, and late in 1841 visited Ulster. The Orangemen of Belfast menaced him with condign punishment if he ventured to appear there. Violence was intended to be offered him on the way. His carriage was to have been waylaid between two high banks which commanded the road, and stones hailed upon it till carriage and occupant were crushed. He escaped only by changing the time of his journey, and to secure changes of horses at the posting-houses was obliged to travel under the name of a popular ventriloquist. His meeting had to be protected with five companies of foot, two troops of horse, and 2,000 police. The windows of his room were broken, and Dawson, Peel's brother-in-law,

vapoured about "every river in Ireland being another
Boyne if necessary." In the autumn of 1842 he
endeavoured to stimulate the movement by appointing
Ray, the secretary of the Association, Steele, the Head
Pacificator, Daunt, and his son, John O'Connell, Repeal Inspectors, to visit the provinces and enrol members. But the missionaries were not more powerful than
their master, and through 1842 the agitation lagged.
Their efforts did, indeed, raise the rent from £45
for the week before they set out to £235 for the week
after their return, but the great stride that was taken
at the end of 1842 and the beginning of 1843 was not
theirs. It was due to two events: the founding of
the *Nation* on October 15th 1842, and the Repeal debate in the Dublin Corporation on February 25th
1843.

The founding of the *Nation* as the newspaper of the
new Repeal movement meant that the younger generation
of Irishmen was willing to cast in its lot with the old.
Davis, poet and patriot, John Blake Dillon, C. Gavan
Duffy, John Cornelius O'Callaghan, Clarence Mangan, and
J. O'Neill Daunt were the leaders in the enterprise. The
newspaper was instantly successful ; the first issue could
have been sold twice over. The newsvendors clamoured
round the office, breaking in the windows in their
eagerness to procure copies. O'Connell's practical mind
was apt to make the Repeal argument too purely an
appeal to Irish pockets. The motto of the *Nation* was
a saying of Stephen Woulfe, " to create and foster
public opinion in Ireland, and to make it racy of the
soil." O'Connell told the Irish that the Union loaded
them with debts they had not contracted, and deprived
them of the manufactures they had created ; that the
artisans of Dublin had dropped in forty years from

5,000 to 700; the workmen in the woollen trade from
150,000 to 6,000; that Repeal would raise their wages
and lower their taxes. Davis and Duffy sought to make
them feel themselves a nation, talked to them of Brian
Boru, and spelt his name Borhoime; of O'Sullivan,
whom they wrote O'Suillebhain; of Ollam Fodlah, and
Eoghan Ruadh O'Neill. They told them that "Ireland ought to have a foreign policy, but not necessarily
the foreign policy of England." O'Connell had put it
more forcibly, but with the same meaning. "If France
puts England into a difficulty, the first hostile shot that's
fired in the Channel I'll have the Government in my
hand." "England's adversity is Ireland's opportunity,"
was the doctrine of them both.

The Irish Municipal Reform Act had been welcomed
in Dublin by the election of O'Connell on November
1st 1841 to the Lord Mayoralty for 1842. He was
the first Roman Catholic who had filled that office,
and with great tact he negotiated an arrangement by
which it should thereafter be held by Protestants and
Roman Catholics alternately. The sight of their old
leader in that position and the pomp with which he
was surrounded pleased and inspirited the people of
Dublin. In 1843 O'Connell, now an alderman, decided to attract attention to the question of Repeal by
a debate in the Corporation, and on February 25th he
brought on a motion in its favour. A great crowd
gathered in the Assembly House in William Street, and
a still greater in the street outside. O'Connell spoke
for upwards of four hours, and delivered a speech,
which, even among his, had no superior. He arranged
it, as was his favourite manner, under heads, and
covered the whole ground with a masterly command
of figures and arguments. He declared the Irish fit

for an independent parliament, entitled to it by im-
memorial constitutional right, and robbed of it by
bribery, menaces, and force, by the craft of Pitt, and the
cruelty of Castlereagh. He affirmed that the Irish Parliament could not by any contract bargain away its own
existence, and that in any case the Union was morally
void, being procured by fraud and duress. He went
through a vast parade of statistics to show the increase of absenteeism which the Union had caused,
and the consequent decay of trade, and painted a glow-
ing picture of the wealth, peace, and dignity which
would accrue to Ireland from the presence of a Parliament in College Green. Isaac Butt, then a rising
junior barrister, a professor in Dublin University, and
formerly editor of the *Dublin University Magazine*,
replied in a speech of almost equal merit. The debate
lasted for three days. In an assembly of Irishmen glad
to be convinced, O'Connell's argument carried all before
it. He made a triumphant reply, and carried his
motion by 41 to 15.

From that day the Repeal Association and its work
grew apace. The average rent in January 1843 had
been about £150 per week ; for the last week in February it was £342, for the second in March £366, for
the first in April £473, for the last £683, for the last
week in May £2,205, for the third in June £3,103, for
the entire year £48,400. The priests, headed by the
Bishops of Meath and Dromore, and finally by Archbishop MacHale, joined the Association. O'Connell's
rash prediction that "1843 was to be the Repeal year,"
seemed in a fair way to be realised. Meetings were
arranged for every county; the Association met in
Dublin twice a week ; the old room on the second floor
of the Corn Exchange, which had served the Catholic

Association, was but eight yards by sixteen in size, and rudely furnished; 400 persons overcrowded it. A large hall was projected to hold first twice as many, then 1,200, finally 5,000. With grim humour they obtained a site from an anti-Repealer, concealing the object of the bargain till the contract was signed. The hall was completed and opened in October, and un-couthly called Conciliation Hall. The business of the Association became enormous. In 1841 its staff of clerks had been 9; in 1842, 7; by the end of 1843 they numbered 48. Everything was conducted with the regularity and routine of a great counting-house. There were 58 folio volumes of documents containing 44,000 separate papers, 40 quarto volumes of letters, and 22 folio volumes of vouchers for subscriptions, containing 33,000 vouchers. There were cash books, day books, minute books, and scrap books fully indexed; lists of the three classes of members; lists of American contri-butors. A Repeal police was instituted, over which a " Head Pacificator," Tom Steele, presided. If tumult broke out in any district in Ireland, any rising of " Terry Alts," or conflict of " Gows " and of " Po-leens," it was the business of the local Repeal police, or, if necessary, of the august Head Pacificator himself, to repair to the spot and compose the quarrel. Arbitra-tion Courts were established, which soon threatened to leave the courts of the Queen nothing to do. The card of membership, which had hitherto been plain and busi-ness-like, expanded, in deference to the national aspira-tions, into a document highly emblematic of Ireland's history and Ireland's wrongs, the design of Mr. John Cornelius O'Callaghan. Seventy thousand of them were issued during the year. A host of little books upon Irish history, Irish poetry, and Irish art, poured from the press of James Duffy. O'Connell's activity was incessant and marvellous in a man of his years. From meeting to meeting he travelled in the year some five thousand miles. Beside presiding at the public and committee meetings of the Association, and directing, if not executing, the greater part of its business with vast forethought and attention to detail, he attended in March three, in May six, in June nine, in July three, in August five, in September three huge meetings, and his admirers were never content with a short speech from him. A series of meetings, which the *Times* dubbed "Monster Meetings," was projected and carried out. The number of persons attending them could only be guessed, and must have been grossly exaggerated, but it is certain that enormous crowds gathered almost day after day in different parts of Ireland to agitate for Repeal. In April nine meetings were held, at which it was estimated 620,000 persons attended; one meeting of 110,000 was held at Limerick; and two of 150,000 at Kells and Carrickmacross respectively. At eleven meetings in May two millions and a quarter persons were present; they included one of 170,000 at Sligo, one of 150,000 at Mullingar, one of 260,000 at Longford, one of 300,000 at Charleville, two of 400,000 at Armagh and Cashel respectively, and one of 500,000 at Cork. Two millions and three-quarter persons attended nine meetings in June, at the least of which 100,000 were present, at two 300,000, at two 400,000 and upwards, and at one in Clare 700,000. There were three meetings of 300,000 in July, and one of 500,000. On August 15th, 750,000* persons assembled at Tara,

---

* Daunt, in his *Recollections*, puts the number at 1,200,000. If that were so, three-fourths of the adult males of Ireland must have been present.

in Meath, and on the same day 300,000 more at Clon-
tibret in Monaghan, and the series was closed by two of
400,000 each at an interval of a week at Lismore and
the Rath of Mullaghmast.

These numbers were probably no more than the
sanguine guesses of triumphant enthusiasts. What was
more extraordinary, and to the Government more
ominous than even these numbers, was the complete
orderliness of the meetings. They were held in the
open air, and even under cover not a tenth of those
huge multitudes could have heard the speaker's voice.
They were held in the heat of summer, and the dust
and pressure of so many persons must have aggravated
the thirst natural to the season of the year. Yet the
tedium of standing and hearing nothing did not produce disorder, nor did fatigue and exhaustion lead to
drunkenness. The meeting at the Hill of Tara was a
sight peculiarly solemn and affecting. Tara was the
coronation place of Irish kings ; the day, a feast of the
Virgin Mary of peculiar sanctity. All night long the
people gathered by thousands at the hill, and bivouacked
under the open sky. In the morning so vast a crowd
covered the place of meeting, that there was no one
place from which the whole of it could be surveyed.
Dublin was denuded of public conveyances. It seemed
deserted by its inhabitants. For miles along the roads
leading to the hill carriages were drawn up and horses
picketed by the wayside. No one was left to watch
them ; yet they suffered neither theft nor injury. If the
gathering was a triumph for O'Connell, it was a still
greater triumph for Father Mathew. Three-fourths of
the crowd were pledged teetotallers. From dawn till
noon at forty altars priests were celebrating mass under
the summer sun, and over the heads of kneeling thou-

sands the bell tinkled, the smoke of incense quivered, and the Host was held on high. Towards noon O'Connell came, attended by a procession of ten thousand horsemen, mustered by marshals in orderly battalions. Forty-two bands raised a discordant note of triumph. The crowds made way for the Liberator, but so great was the press, that he was two hours in passing the last mile. When the platform was reached he delivered a speech, but it was not his speaking that produced the effect of the day. That silent orderly crowd was ten times more eloquent than he, a disciplined army obedient to his beck and nod. At Tara the uncrowned king assembled his subjects; on October 1st at the Rath of Mullaghmast his subjects offered their king a crown. Duffy suggested that a quaint and uncomely cap, which was part of the traditional garb of an independent Irish king, should be again brought into use. At the conclusion of the meeting a deputation consisting of John Hogan, an Irish national sculptor, Henry MacManus, an Irish national painter, John Cornelius O'Callaghan, the designer of the national symbolism of the members' card, and his brother Mark, solemnly advanced through the crowd, and gravely crowned O'Connell with the Irish national cap. The proceeding, in itself so ridiculous and theatrical, appeared in the tense state of public feeling, to be nothing short of sublime.

For fifteen months the agitation had been proceeding unchecked; for seven it had been of the most formidable proportions. The apprehensions, which the sight of these unarmed armies of disciplined men excited in the minds of ministers, were justified by the language which O'Connell and his followers publicly employed. Davis, the poet of the *Nation*, in lines which, though often unpolished, were singularly terse and fiery, was rousing a spirit of antagonism to England, and inculcating the duty of the struggle to be free, in language which was meaningless if it did not advocate an ultimate appeal to force. The whole teaching of his colleagues of the " Young Ireland " party was instinct with the feeling that, although the gift of freedom might perhaps be accepted if extorted by mere menaces, it was hardly worth having unless won by force of arms. From the point of view of Her Majesty's Government, responsible for peace and order and for the dominions of the Crown, this was sedition, a veiled incitement to rebellion ; and yet O'Connell, who viewed the growing power and unfamiliar tone of the *Nation* with jealousy, and endeavoured to check it by private remonstrance, in public thought it necessary to echo its language. On May 9th, questions were put in the House of Lords by Lord Roden, Grand Master of the Orangemen, and by Lord Jocelyn, his son, in the House of Commons, as to the intentions of the Ministry. Peel seized the opportunity of delivering an ultimatum in reply.

There is no influence [said he], no power, no authority, which the prerogatives of the Crown and the existing law give the Government, which shall not be exercised for the purpose of maintaining the Union, the dissolution of which would involve not merely the repeal of the Act of Parliament, but the dismemberment of this great Empire. . . . I am prepared to make the declaration which was made, and nobly made, by my predecessor, Lord Althorp, that deprecating as I do all war, and especially civil war, there is no alternative which I do not think preferable to the dismemberment of this Empire.

The words were weighty ; their meaning was not to be mistaken. To some of the Irish they sounded the knell of their hopes, to others the tocsin of a welcome war. O'Connell interpreted them to mean that agitation for a political object, however unanimous, and however constitutional, was to be met with a cold and resolute denial.

I belong [he cried] to a nation of eight millions, and there is besides a million of Irishmen in England. If Sir Robert Peel has the audacity to cause a contest to take place between the two countries, we will put him in the wrong, for we will begin no rebellion; but I tell him from this place that he dare not begin that strife against Ireland.

The meaning of the words was obvious. They meant that, however peacefully disposed, events might come in which he would be prepared to declare war. The people so understood him ; already the *Nation* was writing about " being ready for death, for liberty."

They talk of civil war [he said on another occasion], but while I live there shall be no civil war. But if others invade us, *that* is not civil war, and I promise them that there is not a Wellingtonian of them all who would less shrink from that contest than I, if they will enforce it upon us. We are ready to keep the ground of the constitution as long as they will allow us to do so, but should they throw us from that ground, then *vae victis !* between the contending parties.

At the meeting at Cashel on May 23rd, after his accustomed panegyric upon the beauties of Ireland, he went on, " Where was the coward who would not die for such a land ? . . . He did not like fighting, but let their enemies attack them if they dare." Nor was this the mere ebullition of impassioned oratory. John O'Connell, his most trusted son and henchman, wrote to the *Morning Chronicle* : " We will not attack ; I do not say we will not defend."

The Government began to act. On May 23rd Sir Edward Sugden, Lord Chancellor of Ireland, a profoundly learned lawyer, but an indiscreet statesman, dismissed from the magistracy Lord Ffrench, O'Connell, his son John, and thirty-one others. The Irish promptly took up the challenge. ' The "rent" trebled in a week; it leapt from £700 to £2,200 ; Smith O'Brien and many other Irish Whigs resigned their commissions of the peace. A crowd of new members joined the Association. It was then that O'Connell established the Arbitration Courts, which quickly spread throughout the country. The English Whigs censured the Chancellor's act; Russell declared that Repeal was as fit to be discussed in a constitutional manner as any other topic; and the Whig lawyers condemned the legality of the proceeding. The Government, however, kept to its course. The Irish Arms Act was expiring; they had proposed to renew it with increased severity, and they pressed it steadily upon the House of Commons. Whigs, Radicals, and Irish combined to resist it; they fought it line by line; it remained three months in committee. Nor was it by the Ministry alone, or in Ireland alone, that civil war was expected and designed. From America came the news that Tyler, the President of the United States, while declining to attend a Repeal meeting, had declared himself the strong friend of Repeal. Sir Charles Metcalfe, Governor of Canada, reported to his superiors that if any aggression took place upon Ireland he could not answer for the peace, perhaps not even for the security of the Dominion. In France the Radicals, with Ledru Rollin at their head, were openly projecting armed assistance for the Irish. Military plans began to be openly discussed. It was pointed out how defensible a country Ireland was ; cavalry would be powerless ; for in Ireland rough stone walls took the place of hedges and made each field a redoubt. The art of manufacturing pikes was explained. O'Connell told his hearers at Kilkenny on June 8th :—

They stood that day at the head of a group of men sufficient, if they underwent military discipline, to conquer Europe. Wellington never had such an army. There were not at Waterloo, on both sides, as many brave and energetic men. However, they were not disci-

plined, but tell them what to do, and you would have them disciplined
in an hour. They were as well able to walk in order after a band
as if they wore red coats. They were as able to be submissive to the
Repeal wardens, or anybody else told to take care of them, as if they
were called sergeants or captains.

Three days later, at the meeting at Mallow, he
crowned all his utterances with his celebrated "Mallow
defiance":—

Do you know [he exclaimed], I never felt such a loathing for
speechifying as I do at present. The time is coming when we must be
doing. Gentlemen, you may learn the alternative to live as slaves or
die as freemen. . . . In the midst of peace and tranquillity they are
covering our land with troops. Yes, I speak with the awful determination with which I commenced my address, in consequence of news
received this day. . . What are Irishmen that they should be denied
an equal privilege? Have we not the ordinary courage of Englishmen? Are we to be called slaves? Are we to be trampled under
foot? Oh! they shall never trample on me, at least! I say they may
trample on me, but it will be my dead body they will trample on, not
the living man!

Never was man more skilful than O'Connell in so
measuring his language as to convey the most inflam-
matory impression in still peaceable words. Never did
any man so hold a whole country in check upon the
very verge of civil war without suffering it to break the
peace. But, elated with the delirious enthusiasm of
1843, he had been carried too far. It was the theory
of Davis and his followers, that, if necessary, the Irish
ought to fight for their freedom. The Irish accepted
the theory; they were eager to fight; and they understood
O'Connell's words, as Peel understood them to mean,
that he would, when the time came, lead them to battle,
and they rejoiced at the prospect and had no fear of its
issue. "At any moment that Mr. O'Connell had chosen

during that year," writes John O'Connell, " and indeed for long afterwards, he could have raised them in insurrection as one man throughout the entire country, and however bloody, wasting and desolating might have been the struggle, it is utterly impossible but that the result would have been a violent separation from England. There was a spirit abroad among the people which would have made millions among them prefer death to submission again to England." They imagined they could drive the English into the sea.

It is hardly conceivable that O'Connell could have hoped for any such issue ; it is difficult to see how he allowed himself to encourage such a temper in the people of Ireland. If he meant what he said he was preparing for rebellion ; if he did not, he was playing with fire, and risking the lives and liberties of his fellow-countrymen for a little idle rhetoric. The truth probably lies between the two suppositions. It acquits him of folly if not of guilt. He recollected 1828 and how his present opponents, Wellington and Peel, had succumbed, sorely against their will, to the peaceful menace of unanimous agitation. He thought the same tactics would succeed now. He could not believe that Peel meant to go to any lengths in defence of the Union. He was counting on the surrender of the Government.

But he had sadly mistaken his men. Peel had yielded in 1829 because the House of Commons was divided and because the best of the English were in agreement with the Irish. With a united House of Commons he was not the man to flinch. Wellington had yielded because in face of imminent civil war he was told the troops were no longer to be trusted. There were no Repeal regiments now, and if the Irish must

11 *

come to blows with the Empire the lesson would be short, certain, and lasting.

The Government quietly took their measures. They masked each meeting with dragoons, but did not interfere with it. The Duke had poured 35,000 troops into Ireland. Barracks had been fortified, martello towers put in repair, forts loopholed, stores accumulated. Ships of war lay in the rivers; more troops were in readiness in the west and north of England. If there was to be a conflict he was ready. The Repealers felt that the series of monster meetings must be brought to an end; their novelty was wearing off; autumn was fast vanishing. It was decided to conclude them with one beside which the others, gigantic as they were, should sink into insignificance. It was to be held at another of the historic spots of Ireland, at Clontarf, a few miles from Dublin. To it the people were to be gathered from every part of Ireland and from England and Scotland across the sea. Nine-tenths of the grown men of Ireland were Repealers; it was to be an awe-inspiring proof of the unanimity of the Irish race. A platform was set up and minute directions given for the gathering of the host. One slip they made, but only for a moment. One of the secretaries, Frank Morgan, a solicitor, issued a placard summoning and directing what he called the "Repeal Cavalry." The expression was not very obnoxious, but it was indiscreet, and the placard was at once called in. The Government made no sign, and it was thought they would allow this last meeting to pass as they had tolerated so many of its predecessors.

The meeting was to be held on Sunday, October 5th. Already steamers were arriving laden with the Repealers of Glasgow and Liverpool, when the *Dublin Mail* announced on the Friday that the meeting would be forbidden. It was known that the Irish Privy Council was assembled to receive a despatch from England. Still the Government uttered not a word. But soon troops began to be moved down upon Clontarf. On the following day the guards at the barracks and at Dublin Castle were doubled. The guns at the Pigeon House Fort and the batteries of the ships in the river were trained upon the place of meeting. The *Rhadamanthus* and the *Dee* arrived from England with the 34th Regiment of Foot and the 87th Royal Irish Fusiliers. The 5th Dragoons, each man equipped for active service, with food for twenty-four hours, moved towards evening to Clontarf. Close by, at Conquest Hill, were the 11th Hussars and the 54th Foot, and a brigade of the Royal Horse Artillery, with four six-pounders. The 60th Rifles commanded the ground, and each man had sixty rounds of ball cartridge.

From an early hour on that Saturday the Committee of the Association had been in session, fitfully transacting its business, and expectant, amid the news of these preparations, of some word from the Castle. The room grew crowded. At last, at half-past three a messenger burst in with a copy of the proclamation in his hand wet from the press. The meeting was forbidden. There was no time for deliberation. Less than two hours of daylight remained. Already the people were beginning to approach Clontarf. It had to be decided on the instant whether the proclamation should be obeyed or defied. The habit of a lifetime determined O'Connell to obey. But it was not enough passively to yield; the people must be warned in time and time was scant. O'Connell did not talk; he acted. Peter Martin was sent to pull down the platform, which had been erected at Clontarf. Twenty or thirty gentlemen were despatched through the surrounding country in pairs to warn the gathering crowds. By dawn O'Connell's proclamation, commanding obedience to the proclamation, was posted in every village within twenty miles of Clontarf. The meeting was abandoned ; the Government was victorious. If the meeting was legal, as O'Connell said it was, the Government had "invaded" the Irish and O'Connell *had* " shrunk from the contest." In the sight of the whole people of Ireland, he had flinched from his word.

CHAPTER IX.

LAST DAYS.

1843-1847.

The trial—The judgment of the House of Lords—The Federal controversy—The conflict with Young Ireland—Alliance with the
Whigs—The Famine—Last days and death.

UNCONDITIONAL submission to the proclamation of the
Government was undoubtedly the only course open to
O'Connell, whether as a man of sense, a humane Irishman, or a loyal subject of the Queen, but for the time
being it was a severe blow to his hopes, his self-esteem,
and his *prestige*. Nothing less than the devotion of the
Irish to their trusted leader could have kept them
faithful to him, so bitter was their disappointment. He
had conducted agitations for a generation past against
governments of every temper and description. He had
baffled the law officers of the Crown, laughed at statute
after statute, defied the Executive again and again, with
consummate dexterity. He had said, and he still maintained, that the Clontarf meeting was perfectly legal;
he had announced that he would resist by force any invasion by the Government of the people's legal rights,
and after all his defiances, he had turned his cheek to
the smiter. Between the leaders of the Young Ireland

party and O'Connell's henchmen for long no love had
been lost. The young men now began to think that
their chief was superannuated, and that his hand had
lost its cunning.

Still the matter was far from being hopeless. In the
summer O'Connell had formulated a plan for an assembly, which was to be the germ of an Irish House of
Commons. He argued, somewhat pedantically it is
true, that, as Parliaments were originally summoned by
the writ of the Sovereign, it needed now no statute to
create an Irish Parliament. A little wax and parch-
ment, a royal summons to counties and boroughs to
send persons to advise the Crown, would suffice. He
proposed to collect such a body of advisers beforehand ; to bring together in Dublin an amateur House of
Commons, as he had established throughout the country
a volunteer judiciary. The Repealers of each locality
were to subscribe £100, and to select someone in whom
they had confidence, not to represent them, since that
would have infringed Lord Clare's Convention Act, but
to be the bearer of the £100 to Dublin. These agents
for the transmission of money, finding themselves for-
tuitously in Dublin, were to meet, to debate, to resolve,
to comport themselves like the delegates that they were
and the members of a House of Commons that they
hoped to be. Their number was to be 300; it was a
number instinct with the recollections of independent
Ireland, the number of Charlemont's assembly, the
number of Grattan's Parliament, the number of the
Dungannon Convention. Here was a plan still remaining to be tried.

There was this, too, to encourage the Repealers. The
Irish Whigs had hitherto stood aloof from their movement. They were fully alive to the grievances, which

remained unredressed ; they were no longer sanguine
that they ever would be remedied under existing constitutional arrangements. But their leaders were men of
high rank and ancient family, such as the Duke of
Leinster and the Earl of Meath. They could not consent
to throw in their lot with O'Connell and Barrett and
Steele, or to support Repeal pure and simple. But the
Federal idea was gaining ground among them and
Federalists were always possible Repeal recruits. Sharman Crawford had put forward a scheme for a subordinate Irish assembly to manage Irish affairs, and an
Imperial legislature for Imperial affairs. Ross, member
for Belfast, and Caulfield, a son of the Lord Charlemont who was a leader of the Volunteers in 1782, were
of the same opinion. Smith O'Brien, than whom no Irish
member was more esteemed for his family or for his
integrity, had moved in July that the House of Commons should go into committee to consider the state of
Ireland. An excellent case had been made out for Irish
reforms. The Whigs had supported him ; the debate
had been carried on for five nights ; and the rejection
of the motion brought the Whigs so much the nearer to
Repeal.

Everyone was anxious to hear what O'Connell's next
step would be. The next Association meeting was attended by a dense crowd. He spoke long, but to little
purpose. Nothing was made of the Convention scheme ;
nothing of the Whig accession. He proposed to hold
simultaneous meetings in every parish, as had been done
in 1828 ; the Government could not break up a thousand meetings in a day. He had also a vague scheme
for a joint stock company, which was to benefit Ireland
in some unexplained way by jobbing in Irish mortgages.
The disappointment of the Repealers was intense ; their

leader had lost his nerve. Their enemies were openly
exultant, and the Government struck another blow.

On October the 14th O'Connell, his son John, Ray,
Secretary of the Association, Steele, its Head Pacificator, Barrett, editor of the *Pilot,* Gray, editor of the
Freeman's Journal, and Gavan Duffy, editor of the-
Nation, were called upon to give bail to answer infor-
mations, which had been sworn against them, for a conspiracy to raise sedition and to excite disaffection in
the army.   The indictment was sent up before the
Grand Jury on November 2nd; they deliberated for
six days and found true bills on the 8th.   The indictment was an instrument of portentous size and impene-
trable obscurity.   It set out at full length resolutions,
speeches, and newspaper articles.   It was one hundred
yards in length; it occupies fifty-five close-printed folio
pages in the Appendix to the Traversers' case in the
House of Lords.   There were eleven separate counts;
forty-three overt acts were alleged; and all the traversers were charged with conspiring together to commit each act, and with a general conspiracy to commit
general seditious acts.   It was a masterpiece of intricate
alternative pleading.   It is too much to say that it was
intelligible.

A vast array of counsel was retained on either side.
The Crown had a dozen barristers to represent it—
the Attorney-General, T. B. C. Smith, afterwards
Master of the Rolls, the Solicitor-General, R. Wil-
son Greene, afterwards a Baron of the Exchequer,.
Brewster and Napier, both subsequently Lord Chan-
cellors and others.   The traversers had an equally bril-
liant array—Sheil, Pigot, afterwards Chief Baron,
Monahan, afterwards Chief Justice of the Common,
Pleas, Whiteside, afterwards Chief Justice of the Queen's.

Bench, O'Hagan, subsequently Lord Chancellor, O'Loghlen, subsequently Judge - Advocate - General. From the first the Irish Repealers made up their minds that the accused would not have a fair trial, and their newspapers encouraged the belief. Unfortunately the unscrupulous zeal of the minor officials of the Crown converted their prejudiced apprehension into a lamentable truth, and it must be owned that the counsel for the Crown availed themselves of every technical objection with illiberal pedantry.

The trial was to take place at bar, but it could not well be held until the jury panel had been revised. Shaw, the Recorder of Dublin, member for Dublin University and a Privy-Councillor, was the officer before whom the list was revised. He had made frequent and strong complaints of the incompleteness and inadequacy of the list of persons qualified to serve as jurors. The revision was now at hand. The special jury panel ought to have contained all peers and eldest sons of peers, all esquires and all merchants, whose property was worth £5,000. The existing panel showed but 388 special jurors' names, an obviously insufficient number, and of these, 70 were dead or disqualified. At least 300 Catholics must have been entitled to have their names on the list; there were but 23. The returns of the collectors of Grand Jury cess showed over 11,000 houses in Dublin rated at the amount which qualified for the common jury list. Presumably there ought to have been a common jury list of at least 9,000 names. The existing list contained but 5,000, and was besides scandalously incomplete in other respects. These facts were notorious. From such a jurors' book in such a case a panel could not be struck. The trial was postponed till January 15th, 1844.

The revision took place. The Recorder enlarged the list of special jurors from 388 to 717. On January 4th the parties attended before the Clerk of the Crown to strike a jury. It was pointed out on behalf of the traversers that the names of 60 persons, wealthy and respectable men, which had been entered by the Recorder in the list of special jurors, had been somehow omitted from the list, from which it was now proposed to strike the panel. The Clerk of the Crown decided that he had come there not to argue but to strike a panel and a panel should be struck. The ballot produced the names of forty persons; eleven were Roman Catholics. One by one Kemmis, the solicitor for the Crown, struck them off. The jury finally consisted of twelve Protestant tradesmen, of whom one was an Englishman. The Court consisted of Chief Justice Pennefather and three puisne judges, Burton, Crampton and Perrin. All were Protestants, two were Tories, one was an Englishman.

The 15th came. Business in Dublin was suspended. Huge crowds thronged the Four Courts. O'Connell arrived at the Court in semi-royal state, riding in the Lord Mayor's coach and attended by the Dublin aldermen in their robes. He took his seat in Court in wig and gown. The judges entered, the jurors were called. When the first person called came to the book to be sworn, counsel for the traversers interposed with a challenge to the array and pointed to the omission of the sixty names. The Attorney-General put in a demurrer; he admitted the fact, and argued that it was immaterial in law. The Court sustained the demurrer. On the 17th the jury were sworn, and the case proceeded at a length worthy of the indictment. The Attorney-General occupied two days in opening his case; the evidence for the Crown occupied seven days; the speeches for the traversers ten; the reply of the Solicitor-General three. O'Connell was the last of the traversers to speak and his speech was a failure; it was feeble and ineffective. Late on the afternoon of the twenty-third day the jury retired. It was a Saturday, and the hours wore on into the night; but no one left the Court while the jury were out. Shortly before twelve they returned. They were agreed as to the substance of their verdict, but had a natural difficulty in adjusting it to the case of nine traversers, eleven counts, and forty-three overt acts. Before this nice matter could be set right midnight arrived. All was in doubt. The Attorney-General was of opinion the jury must undergo further incarceration and give their verdict on Monday; he doubted if the verdict could be taken in the small hours of Sunday morning. The judge directed that the jury should remain together till Monday and proposed to adjourn. Another learned gentleman doubted if the Court could now adjourn; it would be the performance of a judicial act on Sunday, a *dies non*. The judge had had doubts of his power to take the verdict and let the wretched jurymen go to their homes; he had none of his power to adjourn and go to his own. The Court rose.

But practically the verdict was known. The Government had a steamer in readiness at Kingstown; it sped away with the news at once, and the *Times* had the verdict printed in London at the time it was being formally delivered in Dublin. O'Connell, Barrett, and Duffy were found guilty on the whole of the first three counts, except as to the charge of acting " maliciously and seditiously "; on the other counts there was a general verdict of guilty against all. Sentence was deferred until the following term. Parliament was then in session. O'Connell only

waited for a meeting of the General Committee before
setting out for London. But at that meeting he startled
his followers by the tone which he adopted ; in truth, the
verdict and the certain prospect of imprisonment might
well quench the spirit of a man on the verge of his
seventieth year. He urged a complete submission ; he
proposed to abandon the Arbitration Courts, and he
recommended the dissolution of the Association and its
reconstitution in some other and less obnoxious form.
The young and fighting wing were up in arms. They
had with difficulty acquiesced in the policy of abandoning
the Clontarf meeting ; now they threatened, rather
than acquiesce in the dissolution of the Association, to
split the party. Smith O'Brien, who had now become an
avowed Repealer and a member of the Association, was
of the same opinion. At last a compromise was arrived
at. In the late trial the articles in newspapers, though
unauthorised by and unconnected with many of the
traversers, had formed the most serious evidence against
them. For the security of the Association all the edi-
tors of newspapers resigned their membership. Notice
was sent to the Arbitration Courts that they must no
longer have any connection with the Association.
Severed from the parent stem they speedily perished.

O'Connell crossed to England, and was enthusiastically received by the Liberals. He addressed large
meetings at Liverpool, at Manchester, at Coventry, at
Birmingham. A great banquet was given in his honour
at Covent Garden theatre. He entered the House of
Commons during an Irish debate, and was hailed with
enthusiastic cheers. In Parliament strong opinions
were expressed against the course of the trial by Sir
Thomas Wilde and other eminent lawyers. But in spite
of it all two adverse and significant facts appeared.

The Radicals were eager for Reform; they were hostile
to Repeal. The official Whigs held themselves aloof
altogether.

The day of sentence at length arrived. Efforts had
been made to disturb the verdict. A motion was made
at the beginning of term for a new trial on the ground
of misdirection, but it was refused. On May 30th
the traversers were called up. As he entered the
Court, O'Connell was received with vociferous applause. The traversers were called upon, and
Mr. Justice Burton pronounced the sentence of the
Court. He and O'Connell had been old friends and
companions on the Munster circuit and old rivals at
the bar. As his judgment proceeded, he was painfully
affected and even wept. The sentence upon O'Connell
was imprisonment for twelve months, a fine of £2,000,
and security in £5,000, his own and another's, for his
good behaviour during seven years. The other traversers were sentenced to nine months' imprisonment and
£50 fines. When sentence had been delivered, O'Connell rose, and briefly said that justice had not been
done him. His words were caught up with cheers for
Repeal by the audience in Court, which were repeated by
the crowd outside. The prisoners were then removed,
escorted by a silent multitude, to Richmond Gaol.

In the matter of their imprisonment they were treated
with the utmost leniency. It had been privately com-
municated to them, that they would be permitted to
choose the place of their confinement. Fitzpatrick had
occupied himself with inquiries about the gaols of Ireland, and had ascertained that Richmond Prison was a
commodious and convenient gaol. It had the great
recommendation of being under the control of the Corporation of Dublin, who could be counted on even to

strain the law in order to treat them as honoured guests, not as condemned criminals.

The prisoners were delivered into the custody of the governor of the gaol, and their names and descriptions entered in the usual way in the prison register, where they may still be seen. The Board of Superintendence was holding a meeting in the prison, and sent for O'Connell. As he entered all rose to receive him. He was informed that every possible concession would be made to the comfort of the prisoners, if they would give their *parole* not to misuse the indulgence by turning it into a means of escape. The pledge was given; the officials were permitted to let their private houses to the prisoners; the garden of the gaol was placed at their disposal. They were catered for from outside, they received their letters and visitors, and entertained guests as if they were in their own homes. The only persons who were refused admittance were the mayors of Cork, Waterford, Limerick, Kilkenny, and Clonmel, who came in state with their aldermen and town councillors to present addresses to O'Connell. The Roman Catholic bishops undertook in terms the duty of saying a daily mass for O'Connell's benefit, and eagerly competed with one another for the honour. Visitors to the gaol found him walking placidly in the garden with his grandchildren about him playing among the flowers, and his fellow-prisoners engaged in various pastimes, in conducting a gaol journal, the *Prison Gazette*, which chronicled meetings held at the hillocks in the garden, which they nicknamed the Hill of Tara, and the Rath of Mullaghmasts, or in the more serious business of advising those who remained at liberty and were carrying on the work of the Association.

Meantime, proceedings had been taken for bringing

the trial on appeal to the House of Lords by writ of error. O'Connell to the very last had little expectation that this forlorn hope could succeed. His attention was concentrated on the proceedings of the Association, which were being carried on under the leadership of Smith O'Brien, and upon the conduct of the people at large.

> The people [he said] are behaving nobly. I was at first a little afraid, despite all my teaching, that at such a crisis they would have done either too much or too little; either have been stung into an outbreak, or else awed into apathy. Neither has happened. Blessed be God! the people are acting nobly. What it is to have such a people to lead! In the days of the Catholic Association I used to have more trouble than I can express in keeping down mutiny. I always arrived in town about October 25th, and on my arrival I invariably found some jealousies, some squabbles, some fellow trying to be leader, which gave me infinite annoyance. But now all goes right; no man is jealous of any other man; each does his best for the general cause.

The English lawyers, however, who had now been engaged for the prisoners, knew better than O'Connell that any points of law that could be raised would be fairly heard by the House of Lords. They assigned error on no less than thirty-four grounds. There was error in the composition of the jury, error in the inextricable intricacies of the indictment, error in the verdict, and error in the judgment. The jury was unlawfully chosen; the indictment in some cases said too little, for it did not name the persons whom it was alleged the prisoners had conspired to intimidate; and in others it said too much, for it charged the same and only conspiracy over and over again; the verdict, which found them guilty of conspiracy, was so framed as to acquit them on its face of having conspired in common, which was essential to the existence of the offence; the judg-

12

ment ingeniously sentenced each to imprisonment until all had paid up the amount of their fines.

If the original indictment was formidable, the indictment against it on appeal was no less so. According to custom, the House of Lords stated questions for the opinion of the judges, and Tindal, Chief Justice of the Common Pleas, attended to read their opinion to the House. The judges differed in opinion, but a majority were against the appeal, and in particular, with little hesitation, they held that the defect in the jury panel, since partiality was not alleged against the sheriff, did not invalidate the subsequent proceedings. The House gave judgment upon September 4th. Five law lords had heard the case, Lyndhurst, the Chancellor, Brougham and Cottenham, ex-Chancellors, Campbell, ex-Chancellor of Ireland, and Denman, Lord Chief Justice. The judgments of the first four had been accurately forecast; they were evenly divided. Denman, indignant at the incompleteness of the jury panel, turned the scale in favour of quashing the whole proceedings. If the omission of sixty names was immaterial, he said, why should not the sheriff have been at liberty to add sixty names? The persons who had tried O'Connell were not truly jurors at all. If sheriffs were to do their duty thus, then trial by jury was "a mockery, a delusion, and a snare." Upon the judgments of the law lords the proceedings were to be quashed. In strict law any member of the House of Lords was entitled to vote upon the question, for formally the judgments in the House of Lords are speeches in support of or against a motion. Some lay peers, alarmed at the prospect of O'Connell's release, proposed to vote and carry Lyndhurst's motion against their enemy. Then Lord Wharncliffe rose, deputed by the

Government, and with grave dignity appealed to them
not to violate the now well-established custom of the
House, which was to leave the decision upon questions
of legal process to the peers who were learned in the
law. The peers bowed to his appeal to their sense of
fairness; they overcame their prejudices and withdrew,
and their enemy went free.

Away posted Ford, O'Connell's solicitor, to Holy-
head with the news in his pocket. A steamer, the
Medusa, was in waiting to carry him to Dublin. Eagerly
expecting the issue, were it good or evil, thousands
crowded the Kingstown pier on her arrival. In
an instant all was rejoicing. The engine that brought
the messenger up to Dublin was decorated with a flag,
"O'Connell is free," to spread the news by the wayside. Away rushed Ford to Richmond and dashed
into O'Connell's dining-room with tears and ejacula-
tions. "Fitzpatrick," said O'Connell, reverently, "the
hand of man is not in this. It is the response given by
Providence to the prayers of the faithful, steadfast people
of Ireland." That night he left the prison and walked
home to Merrion Square; as they met him in the streets
the people stared at him as if he had risen from the dead.
But no quiet home-coming could satisfy his admirers.
From end to end of Ireland the news had been expected,
and bonfires telegraphed from hill to hill, that the news
was good. Next day the prisoners returned to gaol to
be formally escorted home by a vast procession. O'Connell, mounted upon a grotesque triumphal chariot, with
a harper in ancient Irish garb harping patriotic tunes
before him, and all the trades of Dublin marching before
and behind, was drawn amid thunders of applause
through the streets to his home.

But although few at first believed it, in those few

12 *

months of his imprisonment the whole scene changed. The eyes of all Europe had been fixed upon the trial, and the trial had been represented as the struggle of innocence against a legal system and a bench of judges, which were nothing but tools in the firm grip of the English Government, and now in the sight of all the world the highest English tribunal had shown its independence of the Government, by giving a just judgment upon a passionless point of law. It was a signal proof to the Irish people that English justice was justice indeed. The sympathy of the spectators was changed; but the actors were changing too. While O'Connell was in prison the forward party had obtained a greater control over the machinery of the Association, and had become more confirmed in the belief that the struggle must, if necessary, be decided by an appeal to the sword; and unhappily, while these ardent spirits were becoming more and more fiery, O'Connell's power of controlling them was fast diminishing. While he lay in gaol, he was attacked, secretly but certainly, by that disease of which less than three years later he died.

The Federal idea had been steadily gaining force among the Protestant gentry of Ireland and the English Whigs, until it became elevated almost into an avowed object of their policy. Nassau Senior had propounded in the *Edinburgh Review* a scheme for an "itinerant Parliament." Occasional sessions of the Imperial Legislature were to be held in Dublin. Lord John Russell corrected the proof sheets of the article. The project met with some favour. Many years afterwards it was alleged, on the authority of one who afterwards became a Whig Cabinet Minister, and was not denied by Russell, that the Whig leaders actually resolved to offer O'Connell "an alliance, on the basis of conceding to Ireland a Parliament administering Irish affairs under a system of federal union with Great Britain." Mr. Hatchell was sent to Dublin to sound the Irish Repealers upon the subject. Even if this rumour were, as it probably was, an exaggeration, it was clear that as a *via media* Federation would command no little support. O'Connell was disposed to forego Repeal, of which he now knew the hope to be so shadowy, for the solid benefits, which the English were willing to bestow as soon as the *inertia* of their unfamiliarity with Ireland was overcome. Upon his release from prison he wrote on October 14th to the Repeal Association a letter, in which, after disclaiming any more monster meetings, and keeping silence about his plan for a Convention in Dublin, he said :—

For my own part I will own that since I have come to contemplate the specific differences, such as they are, between simple Repeal and Federation, I do at present feel a preference for the Federation plan, as tending more to the utility of Ireland and the maintenance of the connection with England than the proposal of simple Repeal. But I must either deliberately propose or deliberately adopt from some other person a plan of Federative Union, before I bind myself to the opinion which I now entertain. . . . The Federalists cannot but perceive that there has been on my part a pause in the agitation for Repeal since our liberation from unjust captivity.

The letter fell like a bomb upon the party which found voice in the *Nation*; to them it seemed, that to abandon Repeal, after all the great things that had been said of it for years past, was pusillanimous. It made Ireland contemptible. Duffy issued a temperately worded manifesto, in which he declared that a voice in the Imperial destiny of England was a poor compensation for a little limitation upon the Irish claim to have the sole control of the individual destinies of Ireland; nothing could satisfy him but the restoration of Ireland's ancient and historic constitution. Smith O'Brien was as yet mute. O'Connell wrote to him on the 21st a letter, in which he dwelt on the importance of their common agreement and propounded a Federal plan, of which he said :—

While all matters of taxation, commercial and ecclesiastical policy, as well as the general taxation and expenditure of the United Kingdom, would by such an arrangement remain, as now, within the exclusive control of the Imperial Legislature, such matters as the regulation and disposition of local taxation, the relief of the poor and the development of the natural resources of the country would be provided for by the local assembly, which must necessarily be better qualified to discharge such functions.

We utterly disclaim any intention of rendering the proposed measures in any degree subservient to the severance of the legislative connection between Great Britain and Ireland, which, thus reformed, we shall deem it our duty, as we believe it will be our interest, by every means in our power to maintain.

But it speedily became apparent that except among his own sycophants, who would have accepted any policy from his hands, O'Connell's suggestion of adopting Federation found no favour. The Protestants, who followed Sharman Crawford, personally distrusted him. The English Whigs, unaware, perhaps, of any change of opinion among their leaders, adhered to the Whig cry of Reform but no Repeal; the Irish Repealers, one and all, denounced any concession. O'Connell felt that the reins were slipping from his grasp. It was not thus that in the heyday of his powers his suggestions were disputed; unfortunately, too, it was not thus that he had been accustomed to crush a mutineer. He recanted. He returned to Dublin from Darrynane amid the usual signs of enthusiasm and popularity, banquets, addresses, and torchlight processions. He attended the Association meeting on November 25th, and practically announced that his Federalism had been a temporary ruse adopted to attract the Federalists, a tub to catch

a whale. If they assented they would have been drawn
into the Repeal circle ; if they refused they would have
been made to appear opinionated and in the wrong.

After the liberation of the state prisoners [he said] advances had
been made to him by men of large influence and large property, who
talked of seeking Repeal on what they called the Federal Plan. He
inquired what the Federal Plan was, but nobody could tell him. He
called upon them to propose their plan, the view in his own mind
being that Federalism could not commence till Ireland had a parliament of her own, because she would not be on a footing with England
till possessed of a parliament to arrange her own terms. The Federalists were bound to declare their plan, and he had conjectured that
there was something advantageous in it, but he did not go any further ;
he expressly said he would not bind himself to any plan. . . . He had
expected the assistance of the Federalists, and opened the door as
wide as he could without letting out Irish liberty. But [said he,
snapping his fingers], let me tell you a secret ; Federalism is not
worth *that.* Federalists, I am told, are still talking and meeting. . . .
I wish them well. Let them work as well as they can, but they are
none of my children—I have nothing to do with them.

In truth, O'Connell's position in relation to Repeal
never had been the same as that of the more advanced
and fanatical of his party. His rooted belief was that
no political advantage was worth having at the cost of
shedding one drop of blood. They were not far from
thinking that Irish liberties were not worth having
until they had been baptized with English blood shed
by Irish hands. There could be no lasting union between two such views. O'Connell's practical mind
shrank from rejecting present boons when nothing
better could be got ; he knew that when a peaceful
agitation had missed fire, as the Repeal agitation had, to
prolong it was to be ridiculous ; for criminal he would
not be, and prolonged agitation of the pattern of 1843
would either lead him to the crime of rebellion, or
would fritter itself away. He was looking anxiously
round for a practicable policy and a practicable goal.

He knew his countrymen better than the Young Ireland party did, and saw that they did not walk in processions and pay Repeal rents—the rent, which had averaged £500 a week during the trial, had risen to £2,500 and £3,000 a week during the imprisonment—for nothing. They looked for legislative advantages, and expected to feel the advantage in their pockets. A boon such as that must be obtained peacefully and from England. But to the Young Ireland party a boon from England seemed no better than a penny tossed to a beggar, and they detested the policy which accepted it. When the Repeal party was thus on the verge of breaking up, Peel accelerated the process by offering remedial legislation to Ireland. His mind had been much impressed with the debate on Smith O'Brien's motion in 1843. There had been another long debate on the causes of Irish discontent on Russell's motion in the spring of 1844. The Devon Commission, appointed in 1843, conducted an exhaustive inquiry into the Irish land question in 1844, and reported early in 1845. Peel, now informed upon the question, braved the fanaticism of some of his party, and proposed substantial reform. The Irish were to be educated. For the benefit of the priests the Maynooth grant was almost trebled, and was made permanent and placed beyond the reach of controversy; for the laity it was proposed to establish three Queen's Colleges at a cost of £100,000, and to endow them with £7,000 a year, and the education given in them was to be secular.

O'Connell was in some difficulty in the matter. Through Mr. Petre, an unaccredited agent, backed by the powerful influence of the agent of the Austrian Monarchy, the Government had succeeded in obtaining from the See of Rome a letter from Cardinal Fransoni,

Prefect of the Propaganda, to Archbishop Crolly, deprecating the lively part which Irish priests were taking in political agitation. Most of the Irish bishops evaded the monition by interpreting it as a warning against excessive zeal on the part of their clergy, but a minority deferred to it by withdrawing all ecclesiastical support from the agitation. Now the Maynooth grant was likely still further to alienate the priests. And yet it was difficult to oppose it.

As time progressed, however, he became decidedly hostile to the Government plan of provincial colleges. The Bill was introduced on May 9th, and was well received by the House of Commons. In Ireland some of the bishops, the Young Ireland party, and the Protestants, also welcomed it. In the General Committee, in spite of O'Connell's opposition, a majority was favourable to it. He was impatient of such a result. Davis suggested that to avoid the spectacle of open divisions the question should not be dealt with by the Association at all. O'Connell would have none of the suggestion. He brought it before a full meeting in Conciliation Hall. Sir Robert Inglis, member for the University of Oxford, had stigmatized the projected colleges as " godless colleges." This was said from the extreme Protestant point of view. O'Connell thanked him for teaching him that word, and, as a Catholic, denounced them too as " godless." His son John, a poor-spirited bigot, who aspired to be his successor, and already possessed a great influence over his father's mind and the proceedings of the Association, followed in the same tone. O'Connell proposed Catholic colleges in Cork and Galway, and a Presbyterian college in Belfast. To the Young Ireland men, who cared for nothing except as a means to Repeal, and for

that end were ardently working for a union of Catholics-
and Protestants in one party, this seemed madness. It
had been bad enough when O'Connell treated the Federalists with discourtesy, not to say contempt. To see
all their efforts at union destroyed by this rekindling of
religious strife was more than they could bear. They
openly dissented from their leader in the Association
Hall. At a subsequent meeting, what had been merely
the cut and thrust of debate, became the blows and
wounds of personality. O'Connell denounced the Bill
as "execrable," and prejudicial to "faith and morals."
A clever but dissolute free-lance named Conway rose
and attacked Davis and his party, declaring that their
indifference to the perilous character of the Bill was
only part of their general indifference to religion. Some
of them were Protestants; in an assembly consisting
principally of ardent Catholics the hit told. O'Connell
so far forgot himself as to wave his cap round his head
in unrestrained applause. Davis denied the charge.
O'Connell came into collision with him, and used words
which, whatever Davis might do, his followers could not
forgive :—

The principle of the Bill [said he] has been lauded by Mr. Davis,
and was advocated in a newspaper professing to be the organ
of the Roman Catholic people of this country, but which I emphati-
cally pronounce to be no such thing. The section of politicians styling
themselves the Young Ireland party, anxious to rule the destinies of
this country, start up and support this measure. There is no such
party as that styled Young Ireland. There may be a few individuals
who take that denomination on themselves. I am for Old Ireland.
'Tis time that this delusion should be put an end to. Young Ireland
may play what pranks they please. I do not envy them the name
they rejoice in. I shall stand by Old Ireland, and I have some slight
notion that Old Ireland will stand by me.

The deed was done. Though Davis and O'Connell
became reconciled before the meeting separated, there

could after this be no peace between the Young Ireland
and the Old.

O'Connell had always been intolerant of any opposition to his will among his followers, though with combined good nature and good sense he had never been
jealous of expressions of mere verbal dissent. The feud
between him and The O'Gorman Mahon arising out of the
Clare election of 1830 remained open for several years,
and about 1833 O'Connell refused him admission to his
National Trades Union. Galway, one of the Repeal
members, had voted with the Government in one of the
divisions upon the Coercion Bill of 1833. At the earliest
opportunity he was drummed·out of the party. But
now O'Connell had far more cause than pique or
jealousy to turn him against the party of the
Nation. Davis died, and they began to get somewhat
out of hand. Some newspaper had pointed out the
military advantage, in case of a rebellion, of the projected system of Irish railways; it brought all Ireland
within a few hours of the garrison of Dublin. Mitchell
replied with an article in the *Nation*, explaining to hypothetical insurgents the best modes of disabling the railways. O'Connell openly disapproved of the article.
The Government prosecuted Duffy, the editor of the
Nation. O'Connell declined to say anything in his
defence.

Soon it became clear that the old agitation for Repeal
was abandoned and that O'Connell was returning to the
policy of supporting the Whigs, which he had pursued
from 1835 to 1840. During the autumn of 1845 he
had, at various provincial meetings, pressed for the formation of a Parliamentary party. He called for the
return of sixty-five Repealers at the next General Election. In particular he warned Sheil that he must

accept the Repeal pledge or lose his seat. In December, during the crisis when Russell attempted and failed to form a Ministry and Peel was compelled to resume the Government, he made a long speech in the Repeal Association, unmistakeably offering the Whigs the support of the Repeal party in return for a very moderate programme of Irish reform. In May 1846 he attended a meeting of Lord John Russell's followers at his house in Chesham Place. At the end of June Peel fell and O'Connell entered into an alliance with the new Whig Ministry. Ministers with Irish seats were not to be opposed; one of them was Sheil, who sat for Dungarvan. He was the new Master of the Mint. The patronage of Ireland was in return to be at O'Connell's disposal as it had been under Lord Melbourne's Administration. This brought the conflict with the Young Ireland party to a head at once. O'Connell had ceased to be willing to tolerate them; they would follow the banner of no captain of Whig mercenaries. By tactics, adroit but disingenuous, O'Connell contrived to let Sheil's election pass without opposition. The Young Ireland party considered this a disgrace to the cause of Repeal. But they were most anxious not to abandon the Association. John O'Connell was scheming for the succession to his father: Elijah's mantle was to fall upon him. He wished to be not less an autocrat than his father was, and therefore he was anxious to expel the Young Ireland members, to crush the *Nation,* and leave himself without check or rival. They were equally anxious to thwart this plan. O'Connell, himself sincerely alarmed at the tone, or what he believed to be the tone, of the *Nation,* was now worked upon by his son to take steps to assert his own authority and to drive the party of the *Nation* into secession. He proposed the adoption by the Associa-

tion of a report, pledging its members to a renunciation·
of the use of physical force in the agitation under any
circumstances whatever. The pledge was a purely gra-
tuitous one. As an abstract theorem of politics, it was.
maintained by none but Quakers, and hardly acted on
by them. O'Connell himself had a thousand times.
over used language in flat contradiction of it. As a
motion of immediate expediency, it was unnecessary,
because, in spite of Mitchell's article, nobody was at
present advocating the employment of physical force.
But it was a stroke of very great ingenuity. To oppose
it for its own sake looked seditious, and, coupled with
the existing charge of infidelity, was certain to alienate
the Roman Catholic clergy. To oppose it on the
ground that it was needless and irrelevant was to expose
its opponents to the charge of a pedantic or vexatious
hindrance of the policy of the Liberator. Meagher, a
lad of fiery eloquence, whose subsequent speech
upon this pledge earned him the title of Meagher
"of the sword," made matters worse by charging one
of O'Connell's henchmen with having sought and obtained
a Government place, a charge all the more unpalatable
for being true. The adoption of the pledge was carried
all but unanimously. The Young Ireland party did not
instantly retire, but it only needed a little discourteous
interruption and hectoring from John O'Connell to
drive them out. The Association was purged of its forward party, and O'Connell was free to act up to his
parliamentary alliance with the Whigs. But the secession reduced the Association to impotence and O'Connell did not live to serve his allies.

While these dissensions and intrigues were proceeding
in Dublin and London, Ireland was passing through the
very darkest of her many hours of suffering. The Irish

people, which had multiplied beyond the normal capacity of the soil to support it, had come to depend for its existence upon a single root. The potato was a crop more abundant, more easily cultivated, and more nutritious than any other. But it is unfortunately liable to the attacks of a disease, which, unforeseen and beyond the reach of any remedy, destroys the entire crop with unexampled rapidity. In October 1845 this disease made its appearance and spread slowly. Soon the people of Ireland were starving by thousands. But Ireland's adversity was England's opportunity, and the helping hand of public and private charity was nobly held out for her succour. It was hoped that the crop of 1846 would be a full one; instead of being a full one it perished with an almost instantaneous blight. In July the traveller from Cork to Dublin found the crop all around him luxuriant, plenteous, and sound. A week later he returned through a country covered with rotting vegetation and sickly with the smell of decay. Where thousands had wanted the autumn before, scores of thousands died of hunger in 1846, and scores of thousands more of the fever and pestilence which followed in the track of famine. It was a misery that mocked the powerlessness of agitation. O'Connell's mind was distressed by the dissensions in the Association, by the rash and daring projects which he believed the Young Ireland party entertained, by the disappointment which had fallen upon the rosy hopes of 1843. But beside the famine these were light matters. When he went in the autumn to Darrynane, he passed through a country that seemed accursed; where he had been accustomed to see crowds of rejoicing and triumphant supporters, he met troops of haggard and wasted wretches, whose sufferings were beyond human help.

It was to this all his agitation had brought him. After fifty years of effort and thirty years of triumph, he felt that he was passing from the scene with nothing but distress to cloud his present, and no cheering hopes of the future to console him. He was going down to his grave, and there

> Vestibulum ante ipsum primisque in faucibus Orci
> Luctus et ultrices posuere cubilia Curæ:
> Pallentesque habitant Morbi tristisque Senectus
> Et Metus et malesuada Fames ac turpis Egestas
> Terribiles visu formæ.

His end, indeed, was now near at hand. In addition to the woes of his country which he saw around him, his faculties had long been decaying under the strain of private anxieties. He was now visibly a broken man. Shortly before his imprisonment, though all but seventy years of age, he had fallen deeply in love with a girl hardly out of her teens, an Englishwoman and a Protestant. Her persistent refusals to marry him allayed neither his passion nor his disturbance of mind. His religious austerities increased; his family began to fear that he might take the Trappist vows. Fierce attacks were made on him for his inveterate habit of controlling the expenditure of the Repeal Association, without permitting the accounts to be published. He disdained the imputations upon his honesty, but he could not forget that the best friends of the cause condemned his refusal to publish the accounts. During the misery of the famine the *Times* sent a special correspondent to investigate the condition of his estates about Darrynane, and published a very dark account of his conduct as a landlord. The warfare of contradictions, which this entailed, was very harassing to his health. His physical

powers now gave way. He paid his last visit to Darrynane in September 1846 ; his once upright figure was
bent ; the vivacity of manner and the elasticity of foot-
step, which had long been remarkable in him, were
gone ; he shuffled rather than walked into his house.
On the 26th of January 1847 he left Ireland for the
last time and the darkness of the hour was accentuated
by the fact that on the steamer, among his fellow-pas-
sengers, there chanced to be a Protestant clergyman and
a Catholic priest, both visiting England to beg alms
for their starving parishioners. He appeared in Parliament on February 8th, and solemnly warned the Government that they little realised how great was the
misery and disaster impending over Ireland. A quarter
of the people must die if the House would not save
them, and that could be done only by some great
act of national charity. It was a solemn appeal and
the House listened to it with respect, but the change
in O'Connell himself was distressing. His eloquence
was gone. He appeared to be " a feeble old man mut-
tering at a table " ; his figure was shrunk ; his once
splendid voice was so feeble that it could scarcely be
heard. He was but the wreck of himself.

He went to Hastings to recover a little strength and
then to Folkestone. But he knew he was a dying man,
and he was eager at all hazards, before he died, to reach
Rome, the sacred seat of his Church. He embarked
amid a great crowd, and on March 22nd reached Bou-
logne. He was visited at his hotel, the Hotel des
Bains, by the Abbé van Drival, a canon of Arras. He
was wearing his green and gold Liberator's cap, but he
was feeble, full of the preoccupation of death, full of the
fear that he had not strength to reach Rome. The
Abbé wished him better health. " God's will be

done," said O'Connell in an inexpressibly solemn tone.

Sa tête [says the Abbé] était enorme, sa face carrée comme la face d'un lion; ses traits étaient fortement marqués; le feu jaillissait de ses yeux pourtant. . . . Il était évident qu' O'Connell était alors préoccupé sans cesse d'une seule idée, qui ne le quittait plus, et dont on m'avait recommandé de ne lui point parler, les malheurs d'Irlande, les folies d' O'Brien.*

Travelling by slow stages he reached Paris on the 26th. At the Hôtel Windsor great numbers of persons came to visit him, among them Montalembert and De Berryer. He consulted Doctors Chomel and Oliffe and was told that he was dying of a lingering congestion of the brain of two or three years standing. By slow degrees he was brought by Nevers, Moulines, and Lapalisse to Lyons, which he reached on April 11th. There he was detained for several days by frost and snow. The people took the liveliest interest in his welfare; prayers were said for his recovery in all the churches. If he walked abroad, crowds gathered round him, but, oppressed by melancholy, his head hung down, moving by slow and painful steps, he did not notice them. He left Lyons on the 22nd, and passing through Avignon, reached Marseilles on May 3rd. The day but one after he sailed for Genoa, and on arriving went to the Hôtel Feder. He never left it alive. He was attended by Dr. Miley of Dublin as his chaplain, and his faithful valet Duggan. He was soon very ill; leeches were applied but gave him no relief. Presently he became delirious, and was oppressed with a haunting fear that he might be buried before life had really left his body. For some days, with occasional intervals of consciousness, he remained in this condition. At dawn on the

* *O'Connell et le Collège Anglais   St. Omer,* par Louis Cavrois, Arras, 1867.

morning of the 15th, the Cardinal Archbishop of Genoa, though in extreme old age, came at a hasty summons and administered the last sacraments of the Roman Church. "All Genoa was praying for him." His last hour had indeed come; at half-past nine that night he died.

His will directed that his heart should be removed and buried in Rome. His body was taken to the hospital on the day after his death and embalmed. His heart was placed in an urn and taken to Rome, and there, with many pompous obsequies, placed in the Church of St. Agatha, where there is a monument to him representing him at the bar of the House of Commons refusing the old Parliamentary oath. His body was brought to Ireland and reached Dublin in August. It was received with almost royal honours and was buried on the 5th in Glasnevin cemetery. In 1869 an Irish round tower, 165 feet high, was erected to his memory and his body was then removed to a crypt at its base.

CHAPTER X.

DOMESTIC LIFE AND CHARACTER.

His wife and family—His domestic life and amusements—His personal piety—His appearance—His oratory—His political character and achievements.

O'CONNELL lived from his thirtieth to his latest year full in face of the public. The law courts, the platform, or the House of Commons, claimed all his energies and most of his time. Though devotedly attached to his family and his domestic life, they formed but a small part of his existence. He married on June 23rd 1802 a distant relative, Mary, daughter of Dr. Edward O'Connell of Tralee; the marriage, which was contrary to the wishes of his uncle Maurice, was celebrated privately in Dame Street, Dublin, in the lodgings of James Connor, the bride's brother-in-law. Maurice O'Connell was at first deeply offended at the match, but presently became reconciled to it. Of this marriage a numerous family was born: four sons, Maurice, Morgan, and John, all at different times members of Parliament, and Daniel; and three daughters, Ellen, who married Christopher Fitzsimon, Catharine, who married Charles O'Connell,

18 *

and Elizabeth, who married Nicholas French of Fort
William, Roscommon. Surrounded by his family, he
took the little distraction that he allowed himself from
his profession and his agitation. His life was sternly
laborious and punctiliously methodical.

He told me [says Mrs. Nicol] that for twenty-five years of his life he
rose soon after four, lighted his own fire, and was always seated at
business at five; at half-past eight one of his little girls came by turns
to announce breakfast; gave an hour to that. At half-past ten he set
off to the Court-house, walked two miles there in twenty-five minutes,
always reached the Court five minutes before the judges arrived.
From eleven to half-past three was not a minute unoccupied; at half-
past three he returned, taking the office of the Catholic Association
on his way. He always went in (the regular meetings were only
once a week), read the letters, wrote a sentence or two in reply, out of
which his secretary wrote a full letter. Returned home, dined at
four; with his family till half-past six, then went to his study;
went to bed at a quarter before ten, his head on his pillow always
at ten.

After he gave up practice at the bar, about the time
when he entered Parliament, he was less stern with
himself, and the family breakfast hour became ten.
But it was at Darrynane that his real moments of hap-
piness were passed. It had been the home of his boyhood, and it was the solace of his old age. He found
in wandering upon the Atlantic shores, or among the
mountains of Kerry, food at once for his imagination
and for the vein of melancholy that ran through his as
it runs through all Irish natures. His enjoyment of
nature in contrast to the sordid business, in which he
was obliged to spend so much of his time, was keen. In
1829 he wrote regretfully to a friend of his night journey through the Kerry Hills from Darrynane to Cork to
defend the Doneraile prisoners: "At ten that morning,
after that glorious feast of soul, I found myself settled
down amid all the rascalities of an Irish Court of Jus-

tice." To the Kerry sport of hare-hunting with beagles among the hills, he was passionately attached. His pack was famous all over Ireland. At night he would go round his drawing-room and ask his guests, " Are you for the mountain in the morning? " and gave orders for the huntsman to call the sportsmen at 4 a.m. Equipped with a long wooden staff, he followed his dogs on foot, even in his old age, with extraordinary vigour and fleetness. While his companions beat for game, he would hold a hasty court to arbitrate upon the quarrels of his tenants, and would break away from them to cheer on his beagles, and pursue the chase from one hill-top to another. Breakfast was brought out to the hillside, but the party,' however fasting, was not allowed to sit down till two hares at least had been killed. At breakfast he eagerly devoured the contents of his post-bag ; but when the time came for starting the hunt again, he impetuously strewed the grass with the letters and newspapers that he threw away. In such hard sport his day was spent, and at dark he would return home the freshest of the whole party. When he refused to be Chief Baron, "I don't at all deny," said he, "that the office would have had great attractions for me. There would not be more than eighty days duty in the year. I would take a country house near Dublin and walk into town, and during the intervals of judicial labour I 'd go to Darrynane. I should be idle in the early part of April, just when the jack hares leave the most splendid trails on the mountains." In 1840, when he was sixty-five, he wrote to his son John that he had killed five hares in one day, and it was always to Darrynane that he turned whenever he could snatch a brief respite from the toils of agitation.

There he kept almost open house. His relatives

alone were very numerous, for he had twenty-one
uncles and aunts, and seven married sisters, and was
kind to all his kinsfolk; but visitors from abroad, and
even the casual tourist who passed his door, were hos-
pitably received. His table was generally laid for thirty
at Darrynane. In Dublin he lived for nearly forty
years at 30 Merrion Square south, and there he loved
to make a handsome figure. He set up his carriage when
he had been a few years at the bar, and his green coach
and his footmen in green liveries were a striking sight
in the streets of Dublin. He was burthened, too, with
the expense of a house in London during the session of
Parliament. Generally he lived in Langham Place, but
in 1832 he had a house in Albemarle Street, and in
1835 at 9 Clarges Street. All these expenses, together
with agitation, elections, and the maintenance of his
sons in Parliament, caused him an enormous annual
outlay, and he was a man habitually careless of money.
He lived in a world where debt was no discredit, and
had little time to spare for the regulation of his private
affairs. Shortly after he was called to the bar he accepted bills to accommodate a friend, which hampered
him for twenty years, nor was he ever free from embarrassments. And yet his means were large. In addition
to his professional income, his patrimony was handsome.
His uncle Maurice died, a childless widower, in 1825,
and left his estates at Darrynane to his nephew. They
were estimated to be worth £4,000 a year, though as to
one-half O'Connell is said to have had only a life
interest. By the death of his uncle, Count Daniel, in
1834 he also inherited a considerable fortune. Fifty
thousand pounds was subscribed for him in 1829 after
the passing of the Relief Act, and the O'Connell Tribute or National Annuity subsequently became an

annual offering. It was managed for him with great skill by Patrick Vincent Fitzpatrick, a wit and *bon vivant* who did not concern himself with politics, and was collected in sums of 10s. and 5s., chiefly from the clergy and middle classes. A day was fixed for its simultaneous collection in chapels and other places, and a writer of repute was employed to compose a eulogy upon its object. Its gross amount averaged £15,000, but the expenses of collection were so heavy as to reduce its proceeds to O'Connell to £10,000.

He was virulently attacked for receiving this tribute, and was called "the big beggarman," and a "paid patriot." But, since the controversies of his lifetime have been calmed, no fair man has condemned him for taking the free offerings of a people, for whose service he had resigned his profession and spent all his energies. Yet he died poor, and left his family little more than a competence. His conduct in money matters was fiercely assailed, and he was charged with mismanagement of the large sums of the Catholic and Repeal Rent which passed through his hands, but not one of these charges could be sustained. It should be remembered that for years he had only to ask, and he might have procured for every one of his male relatives lucrative and easy Government posts. Yet the only offices his relatives held were a stipendiary magistracy held by his son-in-law, and a registrarship by his son Maurice, which was not given at his desire.

Although when first he returned from France he was affected by some sceptical doubts, through all the years of his latter life he was devoutly and sincerely pious. He employed the leisure hours of his first years at the bar in translating Arnaud's Proofs of the Infallibility of the Church. In 1824 and 1826 he engaged in public controversies with Mr. Noel and with Daly, afterwards Bishop of Cashel. His theological learning, however, was small. It was his habit, however busy he was, however late he had gone to rest, in Dublin and in London constantly to attend early mass at some neighbouring chapel, and at Darrynane, his domestic chaplain, Father O'Sullivan, celebrated mass daily at 9 A.M. In August 1838 he performed a retreat of great austerity at the Cistercian Convent of Mount Melleraye in Waterford. To beguile the tedium of his long and wearisome journeys from meeting to meeting, he was accustomed to repeat to himself Latin hymns. That he was unconscious of the edifying effect upon both priests and people of such distinguished piety is not likely; but it would be equally unreasonable to suppose, that he was prompted to it by anything but the natural impulse of a religious mind. In all his correspondence with bishops and clergy and constantly in speaking of them he used language of deference, not to say subjection, which now has a very singular appearance and in his later days gave some offence to the younger generation by whom he was surrounded. Nature had given him, and his foreign education had increased, a hierocratic turn of mind, which made him rest gladly upon the authority of the priesthood, and act with them without misgiving or misunderstanding.

His personal appearance was impressive. He was but half-an-inch under six feet in height, but a roundness about the shoulders, which increased his naturally burly and ecclesiastical appearance, rather diminished his apparent stature. His figure was broad and thick, his step energetic and swift, and in his customary green coat and broad-brimmed hat, striding swiftly along, he was a well-known and remarkable figure about the streets of

Dublin. His mouth and the lower part of his face were beautifully shaped, but his nose was short, and gave to its upper part a rather vulgar appearance. As a young man his complexion was very ruddy ; his eyes were keen blue, and from middle-life he habitually wore a black wig. Such was his face in repose, but when excited or animated, it was extraordinarily mobile, and flashed with every phase of emotion. Humour, pathos, scorn, indignation, hopefulness, or gloom, all seemed equally the natural expression of a face, which instantly reflected every mood of the feeling within. Though he greatly disliked sitting for portraits, many exist. The earliest is a pencil sketch, dated 1810, and engraved in Miss Cusack's life of him. There is also a portrait by Haverty in the National Bank and another by Catterson Smith in the Municipal Chamber at the City Hall, Dublin, and he also sat to Duval and to Wilkie. There are statues of him by Hogan in the Dublin City Hall and at Limerick, by Foley in Dublin, and by Cahill in Ennis.

No doubt there was in his composition a certain rude animalism, almost inseparable from a nature so buoyant, so energetic, so indefatigable. He appears after his marriage to have been engaged in at least one intrigue, the fruit of which was a natural son, who was born about 1820, and to whom and his mother he behaved with considerable neglect. In manner he was obliging, suave, kindly, especially to children, of whom he was very fond. In spite of the violence which he displayed towards his public opponents he was singularly forbearing to private enemies ; he never made use of his powers to their injury, and often employed it for their promotion or advantage.

One so busy as he was from manhood to old age, had naturally scant time for study. He appears to have had little scholarship, and beyond his profession little learning, though his great talent enabled him to put all he knew to the best use. He was an admirer of Dickens, and read novels eagerly but few other books. His speeches owe singularly little to quotation or allusion. For his jest upon Stanley and his seceding companions,

> See down thy vale, romantic Ashbourne, glides
> The Derby dilly carrying six insides,

he is said to have been indebted to Romayne, member for Clonmel; and almost his only other witticism that owes anything to literature is the well-known parody upon Colonels Sibthorp, Percival, and Verny :—

> Three colonels in three distant counties born,
> Lincoln, Armagh, and Sligo did adorn:
> The first in matchless impudence surpassed.
> The next in bigotry, in both the last.
> The force of nature could no further go,
> To beard the third she shaved the other two.

His publications were almost confined to his numerous letters upon public questions, of which perhaps the best is his *Letter to the Earl of Shrewsbury*, in 1842. He also began a work called a *Memoir on Ireland, Native and Saxon*, published in 1843, an extremely amorphous and ill-digested book, which has not even, the merit of being thoroughly accurate. It never got beyond one volume. In 1836 he became, with Dr. Wiseman, part-editor and proprietor of the *Dublin Review*, but whether he took any part in writing for it does not appear. A long article upon his uncle, Count Daniel O'Connell, which appeared in the journals of 1834, is also attributed to him. His knowledge of

French literature was small ; but he spoke French fairly well, though not with perfect ease. In December 1835 he was approached on behalf of the "Lyons conspirators," who were to be tried on a charge of high treason before the French chamber of peers, and was asked to go to France as their advocate. His answer—a refusal —is interesting. He says :—

I am restrained from attempting it by one only motive, the conviction of sheer incapacity to perform that duty efficiently in the French language. It is true that I understand the language well, but I cannot speak it with that abundant fluency, which so important an argument would require. I never write out any discourse beforehand, nor could I do it without utterly cramping the force and nerve of the very limited talent I possess, and my command of the French language is not sufficient to enable me to translate my ideas as I went along in speaking without embarrassing my powers of thought.

But as an orator O'Connell had very great genius ; in oratory he found his natural and constant expression. Yet he had the strength of mind never to give the reins to his tongue for the mere purpose of personal display. In the conduct of a cause he was in every moment an actor ; he affected extreme carelessness to cover his anxiety, indignation to hide a bad case, *bonhomie* to put a witness off his guard, woe to touch the feelings of a jury, and he never allowed himself to make a fine speech at the cost of his client. "Ah!" he said, "a speech is a fine thing, but the verdict is the great thing." Thus playing a part at will, and never, in his most impassioned moments, losing his self-control, he adapted himself with marvellous versatility to every audience and every style of address. In the Crown Court, at *nisi prius*, or *in banco* ; before a mob, a committee, or the House of Commons, he played the *rôle* suited to the place. Where too many of the great Irish barristers had been helpless unless they were appealing to all the noblest passions of humanity, he could argue a right of way case or a nice point upon a criminal indictment, without rhetoric and as a lawyer should argue it.   Before a mass meeting he was a demagogue, bold, rollicking, emotional; in the House of Commons he put off the demagogue and spoke clearly and calmly, except when he dealt about swashing blows with calculated ferocity.   In the conduct of the multifarious business of the Catholic or the Repeal Association, he was rapid, matter-of-fact, and businesslike; and in an after-dinner speech he could draw upon an unfailing fund of wit or pathos to adorn an oration about nothing at all.   Never preparing his speeches, he showed a roughness in his mode of expression, which, though often more trenchant and telling than the most carefully prepared rhetoric, was still oftener inelegant and cumbrous.   In Sheil's often quoted phrase, " He brings forth a brood of lusty thoughts without a rag to cover them."   M. Duvergier speaks of him as " throwing out his opinions in a negligent manner," and N. P. Rogers describes his speaking as " public talk."   He never scrupled to repeat himself; indeed, it was one of his devices to hit upon some telling phrase, which an ignorant audience could carry away, to repeat it over and over again in every form, and to do this at meeting after meeting, until by constant reiteration the public had thoroughly learnt its lesson. This habit of repetition occasionally took odd forms.   He was fond of making gushing allusions in his speeches to his mother, his wife, his children, and his grandchildren. After his wife's death in 1826, he said in one of his speeches: " But that subject brings me back to a being of whom 1 dare not speak in the profanation of words.   No!   I will not mention that name," and so forth.   For once this was all very well; having accidentally reminded himself of his lost wife, the bereaved widower might well check himself thus. But Daunt heard him repeat this impromptu in public speeches several times, and always in identically the same words. To wear one's heart on one's sleeve in this way, and affect to find it painful, strikes the spectator as being curiously inconsistent; yet no doubt each time that he said it, O'Connell, accustomed for thirty years to feel in public, was perfectly sincere, and saw no reason why he should not use over again a passage which had so often proved efficacious before. His readiness and self-possession in controlling an audience were marvellous. During the Repeal year he was anxious to restrain his followers from violent expressions of hatred towards the Government without at the same time giving them offence. "I wish a crow picked Peel's eyes out," bawled an angry auditor parenthetically at one of the great meetings. "I wish a crow," retorted O'Connell instantly, "came and stuffed your mouth with potatoes." On another occasion, when the people were densely packed together, a horse, picketed on the fringe of the crowd, broke loose and caused a panic. There was an alarm that the meeting was charged by dragoons. In a moment a dangerous stampede would have begun. "Stop," thundered O'Connell at the top of his voice, and the crowd stopped instantly and order was restored. At another meeting, which was held in a loft, it had been thought necessary to underpin the floor, to provide for the weight of the crowd. O'Connell was speaking, when word was passed to him that the floor was unsafe, and that the stays were giving way. He calmly finished his sentence, and then said that circumstances rendered it necessary to adjourn the meeting to a plot of vacant land hard by, and asked the people to file out and go there. In a few moments it became plain that this would not be done without a dangerous amount of jostling. Then he quietly told them the state of the case, ordered them to file out right and left, two and two, at the door, and said he would leave the room last himself. The people became perfectly quiet and obeyed his instructions, and though they were three-quarters of an hour in getting out no accident occurred.

But however open to criticism his speeches may be from the point of view of the student of rhetoric, however unfinished or redundant they may seem when read, they produced as they fell from his lips an effect almost unexampled. He was gifted with a superb voice, full as a bell, of wide compass and of great power. He had carefully studied Pitt's speaking, and had attained a perfectly natural and unstudied action. His was the instinct of an orator, never so much at home as when talking with the people at his feet. He had a fine presence, a complete command of telling, nervous language, a rich Irish accent which went to his hearers' hearts, and a finished delivery, and thus equipped, he threw himself into his work and dilated upon the subject which engrossed him with superb and exhaustless eloquence. The peroration of his speech on the first reading of the Coercion Bill of 1833 is a good example of his unprepared and inornate but flowing and affecting eloquence :—

I have now wearied the House. I have not exhausted the subject, nor have I exhausted the deep interest I feel in it. I say, that as far as political agitation is concerned, there is no such case made out, that any dispassionate man, putting his hand to his heart, can say there is evidence to connect it with predial insurrection. Upon inquiring into the subject, facts to the contrary stare you in the face. Is not Ireland in distress? Is she not in want, and suffering

·grievances ?   The noble Lord, the Member for Armagh, exclaims that relief must be given, and you promise relief. Oh yes! if we pass this Bill you will give us a measure of Church Relief! But are you sure of passing that measure of relief in another House? It has little immediate practical benefit besides the abolition of Church-cess. But to secure it, why not adopt the wise motion of my honourable friend and keep your hands off this measure until you have steered the other over the rocks and quicksands in another place ?   I am not ·entering into any compromise. I say that Ireland requires relief, and I ask how do you propose to afford it her? You will not apply any part of the rich revenues of the Church to the relief of the poor. What is to become of them? You can give them nothing; and the ·only thing I can offer them is hope—the hope of a domestic Legislature. You may think that a delusive hope. How are you to show it to be such ?   By anticipating me, by evincing that you are a protecting Legislature—that you are a kind and paternal Legislature. Oh ! instead of that you turn away the look of kindliness, you turn away all benefits and leave the grinding evils. You leave the rack-renting absentees, you leave every misery and grievance untouched; for bread you give them a stone ; you raise the scorpion rod of despotic authority over them, and say that "you must be feared before you ·can be loved." I deny it, Sir. I deny that you have made out a case ; I deny that you have shown that predial insurrection has anything to ·do with political agitation ; I deny the right upon which you found this coercion ; I deny that witnesses have been injured, lately at least, to any public knowledge. If they have, I utterly deny that any juror has been injured during the whole period of this political agitation. Predial agitation subsisted for forty years before political agitation ·commenced. Having thus demonstrated that this measure is by no means necessary, shall I trust the despotic power it confers to hands which I think ought to have no power at all—to statesmen who mingle miserable personal feelings with their political conduct ?   I call upon you, if you would conciliate Ireland—if you would preserve that connexion which I desire you to recollect has never yet conferred a single blessing upon that country—that she knows nothing of you but by distress, forfeitures, and confiscations ; that you have never visited her but in anger ; that the sword of desolation has often swept over her, as when Cromwell sent his eighty thousand to perish ; that you have burdened her with grinding penal laws, despite of the faith of treaties and in violation of every compact, and that you have neglected to fulfil the promises you dealt out to her. You have, it is true, granted Catholic Emancipation ; but nine and twenty years after it was promised, and five and twenty years after the Parliament of Ireland must of

necessity have done so. We know you as yet but in our sufferings and
in our wrongs; and you are now kind enough to give us as a boon this
Act, which deprives us of the Trial by Jury and substitutes Courts
Martial—which deprives us of the Habeas Corpus Act, and, in a word,
imposes on a person the necessity of proving himself innocent. That
Act you give us, and you tell us it will put down the agitation of the
Repeal of the Union. I tell you that until you do us justice you can
never expect to attain your object. The present generation may
perish. Your Robespierrian measures may destroy the existing population; but the indignant soul of Ireland you can never annihilate.
There was a time when a ray of hope dawned upon that country. It
was when the present Parliament first assembled. We saw this reformed House of Commons congregated. We knew that every man
here had a constituency; we knew that the people of England were
represented here; we knew that the public voice not only would influence your decisions but command your votes; we hoped that you
would afford us a redress of our grievances—and you give us an Act
of despotism.

In his situation he fell inevitably into exaggeration, both of praise and of abuse. His eulogies
sometimes were so profusely distributed as to lose
all meaning; but to the leader of a motley combination of highly susceptible followers flattery was a
necessary instrument of command. A passage from a
speech of his in 1813 is characteristic of this mood.
He was praising the newspapers of his party :—

In Ulster we had the *Belfast Magazine*, a work in which all the
elegance of classic taste was combined with all the good feeling of
virtuous sentiment and all the purity of genuine Irish patriotism. . . .
In Limerick there is one of the best conducted and most patriotic
papers in the land, the *Limerick Evening Post*. In Cork the *Mercan-
tile Chronicle*, an admirable paper, most patriotically conducted by
my esteemed friend, Councillor O'Donnell, a member of your board
and a first-rate Irishman. In the *Evening Post* we have a brilliant
advocate, that never ceases powerfully to serve and severely to suffer
for us. In the *Freeman's Journal* and the *Evening Herald* we have
friends who cannot be bought nor intimidated, and whose talents adorn
the cause of their country, which they never cease to promote. But
I must point your vote particularly to the proprietor of the *Evening*

Post. Unseduced by the pleasures and enjoyments of youth, uncontaminated by the selfishness of wealth, unintimidated by the persecutions of power, he seeks to serve you as disinterestedly as he opposes your enemies. . . . I cannot conclude without proclaiming my conviction that Ireland would be free if she possessed a second John Magee.

He was even more extravagant in his abuse of his enemies, and in this matter it is hard to excuse him. Yet he adopted the language of vituperation deliberately, and with a certain relish. It is interesting to know that his paternal grandmother, an O'Donoghue, and locally nicknamed "Black Mary," was pre-eminent, even in Kerry, for her powers of abuse. O'Connell inherited her talent, and employed it, and defended its employment. He thought it gave spirit to a down-trodden class, who under persecution had forgotten that they had rights. "When I was working out Catholic Emancipation," said he, "members of Parliament and private friends used to come to me and say, 'O'Connell, you will never get anything so long as you are so violent.' What did I do? Why, I became more violent, and I succeeded." His language, however, was more than violent; it was irreclaimably coarse. To call the Duke of Wellington "a stunted corporal," Sir Charles Napier "a doldrum general," Lord Hardinge a "one-armed miscreant," had neither wit nor truth to recommend it, nor could such expressions be needed to inspire courage in a people who had proved their valour under those very commanders. It must, however, be remembered how bitterly and remorselessly he was all his life attacked, and what examples of abusiveness he had before him in the most distinguished of his countrymen. His reputation and his life were in almost hourly danger. Whatever may be thought of his conduct in declining challenges, it is certain that, if he had been willing to

14

accept them, duels would have been deliberately forced upon him, and he would have lost his life before he was fifty. More cowardly attempts were made upon him: his carriage axles were tampered with and filed half through ; and in 1825 he was waylaid in county Down, and only escaped the assassins by the accidental breakdown of his carriage and the cunning of a servant. Grattan gave him at once a provocation and an example of abuse in language which even O'Connell could not match. He had described him to Moore as "a bad subject and a worse rebel," but in his irritation at the event of the "securities" controversy, he wrote of him deliberately in an address to the Catholics of Ireland :

His speaking is extravagant diction. . . . his liberty is not liberal,. his politics are not reason, his reason is not learning, his learning is not knowledge; his rhetoric is a gaudy hyperbole, garnished with faded flowers, such as a drabbled girl would pick up in Covent Garden, stuck in with the taste of a kitchen-maid. He makes politics a trade. . . . He barks and barks, and even when the filthy slaverer has exhausted its poison and returns to its kennel, it there still howls and barks within unseen.

His English enemies were better able to preserve their self-respect, but their enmity was no less bitter, and their opposition in its way no less galling. The reporters in the House of Commons misreported his speeches, and when he complained in a speech at the Globe Hotel, they met and resolved not to report him at all. He took his revenge upon them by spying strangers and clearing them out of the gallery. But society placed its ban upon him. Theodore Grenville ceased to visit the house of a friend because he dreaded meeting O'Connell there. Even when he was the trusty ally of the Whigs he was not a guest at Holland House or at Lansdowne House; and in 1840 Guizot, who was anxious to meet him, found it necessary to get Mrs.

Stanley to arrange a dinner for the purpose. After dinner O'Connell, finding other guests were expected, humbly rose to go before they arrived, but was at length prevailed upon to stay.

This merciless warfare, in which he passed his life, this cold and almost contemptuous aversion, which was displayed towards him by those who ought to have been his friends, explain and excuse, though they cannot justify, the extraordinary violence of language, which O'Connell permitted himself to employ. But it was in truth a misfortune to his country, as well as a discredit to himself. In any case, the English must have found him hard to understand, for when first he became a figure in English politics, a Roman Catholic of any kind was unfamiliar to the English, and of the Irish as a people their notions were ill-informed and deeply prejudiced. O'Connell was a fervent Catholic and an Irishman of the Irish. He was Celtic to the very core, though he possessed qualities rare among the Celts, those of patience and self-control. It was vitally important to himself and to Ireland that he should make himself understood by the English, and it ought to have been his study so to comport himself before the English people as to enlist upon the side of Ireland their sympathies, which are deep, and their sense of justice, which is invariable; to disarm their prejudices and compel their respect. Unfortunately, at a hundred points he jarred upon them, offended them, alarmed them. His almost ecclesiastical suavity contrasted with their surly integrity; his peculiar want of sensitiveness and punctilio in the conduct of money matters offended a people peculiarly susceptible upon such points, and obscured his real honesty; his extraordinary vivacity and seeming irresponsibility passed their

14 *

comprehension. A statesman and an orator, a king's counsel learned in the law, and the leader of his people, who could publicly, and without any sense of reserve, engage in a duel of abuse with a fishfag in the streets of Dublin, and enjoy his own and his friends' congratulations upon the happy epithets "whisky-drinking parallelogram" and "porter-swiping similitude of the bisection of a vortex," was to them an unintelligible paradox. Whether he was a blackguard or a buffoon they could not tell, and did not care to ask; but, in their eyes, such a man could not be a trusted statesman. But when, in addition to all this, they found him habitually indulging in language so violent as to be almost impotent, and in menaces of resistance that none but a casuist could distinguish from invitations to rebellion, what had been a prejudice resting upon ignorance deepened into a condemnation prompted by disgust. This was a misfortune for the Irish as well as for O'Connell. He came into English politics late in life, and in spite of the versatility which enabled him to make his power felt in the House of Commons, he was not able to change his modes of action or expression, perhaps not even to see the need of any change. Yet in many respects he was well qualified to have won the sympathy of the English. His opinions in general were just and liberal. His Radicalism, indeed, probably was rather a matter of expediency. It is difficult to suppose that he had any deep zeal for triennial Parliaments or the Ballot, and the Chartists at least, incited by Fergus O'Connor, believed he had none, and mistrusted him accordingly. But he was the advocate of Negro Emancipation, though he knew it was costing his cause much valuable aid in America. He was the proclaimed enemy of despots; he refused the Emperor Nicholas his autograph on that ground, and characteristically let his refusal be known. His opposition to the Poor Law, if mistaken, was generous; he was an early Free-Trader and opponent of the Corn Laws. He attacked flogging in the army; he advocated temperance. Had he only possessed the tact and moderation, which would have won the esteem and respect of the English, the latter part of his life might have been far less barren of results than it was. For barren of results to Ireland his last twenty years in a great measure were. The benefits which the Whigs secured to Ireland no doubt in part were due to him, for although they fell far short of what he desired, it was thanks to his persistent thrusting of Irish questions upon the House of Commons and the people of England that Ireland received so much attention as she did. By incessant reiteration he brought home to the English mind facts which to us are commonplaces but fifty years ago were discoveries. Yet it can hardly be doubted that even without him, and without the necessity of paying in Irish reforms the stipulated price for his support, Liberal ministries could not long have ignored the obvious justice of the cry for reform in nearly every department of Irish life and administration. Melbourne's Irish policy was no triumph of O'Connell's. O'Connell himself did not look upon what his son describes as the " ten years' war " as a period of success. To him the experiment, which he was driven to make, was a failure, and Whig Reform an illusion. Perhaps it was a failure, but to a large extent that was because O'Connell himself was unfortunate, in the impression which he, as representing Ireland, produced upon the English mind. He would not have carried the English with him for Repeal by being more bluff in his demeanour or more courteous in his speech, but it was his

misfortune that he did not perceive how essential it was
to content himself with a policy which a large minority
at least of the English could approve.   Had it not been
for the mistrust which his tendency to cunning excited,
and the repulsion produced by his scurrility, he might
have won for himself and for Ireland an amount of sympathy and support that would have overawed the House
of Lords, and have converted the Whig experiment,
which was far from being the complete failure he
thought it, into an indubitable success.   It is almost
as hard for the Irish to understand the English as
for the English to understand the Irish.   O'Connell's
epoch was a time when the English middle class represented the most liberal instincts of the people, and its
support was all-important to the advocate of a popular
cause.   He unfortunately failed to see that the English
middle class was not to be identified with the Irish
oligarchy.   Led astray by the knowledge of their prejudices, he fell into the error of including them in the
attacks which he made upon the party of Protestant
ascendency.   In this way he ranged against himself and
his country much of the class which formed the best
strength both of Peel and of Melbourne.   It was a
misfortune for both countries.   The Irish were disappointed of their hopes, and they fell into deep discontent.
Personal antipathy to O'Connell alienated numbers of
the middle class from the Whigs.   His support, which
kept Melbourne in power in the House of Commons,
helped to ruin him in the country, and in consequence
an opportunity, perhaps the most favourable that England has had, for satisfying the legitimate desires of the
Irish passed but half employed.

Thus the good and the evil of the career of O'Connell
are so inextricably intermixed, that it is hard to say

whether on the whole it was a benefit to Ireland or not. It falls with a completeness, rare in the lives of men so eminent, into two parts, and the dividing year is 1829. Catholic Emancipation was a victory, which he won in a sense single-handed against the most formidable odds. It was a battle for an entirely just object, and the man who led the Irish to victory in that fight has an everlasting claim upon their gratitude. It is true that Emancipation must have come with the first reformed Parliament, and it ought never to be forgotten that even O'Connell could not have carried Emancipation without the support of the large and powerful body, which advocated it in England and in the House of Commons. None the less it is a boon, nay rather a right, which was secured for the people of Ireland by him. Had his life terminated there, possibly that might have been the better for his fame. In October 1829 he was driving on the mail cart with his brother into Cahirciveen. At a point where the road skirted a precipice, hundreds of feet high and unguarded by any adequate wall, the horses ran away, and O'Connell and his brother jumped out and saved themselves at the cost of some injuries. Had this accident ended fatally, the judgment of posterity upon him must have been one of almost unmixed praise. To have ousted the landlords in 1829 from the leadership of the people was a revolution of the greatest magnitude. It is difficult to regret their fall. It is impossible to be satisfied with their successors. It is a misfortune due to the economic circumstances of Ireland, that she is so deficient in the possession of a middle class. The landlords once ousted, the political leadership fell either into the hands of the priests or, in large degree, into the hands of adventurers. O'Connell's own guiding hand once removed and the influence of both was felt and felt for the worse. Though tolerant himself, he had kindled and fanned the flames of sectarian intolerance, and, although a man of genius, had surrounded himself with partisans of little character and less talent. With many excellent qualities, the priests had not the training which their new position required. As ecclesiastics they would have been better out of politics; as politicians, they had all the instincts of the peasantry, and hardly more breadth of view or knowledge. And the alternative leaders have been even less beneficial to Ireland. But from 1829 he entered upon a course, in which he failed precisely because he did not perceive that the Irish people alone, however unanimous, could not win the contest in which he engaged them. Upon the question of Repeal, he had no supporters in England; for a time the Whigs may have favoured some scheme of extensive local self-government, but all parties in England were united against Repeal, and that one fact placed success beyond his reach. That O'Connell was perfectly sincere in his desire for Repeal cannot be doubted; yet he was always keenly alive to the possibilities of the situation, and personally would have been content with less. But, although he swayed the Irish with an absolute control never possessed by any other leader, whom they have ever had, he was to some extent obliged to float upon their tide. Left to his own judgment he would probably have realised that Reform alone was possible, and would not have jeopardised it by demanding Repeal. Probably, but for the personal slight offered to himself in 1829, he would never have entered upon the agitation for Repeal, which, however much he desired it, he knew to be so difficult of attainment. Even George the Third's opposition to Emancipation, though it did almost more harm than the act of any single man has ever done in England, was less a misfortune to Ireland than George the Fourth's petty spite against O'Connell. The insolent injustice done to him personally he took to be a declaration that Emancipation was as far as possible to be made a nullity. It was a wrong he never forgave. It forced him into a policy of Repeal, which perhaps, except in the intoxication of contact with an enthusiastic multitude, he hardly expected to conduct to a successful issue; and years of agitation in a hopeless cause could not but be prejudicial to Ireland.

O'Connell was the inventor of the whole modern machinery of peaceful agitation, of associations, subscriptions, processions, demonstrations, and organizations, and in his hands it attained a pitch of perfection, which others have only endeavoured to imitate. Of the merit of a system which elicits the expression of the popular will by means of bands and banners, marchings and counter-marchings, teaching the people *pedibus in sententiam ire*, it would be premature to speak. But the invention of these methods and the use O'Connell made of them prove at once his sincerity and the beneficence of his control over his countrymen. The almost pathetic fiasco of Smith O'Brien's rising in 1848, shows, as Mitchell himself admitted, how deeply O'Connell's lessons had entered into the mind of the people of Ireland. That control was won and maintained only at the cost of an endless and wearisome round of speech-making and banqueting, ovations, processions, and demonstrations, of endless and irksome petitions from all sorts of persons for all sorts of services and patronage. At such a price it is inconceivable that O'Connell, "agitator" though he avowed himself to be, could have sought power for the sake of mere popularity or for anything less than that which he conceived to be the good of his country.

No man has ever retained so commanding a position in Ireland for nearly so long a period. For five and thirty years he was so much the first man in his country, that in the eyes of the world he stood for Ireland. He won the admiration and esteem of all sorts and kinds of men, Quakers, Presbyterians, Catholics. Pease was his friend and admirer. Chalmers said of him, " He is a noble fellow, with the gallant and kindly as well as the wily genius of Ireland "; and the dignitaries of his Church entertained for him feelings as warm as were his for them. And his virtues were not confined to the showy arts of the platform. Nothing about him strikes one with more wonder than his vast powers of work and attention to detail. He could carry on the work he had in hand, while attending to the conversation that was going on around him. His patience and his complete mastery of all the details of a question were prodigious. His memory was exceedingly retentive and his capacity for taking pains truly amounted to genius. He spared no effort to conciliate every kind of influence for his agitation and carefully collected and focussed the support of the most dissimilar persons, and by these means gave to his movement a unity and a force which in Ireland were irresistible. In this light even his powers as an orator sink to the second place. If Peel was pre-eminent as a member of Parliament, O'Connell was one of the greatest of men of business. He was indeed a man with the defects of his qualities, impulsive, pugnacious, masterful. But he was, too, a man, of whom Ireland and the United Kingdom have cause to be proud; great as an orator, great as a politician, and, as a man, amiable and upright. It was his fate to have little scope for the statesmanship of constructive policy ; to find his great success balanced by great failure ; to die with so dark a cloud hanging over the country he loved so well. But he served her well and he still lives in her affections, and that is his best reward.

INDEX.

A.

"Algerine Act," the, 68.
Althorp, Lord, 112, 117, 118, 122.
Alvanley, Lord, 56, 128.
Anglesey, Lord, 79, 81, 95, 99, 101, 114.
Arbitration Courts, the, 161, 174.
Association, the first Catholic, 49, 50.
Association, the Catholic, 61–64; collects the rent, 64; suppressed by law, 66; refounded, 68; organized parochially, 74; old Association re-established, 80; finally dissolved, 86.
Association, the General, 137, 140.
Association, the Repeal. *See* Repeal.

B.

Barrett, 169, 170, 173.
Bellew, Sir E., 36, 37, 49.
Black Lane Parliament, 24.

Board, the Catholic, 32, 40
Butler, Charles, 36, 38, 43.
Butt, Isaac, 154.

C.

Canning, George, 38, 63, 74.
Church Temporalities Bill, 113.
Clare Election, the, 75–78.
Clonmel, meeting at, 80.
Clontarf, proposed meeting at, 164–166.
Coercion Bill (1833), 112–113; attempt to renew, 122.
Committee, the Catholic, 29, 32.
Conciliation Hall, 155.
Convention, scheme for a, 168.
Crawford, Sharman, 141, 169, 182.
Curran, 45.

D.

Darrynane Abbey, 2, 191, 192, 196–198.
Davis, 152, 159, 162, 186, 187.

London: Printed by W. H. Allen & Co., 13 Waterloo Place. S.W.

www.ingramcontent.com/pod-product-compliance
Lightning Source LLC
Chambersburg PA
CBHW020121030726
47498CB00006B/2208